IANTHE JER

THE STUDIO (

Ianthe Jerrold was born in 1898, the daughter of the well-known author and journalist Walter Jerrold, and granddaughter of the Victorian playwright Douglas Jerrold. She was the eldest of five sisters.

She published her first book, a work of verse, at the age of fifteen. This was the start of a long and prolific writing career characterized by numerous stylistic shifts. In 1929 she published the first of two classic and influential whodunits. *The Studio Crime* gained her immediate acceptance into the recently formed but highly prestigious Detection Club, and was followed a year later by *Dead Man's Quarry*.

Ianthe Jerrold subsequently moved on from pure whodunits to write novels ranging from romantic fiction to psychological thrillers. She continued writing and publishing her fiction into the 1970's. She died in 1977, twelve years after her husband George Menges. Their Elizabethan farmhouse Cwmmau was left to the National Trust.

Also by Ianthe Jerrold

Dead Man's Quarry

IANTHE JERROLD

THE STUDIO CRIME

With an introduction
by Curtis Evans

DEAN STREET PRESS

Published by Dean Street Press 2015

Copyright © 1929 Ianthe Jerrold

All Rights Reserved

The right of Ianthe Jerrold to be identified as the Author of the Work has been asserted by her estate in accordance with the Copyright, Designs and Patents Act 1988.

Cover by DSP

First published in 1929 by Chapman and Hall

ISBN 978 1 911095 43 9

www.deanstreetpress.co.uk

INTRODUCTION

Today what is known as British Golden Age detective fiction—that published in the period, roughly, between the two World Wars—is most strongly associated with four "Queens of Crime": Agatha Christie, Dorothy L. Sayers, Margery Allingham and Ngaio Marsh. Sometimes Josephine Tey, who wrote a couple of detective novels in this period, is added to the royal company; and advocates have urged as well the case for crowning Georgette Heyer, best known for her witty Regency Romances, though she also wrote some sparkling mysteries (plotted primarily by her husband). Long forgotten, however, is Ianthe Jerrold (1898-1977), despite the fact that her two classic Golden Age detective novels, *The Studio Crime* (1929) and *Dead Man's Quarry* (1930), not only were praised in their day but anticipated the much-admired sophisticated Thirties manners mysteries penned by Sayers, Allingham and Marsh. The reappearance, after eight decades of undeserved neglect, of *The Studio Crime* and *Dead Man's Quarry* should give cause for celebration among classic detective fiction fans everywhere.

Like her contemporary Margery Allingham, Ianthe Jerrold derived her surname from a clever and creative family whose members often lived by their pens. Her paternal great-grandfather, Douglas William Jerrold, was a famed early Victorian-era playwright, conversationalist and journalist (for sixteen years he was a mainstay columnist in *Punch*), who once had been ranked as a literary figure on par with Charles Dickens and William Thackeray; while her great-uncle William Blanchard Jerrold, a journalist and author, had famously collaborated with

French artist Gustave Doré on the book *London: A Pilgrimage.* Nor did the Jerrolds limit themselves, in terms of their creative endeavors, to writing. Ianthe's paternal great-great grandfather, Samuel Jerrold, the first Jerrold of note today, was an actor, a "strolling player," who was said to have reverently kept a pair of the great David Garrick's shoes, which he invariably wore when he made his own dramatic struts upon the stage.

Ianthe's father, Walter Copeland Jerrold, an author and newspaper editor, in 1895 married Clara Armstrong Bridgman, who herself published a number of books, including a once-controversial three-volume life of Queen Victoria (published under the name Clare Armstrong Bridgman Jerrold). After the birth of a son, Oliver, who died as an infant, the couple had five daughters, the oldest of whom was Ianthe, born in London in 1898. Like her sisters—Daphne, Phyllis, Hebe and Althea—Ianthe was named for a character from Greek mythology. Having started writing "as soon as she could hold a pencil," she had newspaper short stories appearing in print before she was ten and by her twentieth year had published two volumes of poetry and a pair of *Strand* tales, "The Orchestra of Death" and "The China Mandarin." After working in a munitions factory during the First World War, she published her first novel, *Young Richard Mast: A Study of Temperament*, in 1923. It was the first of twenty-one novels by Jerrold that would appear over the next forty-three years.

The Studio Crime and *Dead Man's Quarry*, Ianthe Jerrold's two Golden Age detective novels, are superlative examples of the form, manifestly deserving of modern revival. Before the Great War several of the Jerrold sisters had lived at a studio in St. John's Wood, London (twin sisters Daphne and Phyllis were flower painters); and, appropriately enough, it is in St. John's Wood where Ianthe set *The Studio Crime*, in which murder strikes, most memorably, on a fog-bound December night, when a dabbling artist is done to death in his studio. Determining who performed the dark deed proves a tricky question for amateur detective John Christmas, Jerrold's sleuth in both *The Studio Crime* and *Dead Man's Quarry.*

In Jerrold's debut detective novel one can see some resemblance to the romantic Arabian Nights atmosphere in books by the "man who explained miracles," the great mystery writer John Dickson Carr. There is the fog, for one thing, plus a locked door to be dealt with, along with a cryptic message from the murder victim, a lovely vanished lady and a mysterious man in a fez (mysterious men in fezzes pop up, to my knowledge, in two later Carr detective novels, *The Punch and Judy Murders* and *Patrick Butler for the Defence*). At the same time, however, Jerrold sets *The Studio Crime* quite convincingly in a real place, peopled by plausible characters, many of whom on the night of the murder happen to be present, along with John Christmas, at a party in a flat one flight down from the scene of the crime.

Especially memorable is the celebrated novelist and playwright Serafine Wimpole, "a strong and over-energetic woman wearing fine and thin with the approach of middle age." Serafine bears some resemblance to the author, then in her thirty-first year and herself fine and thin, energetic and accomplished. When a man she deeply admires appears to be dangerously implicated in the murder, Serafine becomes emotionally involved in the investigation, as does the reader with her, taking *The Studio Crime* out of the realm of the pure puzzle detective novel—though the puzzle that Jerrold sets for her readers is an excellent one, with an intriguing investigation and clever clues.

John Christmas, the leisured son of department store tycoon Jefferson Christmas, is a likeable gentleman amateur sleuth, drawn along the lines of E.C. Bentley's Philip Trent and possessed of a nose sensitively attuned to scenting baffling mysteries. His friend Laurence Newtree (the celebrated caricaturist), makes a pleasing Watson; and Jerrold's policeman, Inspector Hembrow, is a worthy addition to the fictional ranks of well-intended yet erring British bobbies, stolid yet by no means stupid. Hembrow, we learn, has worked with Christmas before, "during the course of the extraordinary affair known as the Museum murder, which had opened with the discovery in the early hours of the morning of a well-known journalist lying dead under a table in the British Museum reading-room….it had been Christmas who had first detected the forged post-mark which had formed the nucleus of the whole intricate web." In the current case Hembrow again labors mightily, but it is Christmas who deduces and confronts the killer.

The Studio Crime received high commendation back in 1929, with the *Morning Post*, for example, praising the novel's plot construction and good writing. J.B. Priestley was one of the book's contemporary admirers, as were, in more recent decades, two astute crime fiction critics, Jacques Barzun and Julian Symons, who at other times often were at daggers drawn. In Barzun's and Wendell Hertig Taylor's landmark genre reference book *A Catalogue of Crime* Jerrold's first mystery novel was lauded for its "amusing dialogue with sharply differentiated characters," while Symons in his fine anthology *Strange Tales from The Strand Magazine* (wherein is included Jerrold's 1918 short story "The Orchestra of Death") approvingly noted that *The Studio Crime* was "ingeniously clued." That Ianthe Jerrold could bring together in momentary harmony Jacques Barzun and Julian Symons is yet another testament to the exceptional merit of *The Studio Crime*, a jewel of Golden Age detective fiction.

Curtis Evans

THE STUDIO CRIME

CHAPTER I

A PARTY AT NEWTREE'S

"NO, don't draw the curtain for a minute, Mr. Newtree. Do you mind? I like the look of a London fog, when it's fairly thin, like this one, and doesn't hide the street-lamps. That one at the corner looks like a fiery cross with its long rays cutting the fog."

Newtree, who at Miss Wimpole's first word had let go of the curtain with a sort of startled obedience, murmured inadequately:

"Yes . . . " and stood at her side, peering out into the fog and trying to think of something effective to say about it. He couldn't see anything, himself, except a feeble glimmer of light over the gateway of the court and a great deal of unpleasantly yellowish darkness; but he knew that if the celebrated Serafine Wimpole found the lamp remarkable, remarkable it must be. Laurence Newtree was a shy man, especially with women, and Miss Wimpole, whom he had not met before, filled his humble heart with terrified respect. It troubled him to think that he was her host and responsible for the entertainment of her and her large, scented, placid, smiling aunt. He couldn't think why Christmas had seen fit to bring these two ladies to the studio, nor why he himself had allowed it. He glanced appealingly at his friend, but Christmas was sitting magisterially on the model's throne, addressing an audience which consisted of Simon Mordby, the psychologist, Mrs. Imogen Wimpole, the aunt, and a lay figure draped in a Chinese robe which gave it, with its bald, featureless head and stiffly bent arms, the look of an old bonze. All of them, except the bonze, who preserved the enigmatic calm of the East, appeared to be enjoying themselves. Laurence envied Christmas his capacity for talking about nothing.

He looked at Miss Wimpole's lamp-ward gazing profile and thought of her plays, her novels, her press-notices, her lecture-tours in the States. . . . These things, combined with her femininity, paralysed him into an oafish silence. Yet at the same time the imp of the perverse, that imp within him which had led him half against his will from a city desk and a competence to Fleet Street and affluence, was noting down with irreverent hilarity the strong salient line of the lady's nose, the long bony curve of the lady's jaw, the cigarette dangling gamin-wise from between unexpectedly full pale lips, the long pointed hands like a mediaeval saint's, the long pointed feet like small canoes.

While the imp was joyfully tucking away an unflattering likeness of the lady in some obscure pigeon-hole in Laurence's complex mind, Laurence himself, his racked brain suddenly perceiving a useful connection between Miss Wimpole's profession of playwright and the state of the weather, was remarking brilliantly :

" It's a bad night for the theatres."

Miss Wimpole did not reply for a moment, but looked dreamily out through the tall studio window into the fog which seemed to move and writhe in dim, drifting shapes like living things. Then she turned and gazing intently at Laurence with her small dark eyes, leant towards him and murmured earnestly:

"It's a bad night for most things. But a good night for crime."

Laurence started slightly at this dark and unexpected pronouncement, and the gold pince-nez to which in a world of horn-rims he was still faithful dropped from his eyes as he stared apprehensively at the lady who had uttered it. Then he saw a twinkle under her crooked black eyebrows and a little line which might once have been a girlish dimple in her thin cheek. With relief rather than mortification he thought:

"She's laughing at me."

Serafine's twinkle became a wide and sudden smile, as jolly as a schoolboy's. She stood up and gathered her brilliant Chinese shawl around her thin shoulders.

"Seriously, Mr. Newtree," she said, and her clear, penetrating voice cut across and stilled the chatter at the other end of the studio, "it *is* a good night for crime. Don't you often think that if you were going to commit a murder you'd choose a foggy night?"

"I—I—no, I can't say I've ever thought about it," stammered Laurence, and was relieved to see his friend John Christmas approaching them with an amused smile.

"Personally," said Christmas, "I should hate to murder an enemy in a fog. It seems to me a poor, half-hearted, shamefaced way of doing it. If I had an enemy to murder I should get him alone somewhere in broad daylight and tell him exactly why I was going to murder him and how. We should then part under no misapprehensions, and the affair would be complete, rounded-off, artistic."

"You'd be hanged," said Serafine briefly.

"That's the one consideration," assented John, "that has so far kept me guiltless of blood. What do you think, Laurence? How would you dispose of your enemy?"

"I'm afraid I shouldn't dispose of him at all," said Newtree diffidently, fidgeting with his glasses. "I—I should just keep out of his way if I didn't like him. But I like practically everybody."

Christmas laughed. The contrast between his friend Newtree's acute impish work as a caricaturist and his gentle diffident attitude to the world in general was a constant source of delight to him. John Christmas was a young man with a gift that amounted to genius for making friends with all sorts of people. He had been born under a happy star. He had his fair share of good looks, the good humour born of perfect health, the free, natural good manners of one who delights in his fellow-creatures and that alert and sympathetic sort of mind to which the meaning of the word "boredom" is unknown. He had sought out Newtree in the first place to buy the original of Newtree's brilliant caricature of his father, Jefferson Christmas, head of the Christmas Stores, that steel and stonework colossus of the West End; and he had soon added him to his large collection of friends. Of all these, Serafine was his oldest and perhaps his dearest. In his early twenties he had frequently asked her to marry him. But her persistent refusal to take him seriously had gradually worn the romantic gilt off their friendship, and now in his thirtieth year their relationship was more like that of favourite nephew and young indulgent aunt than any other. Now, at Newtree's deprecating " I like practically everybody " their eyes met with a twinkle, and John could see that Serafine liked and appreciated Newtree just as he did.

" And you know," went on Newtree mildly, " you're joking, John. I might say that I'm as incapable of shedding blood as you are yourself."

" I notice," said Christmas with a smile, " that you don't include Miss Wimpole."

Laurence blinked in embarrassment and cast an apologetic glance at the formidable Serafine.

" Oh, well," he stammered quickly. " I don't—I mean, I haven't known Miss Wimpole very—I mean——"

Miss Wimpole gave him a kind smile which added to rather than relieved his embarrassment.

" Mr. Newtree feels quite rightly that he hasn't known me long enough to answer for me," she said reasonably. " I must tell you, Mr. Newtree, that I don't make murder a habit. I only murder under great provocation."

" All murders are committed under great provocation."

It was Simon Mordby who, finding the amiable Mrs. Wimpole a bit heavy in hand, had suggested joining the animated trio at the window. He uttered his dictum with the smooth, unanswerable air of his kind of practitioner. He had a good presence, a suave, creamy voice, an ornate house in Maida Vale and a very large practice, consisting almost entirely of well-to-do and little-to-do women. As he spoke he fixed his wide-apart light eyes on Serafine and smiled a smile at once ingratiating and superior.

" And you are mistaken, Newtree, in supposing yourself incapable of committing a murder. We are all potential murderers."

Mrs. Wimpole closed her eyes like a blissful cat and nodded, as though she found a sad pleasure in this conception of her potentialities. She was a kind, lazy, middle-aged lady with a great deal of time on her hands and no training in any useful way of killing it. The study of psychology was one of her latest hobbies. Serafine, who disliked Dr. Mordby and was tired of being made a subject for amateur psycho-analysis, wished her aunt would go back to astrology or vegetarianism or one of her other more polite and impersonal fads.

"Of course," pursued Dr. Mordby in his best lecture-room manner, "potentialities differ. Now I should say——" He looked at Serafine with his large head on one side and raised himself gently on his toes, a habit of his when talking on his own subject, "I should say that Miss Wimpole's potentialities as a criminal are ex-treme-ly low."

Miss Wimpole's aunt opened her eyes with a slight jerk and looked rather disappointed. Serafine smiled politely. She felt, as usual in the presence of Dr. Mordby, that her murderous potentialities were, on the contrary, rather high.

"She doth protest too much," said the eminent psychologist with a bantering smile. "Your potential murderer does not talk quite so freely about it. He is more likely to have a nervous shrinking from the subject."

"I say," said Laurence Newtree deprecatingly, "aren't we all being rather morbid?"

Christmas laughed, and Mordby transferred his wide fixed gaze to Newtree's face, as if he were sadly measuring that gentleman's potentialities by the nervous shrinking evidenced in his voice.

"It's the fog," said Serafine. "I've noticed that a

London fog always turns people's thoughts in a delightfully morbid direction."

She glanced as she spoke out of the great square-paned window.

"One can imagine that it hides—all sorts of unusual things. It makes the most ordinary things look strange and threatening. At any moment one can expect something sinister to appear. . . ."

She had a clear, flexible voice like an actor's and knew how to give value to her words. Under its spell they all glanced out of the window. And they all saw what she saw—a small patch of whiteness moving through the fog in the quiet courtyard.

Mrs. Wimpole gave a little cry of half-affected alarm and glanced at Dr. Mordby as if for reassurance. He looked out of the window with the same wide, concealing glance with which he looked at his patients, as if he knew a great deal more about the case than there was any need to say. Christmas murmured dreamily:

"It might be a flag of truce from the powers of darkness."

"Yes," said Serafine. "But it's not. It's something quite ordinary. It's a man's muffler."

Even as she spoke they heard the sound of scrunching gravel and a cough.

"Of course," said Newtree in a puzzled tone, as if these flights of fancy were beyond him, "it's Merewether or Steen—or both of them," he added, as two dimly-outlined figures moved past the window and the ghost of a genial laugh was heard.

"Steen!" echoed Dr. Mordby, dropping for a moment his mask of god-like wisdom and looking quite humanly interested. "Is that—*the* Steen?"

" Yes, I suppose so," said Laurence mildly. " Sir Marion Steen."

The surprise on the doctor's face gave way slowly to the look that the mention of Sir Marion's name often brought to the faces of ambitious men—a look far-away yet intent, as if he were doing sums in his head.

" Fancy," said Mrs. Wimpole dreamily, " I read in the paper the other day that he'd just given five thousand pounds towards pulling down St. Paul's and ten thousand towards rebuilding the bungalows round Stonehenge. Or was it the other way about, Serafine? I can't follow all these modern movements. Anyway, it must be very delightful to have so much money."

She gave a faintly envious sigh and relapsed into her usual ruminant silence, preserving her youth and beauty as the latest method was, by sitting quite still and smiling and keeping the mind a blank.

" Now we've seen the worst," said John Christmas jovially, " shall we draw the curtains, Newtree? This fog of yours, Serafine, is worming its way into the room."

He pulled the cord and the Bokhara hangings swung softly together, lighting up the great untidy studio with their rich warm colours and making a bizarre frame for Serafine's black head and sallow face and tall gaunt figure in its yellow shawl. The fog hung thinly in the room, the finest possible mist, up through which drifted here and there the blue arabesques of cigarette smoke. The great open fire in the brick hearth crackled and blazed valiantly as if to dispel with its bright light and homely associations the mystery, the eeriness of the fog. Newtree's old servant pulled aside the tapestry at the door and announced:

" Sir Marion Steen and Dr. Merewether."

It was plain to see, from the servant's interested glance at the elder of the two men, which was Sir Marion, the great financier. But it was Dr. Merewether, a local practitioner, a poor man and without distinction in his profession, who better looked the part. One found it hard to believe, at first sight of Sir Marion's gentle, scholarly, rather dreamy face, that he was one of the great commercial figures of his generation. He had started on the road to millionairedom with a small hardware shop in an east coast town; or so rumour had it, and Sir Marion gave smiling countenance to rumour. The shop had become, in the course of not so very many years, a combine; and the small ironmonger had become the director of a dozen companies, a knight, and a millionaire celebrated for his philanthropy. The Steen homes of rest for the impecunious aged were almost as well known as Dr. Barnardo's orphanages, and the tracts of beautiful country snatched by Sir Marion from the threatening jerry-builder and presented to the National Trust now ran into many thousands of acres. In an uncertain and gullible fashion, the mild-mannered little millionaire was also a patron of the arts, and a fairly familiar figure in the studios of Chelsea and St. John's Wood.

Merewether, on the other hand, had the strong, self-reliant face and assured taciturn manner more often associated with worldly success than failure. A tall, lanky figure with a reserved but observant air and a face that kept in repose a melancholy, but not in the least fretful, expression. A faint ironic smile appeared for an instant in his eyes as Simon Mordby, after an effusive greeting of Sir Marion, gave him two fingers and a patronizing nod with a mechanical: " Well, Merewether, well! " and a quickly-turned shoulder. Dr. Mordby had little use for any member of his own profession, and no use at all for those without money or influence.

Turning aside, Dr. Merewether encountered the reflection of his own faint smile in Miss Wimpole's bright, observant eyes and moved towards her.

"How delightful," he remarked, "to come in out of the fog to the crackle and blaze of a log fire! It is like coming back to life from among the Shades."

"Ah!" said Serafine, "I see that you properly appreciate our London fogs. We were talking about it before you came in, and the way ordinary things become strange and terrible. Was it you or Sir Marion whose white muffler drifted across the courtyard like a small wandering ghost?"

"It was I," replied the doctor with his melancholy smile. "I had an experience of the same kind as I came up the road. I could see the outline of a man moving towards me with what seemed to be an extraordinarily elongated narrow head. It was like some dreadful malformation. I almost crossed the road to avoid meeting him. My flesh positively crept. Yet it was nothing but a man—a foreigner probably, but quite an ordinary harmless fellow-mortal wearing a Turkish fez. An unusual sight, but not an alarming one. He asked me the way to Golders Green," added Merewether pensively.

"Why!" exclaimed Sir Marion, turning from the inspection of a portfolio of etchings, "I met the same man in Greentree Road soon before I caught up with you. And he asked *me* the way to Golders Green!"

"I'm sorry he didn't find me explicit enough. But he didn't seem to be very well acquainted with the English language."

Newtree remarked thoughtfully:

"Some queer friend of Frew's, I shouldn't wonder. Frew has all sorts of queer callers—carpet-dealers and Jew merchants of all kinds. By the way, I've got an invitation to take you all up to his studio later on in the evening to have a look at his collection. He has some of the most wonderful old rugs in the world and all sorts of eastern things. If you'd all care to go . . ."

He looked diffidently round at his guests, and there was a chorus of polite and pleased assent. Only Mrs. Wimpole, turning upon Laurence a reproachful glance from her beautiful, stupid, light-grey eyes, asked plaintively:

"Is it far?"

"Not very," said Laurence with a smile. "Just up a flight of stairs. He has the studio above this one. Rather an interesting chap—seems to have travelled pretty well all over the world. He hasn't been here very long, not more than about ten months. He really has the most marvellous collection of——"

With his feeling that Miss Wimpole was the guest of the evening and must at all costs be kept entertained, Laurence began to address himself to her. He broke off as he found that she was not listening, but was looking aside with a curious, intrigued expression on her plain, lively face. Following the direction of her bright glance he saw that it was Dr. Merewether who had attracted her attention.

Dr. Merewether was standing quite still and looking across the studio. His face was profoundly sad. Standing with his elbow resting on the mantelpiece and his fingers running up into his hair he had the look of a man without hope or spirit who sees through the coloured kaleidoscope of life to some dark perpetual vision of despair. His thin lips were pressed together in a grim line and the deep vertical furrow between his brows looked like the finger-prints of a passing dæmon.

Serafine and Newtree looked at one another without speaking, but each recognized in the other the same curiosity, the same surprise and sympathy. Then, suddenly alarmed to find that he was gazing silently into the strange lady's eyes, Newtree started, dropped his eyeglasses and with a stammer concluded his sentence:

"——the most marvellous collection of Persian rugs. I should especially like you to see——"

Dr. Mordby had manœuvred Sir Marion into a corner and with long suave periods was doing his practised best to impress that gentleman with the social and scientific importance of Dr. Mordby.

"Lord Shottery is very interested in the scheme. You and I, Sir Marion, realize that the science of psychology is practically an unploughed field. Just surface-scratched at present. . . ."

Sir Marion listened with his fresh, gentle face tilted and a pleased, benevolent smile on his lips. He had never outgrown an ingenuous pleasure in his personage-ship. Flattery could draw inexhaustibly on his good humour, but not, as his flatterers were wont ruefully to discover, on his banking-account.

Mrs. Wimpole, opening her placid eyes to find Newtree and Serafine deep in conversation, remarked suddenly and confidentially to Christmas:

"I do wish, John, you could persuade Serafine to have her hair waved and not to wear such *outré* clothes. And not to think so much. It makes her thin and prevents her from getting married. It's no use my talking to

Serafine. I might as well be a pelican crying from the house-tops. . . ."

Laurence, glancing around at his guests, felt that his little party was not going so badly. Their voices rose and fell in a subdued, pleasant hum. No sound of traffic or footsteps penetrated into quiet Madox Court. The studio was a little oasis of warmth and chatter in a world of chill fog and silence.

Suddenly, from somewhere outside the oasis, breaking with uncanny effect across its gay atmosphere, there came a long muffled sound that broke at the end like a gasping cry. Long after it had died away it seemed still to go on, spreading fainter and wider waves of sound through Newtree's studio as a stone spreads ripples in a pond.

CHAPTER II

UPSTAIRS

IN the sudden hush Dr. Simon Mordby's voice went on with an effect of shouting:

" Lord Shottery was much impressed with the scheme. If I may, Sir Marion, I will send you——"

He became suddenly aware that Sir Marion was inattentively gazing upwards and that everybody but himself had fallen silent. He left his sentence hanging in mid-air and looked like the others up at the blank white ceiling. John Christmas was the first to recover himself.

" The pelican crying from the house-tops," he murmured softly. " Listen for the sparrow answering from the wilderness."

Laurence removed his glasses and looked round at the hesitant faces of his guests.

" It sounded to me," he said diffidently, " rather like a chair being pushed back. Frew has a parquet floor. I often wish he'd have castors put on his chairs."

" Why," said Sir Marion gently, as if to help Laurence to dispel any disquietude the ladies of the party might be feeling, " I thought it was a loud yawn. The sort of loud yawn a person gives when he's alone and can take pleasure in yawning."

Mrs. Wimpole, wide-eyed and placid, asked of the world in general:

" What was that? "

And Dr. Mordby, puzzled and rather annoyed at this interruption, of her in particular:

"What was what?"

Serafine said nothing. She was looking from under her lashes at Dr. Merewether, whose self-contained personality seemed to have great interest for her. He was the least excited of the party, remarking with polite professional calm:

"I'll go up and see if everything's all right, Newtree. I know Frew. He's a patient of mine."

Mordby, seeing him move without haste towards the door, began:

"Let me accompany you . . ." but Merewether answered tranquilly:

"No, thanks. It would be too much of an inquisition if two of us went, I think. I shan't be long."

"Tell him to put rubber castors on his chairs," said Newtree cheerily. He still felt that it was his duty to dispel the slight chill, the sense of something wrong which that muffled sound had projected into the studio. His guest s, however, did not seem to want it dispelled. Their talk was desultory, and they watched the door for Merewether's return. W henhe appeared after a moment or two, as composed and leisurely as ever, there was a perceptible disappointment in the faces turned towards him.

"Well?"

"Frew says he heard nothing," said Merewether in his low, deliberate voice. "He said it was probably the wind in the chimney. And he's expecting us all to go up in half an hour or so."

"The wind!" echoed Dr. Mordby. "My dear sir, there's no wind to-night!"

"Tha t," replied Merewether sedately, "is just what I

told him. And he said in that case it was probably a banshee."

"Oh, very likely, very likely!" murmured Mordby absent-mindedly and returned with zest to the conquest of Sir Marion Steen. Otherwise the conversation languished half-heartedly for a moment or two, as if they were all thinking of something else.

"What children we all are!" thought Serafine, half amused, half disgusted. "How we love a sensation! How we hate to be cheated of one!"

She turned towards Merewether, who had gone back to his place at the mantelpiece; and at that moment she herself had a sensation, one of those sensations that were the breath of life to her as a novelist. On the doctor's calm and rather arrogant face there were tiny beads of sweat, and the cigarette he was holding between his fingers was quite flattened out by the pressure of his half-clenched hand.

"Dr. Merewether," she said softly.

He turned towards her with a smooth, courteous movement, and smiled. But at her steady, thoughtful glance a queer expression came momentarily into his eyes—a look half appealing, half inimical, as though he defied her to read his thoughts. Serafine, whose curiosity about her fellow-creatures was insatiable, and who, at first sight of him, had thought the doctor easily the most unusual and interesting person in the room, beckoned him to her side. With a good deal of the novelist's complacent interest in other people's troubles and a little of the sympathy of a kindly if hard-headed woman, she wanted to hear him talk. He came, his face an agreeable if rather melancholy mask.

"Tell me," said Serafine, making room for him on the settee, "something about Gordon Frew. What's he like?"

Merewether paused, then replied expressionlessly:

" Tall, with a black beard."

" Have you read the book about Persia he published a month or two ago? "

" No. Have you? "

" Some of it. I thought it rather dull, to tell the truth."

" Oh."

" What does he do besides collecting rugs? "

The doctor smiled.

" Collects bronzes."

" And? "

" Collects Buddhas."

Serafine laughed.

" And is that all you can tell me? "

Merewether smiled politely, but his glance strayed as though this personal conversation displeased or bored him.

" Why, yes, that's all. I hardly know him, except——" He stopped a moment and went on levelly : " Except in my professional capacity."

" Oh," said Serafine, noting his restless glance and maliciously prolonging the conversation to punish him for it. " Now I'll tell you what you've told me. He's travelled a lot. He's acquisitive, like all of us. He has money, unlike most of us. And—you don't like him."

Merewether said nothing. The lines of his face seemed to harden for a moment. Then a formal, constrained smile appeared upon his lips, and turning with cold politeness towards Miss Wimpole he seemed about to make some aloof, non-committal reply. He paused, looking with a sort of intent absent-mindedness at a carved cornelian ring on his finger, and then said quietly and surprisingly :

" No. I don't like him."

Serafine felt a little embarrassed at this unexpected honesty, and her heart warmed to the doctor. He said no more, and she was rather relieved when Laurence summoned them all to the door. She took John's arm as they all went leisurely up the dim-lit staircase to Mr. Frew's studio. The fanlight over the door was open, and through it the fog drifted thinly in and up the staircase. Serafine sniffed.

"I hate the smell of fog. It's the worst part of it."

"Worse than the murders?" asked Laurence, greatly daring, over his shoulder.

Serafine laughed. The little man was thawing.

On the landing Mrs. Wimpole withdrew her hand from Laurence's arm and stood panting gently with closed eyes.

"Oh dear!" stammered Laurence, almost perspiring with compunction. "I've rushed you up too fast."

"Oh dear no!" murmured Imogen on a fluttering breath. "But if I might . . . just take a rest . . . before going in . . ."

Her voice died away on a sighing breath in which Laurence thought he could distinguish something about the importance of a good first impression. Watching the lady's gentle efforts to regain her composure, he felt an abject fool, and the amused grins he received from Christmas and Serafine did nothing to improve his state of mind.

"If your friend Mr. Frew heard us coming upstairs he'll be thinking we're a gang of burglars. . . ."

"He's probably now barricading the door," said John, "and sharpening a scimitar on the sole of his sandal. Come to think of it, old Merewether has rather a burglarious look about him. Gentleman George on the old lay. . . ."

Serafine looked over the well of the stairs. Sir Marion Steen was treading lightly up, followed at one pace by

Dr. Mordby, who had the solicitous enveloping air of a nurse keeping the draught off a baby. Some stairs behind them came George Merewether, alone and detached from the rest of the party, his hands in his trouser-pockets, looking at the stairs with a slight pre-occupied frown. His soft step, his detachment, something still and secret in his look gave an absurd aptitude to John's frivolous remark.

Taking a very small glass and a very large powder-puff from her handbag and using them with anxious care, Mrs. Wimpole sighed graciously:

"You may knock now, Mr. Newtree."

The great old wrought-iron knocker with which Mr. Frew had replaced the small bar of brass provided by his landlord fell even to the slightest touch with a heavy, ominous, resounding noise.

"How feudal!" said Serafine. "The draw-bridge will be lowered at half-past nine precisely."

"Like the walls of Jericho," murmured her aunt, with some obscure association of ideas lost on her hearers. "But artists are always such original people, aren't they? I mean," she explained gently as Laurence looked puzzled but humble, "there's always something peculiar about their front doors."

"The peculiar thing about this front door," remarked Christmas, after a short expectant pause, "is that it doesn't open."

"Queer," muttered Newtree, and knocked again, diffidently at first, then loudly and repeatedly.

"The whole court must have heard that," said Serafine, but there was no sound on the other side of the door.

Newtree turned a distressed, disappointed face over his shoulder. It seemed as if his little party were going to fall flat after all.

" He did say he was expecting us, didn't he, Merewether? "

" Certainly."

" He must have forgotten and gone out," said Mrs. Wimpole comfortably. " Never mind, Mr. Newtree. Let's go back to your lovely fire."

She shivered slightly and drew her fur stole closer about her fine shoulders.

" I second the resolution," said Mordby with a smile, and there was a slight movement towards the stairs.

" I think I'll just knock again," murmured Laurence. " You see "—he lowered his voice and spoke confidentially to Christmas—" there's a light in the studio."

Inside the studio, as the reverberations of Newtree's attack on the knocker died away, sounded a fine clear note, a soft silvery ping! like the plucking of a wire. In the silence behind that locked door it was a secret, unearthly sound that held them all still and breathless for a moment, looking at one another with startled eyes. Then Merewether said quietly, looking at his wrist-watch:

" A clock striking the half-hour," and there was a movement of relief.

" Come," said Dr. Mordby heartily. " Our friend has forgotten us. Let us forget him. Let us go back to warmth and light and talk and the pleasant things of life in Newtree's studio."

But Sir Marion Steen opposed him.

" I think," he said in his hesitating, apologetic way, " I do really think, considering that the light's still on, and that he was expecting us, and—and one or two other things, that we ought to get into this place somehow. I do really think so."

" The key," said Christmas, stooping to look through,

"is in the lock, so we can't use the ancient and honourable key-hole method."

There was a very slight movement at Serafine's side, as though somebody had given a start. She glanced round, but Dr. Merewether was leaning unconcernedly against the wall and smoking a cigarette.

"What do you think, Merewether?" asked Newtree, deferring to the doctor as the one silent and patient member of the party.

"I?" Merewether raised his brows and smiled. "If I had not seen Frew since we heard that queer sound half an hour ago, I should say: Break open the door by all means. As it is, I hardly like to take the responsibility of advising you to break into his flat. Still, a lock is easily repaired."

"Oh, come along, Mr. Newtree!" said Serafine breezily. "If we're going to smash in the door, let's do it! I can see you're dying to!"

"Dying to? I? Oh, my dear Miss Wimpole!" stammered Laurence, flushing a little at this accusation. "I do assure you. . . . But the whole thing is so very queer! Do you really think we might?"

"Oh, certainly! Why not? However pained Mr. Frew may be over the wreck of his front door, he'll have to be grateful for our solicitude."

"Now my dear young lady," said Dr. Mordby with heavy playfulness, "do you realize that you are advising Newtree to perform a criminal act? Personally, I have no desire to be the recipient of Mr. Frew's gratitude. I think it will be tempered with other less agreeable sentiments."

"Why not simply inform the police?" suggested Sir Marion unheeded, for John, who shared Serafine's dislike of the suave, successful doctor, remarked simply:

" Here goes! " and flung his weight heavily against the side of the door nearest the lock. Laurence impulsively followed suit, and Merewether, having handed his cigarette to Serafine, joined in more sedately. Dr. Mordby shrugged and frowned a little. He was not used to having his advice lightly set aside. He turned towards Sir Marion, but that gentleman had deserted him for Imogen Wimpole, who had taken a seat on the stairs and was endeavouring to feel warm and comfortable by a process of auto-suggestion.

" I don't believe in getting upset about anything, do you? " she was saying in her sweet, plaintive voice. " The latest thinkers say that if one isn't upset there can't be anything going on to upset one. Nothing unpleasant can happen then, can it, if one only——"

Perceiving that the climax of her sentence required a little thought, she abandoned it and relapsed into a beautiful smiling passivity. She jumped slightly, however, when a panel of the door gave way with a loud crack; and gave a little cry as a voice called up the stairs:

" Sir! Mr. Newtree, sir! Is there anything wrong, sir? "

She was reassured when Newtree, disordered and perspiring, stopped his attack on the door to call:

" Well, Greenaway? What is it? "

The old servant came slowly up, stopping respectfully at some distance from where Mrs. Wimpole decorated the staircase. He looked flushed and uneasy and there was a startled interrogation in his eyes.

" I heard the noise, sir, and I thought I'd come and see if I could help. And oh, please, sir! Do you think there's anything wrong? "

Christmas turned to look curiously at the old man.

" We don't know yet, Greenaway. You seem to think there may be. Why? "

The old man looked confused and stammered:

" I, sir? No, I don't know anything about it, sir. Only——" He paused and seemed to cast about in his mind for some explanation for his own agitation. " Only —there was the Oriental gentleman, sir, and——"

" The Oriental gentleman! What Oriental gentleman? "

" The one as came to see Mr. Frew, sir, not long before the young lady came. . . ."

" Dear me! " murmured Sir Marion. " The mysterious Mr. Frew seems to be a man of many visitors."

" Yes, he is, sir," replied the servant, with the faintest note of disapproval in his well-trained manner.

" What young lady was this, Greenaway? " asked John, with a hand through the splintered panel, groping for the lock.

" The young lady that poses, sir."

" Oh, his model! And what time did she arrive? "

" She arrived about ten minutes before the Oriental gentleman left, sir. About twenty minutes to eight. Leastways, when I heard the footsteps coming down I took them to be the Oriental gentleman's, sir. I didn't see him go."

" If the Oriental person, whoever he was, left the court before eight, you needn't worry about him, Greenaway. Because Dr. Merewether saw Mr. Frew alive and well not much more than half an hour ago."

" Oh, in that case, sir," murmured Greenaway, and subsided. But he still hovered anxiously on the stairs with a respectfully uneasy expression on his lined face, watching Christmas who, with his arm through the door, turned the key in the lock with a sharp click. He withdrew his torn coat-sleeve carefully and pushed back the door.

For a perceptible space of time he stood very still on the threshold with his arms outstretched as if to prevent any of the others from crossing it. Then he said in a voice unnaturally level and expressionless:

"He is in. But . . ." and turning a rather pale face over his shoulder, muttered under his breath: "Serafine dear, get your aunt away. And keep away yourself, I should."

"Is he dead?" asked Serafine with silent lips and eyes.

Christmas nodded, and Serafine turned away. As Dr. Merewether drew back a little to make way for her she thought she could feel the dark aura of fear, distress and tense excitement that surrounded his still figure. Her sharpened senses quivered at its contact, and it was with a sickening foreboding at her heart that she led Imogen, gently protesting, down the stairs.

CHAPTER III

AN OPEN WINDOW

THE back window was wide open and the room was full of thin fog. The rich, gorgeous colours of the old rugs that hung upon the walls seemed to swim and melt together in it. A great bronze Buddha in an alcove facing the door rose out of the fine drift as out of a cloud of incense. Mordby made an instinctive movement to shut the window, but Steen checked him.

" Better leave it for the police."

At the end of the long room farthest from the open window Gordon Frew sat at his writing-table. The table was littered with papers, and his head had fallen forward upon them as though he had gone quietly to sleep over his writing. But his arms were outstretched across the table not at all in the comfortable attitude of a sleeper, and his right hand still held a fountain-pen. He wore an amber-coloured dressing-gown, embroidered on the back and sleeves with strange flowers and birds of paradise in gilt and green. But in one place the embroidery was dyed dark crimson with a dye that seemed to have run into the amber silk . . . on to the brocade upholstery of the chair . . . on to the Persian prayer-rug on the floor.

" Look! " whispered Newtree. " The knife! "

From the embroidered silk under Frew's left shoulder-blade, where the crimson stain was deepest, protruded the long brass handle of a knife.

It was strange how silent the five men were as they approached that quiet figure. Even Mordby had nothing to say. There were no outcries of surprise, no exclamations of horror. It was as if the fog had laid stealthy fingers upon their lips and silenced them, as if they had stumbled here in this bizarre rich room upon the very fount of that evil of the fog of which Serafine had half-jestingly spoken. No one said a word until Dr. Merewether had lifted the heavy body in his arms and laid it back upon its chair. Then Laurence at least recoiled with a gasp of horror from the fixed open eyes and mouth that, staring upwards, seemed so dreadfully to accuse some invisible being.

There was revealed the firm fleshy face of a man in the prime of life, with dark strong beard and hair wired with grey; a face dreadfully white with white lips which showed square, yellowish teeth. The spatulate hands fell limply at each side of the chair, and the gold fountain-pen dropped to the rug.

Looking down upon that stony face, Merewether said in a low, steady voice:

"He's dead. There's nothing to be done for him."

Mordby muttered:

"The police . . ." and looked distractedly round the room for a telephone.

Although Merewether had spoken so quietly, he did not look the part of the inured, impersonal doctor. Glancing at him, John noted that small drops of sweat were standing on his forehead and that his eyes, which should have been so calm and professional, held an expression of intense anxiety, as though he were suffering torture.

Mordby, whose nerves were all on edge, cried irritably:

"Oh, this fog is horrible! Can't we shut the window? Oh, damn the exchange! Hullo! Hullo! Yes, the police, I tell you! Madox Court, Hurst Road!"

The study of nervous disorders had not, it seemed, had the effect of making the student immune from them. Or perhaps it was the fashionable doctrine of the evils of repression which prevented the fashionable doctor from repressing his excitement. He clung with frenzied desperation to the telephone, as though it were a galvanic battery, and when at last he tried to hang up the receiver, dropped it with a clatter on the table.

"Well?" he said then, turning sharply upon Merewether, who had finished his examination of the body and was standing quite still as though on guard over the dead. "What's the verdict?"

Merewether answered very quietly:

"Mr. Frew is dead. It is quite impossible that he should have killed himself. He has been murdered. About half an hour ago. By a long knife passed under the left shoulder-blade into the heart."

"Half an hour ago! That's an alibi for all of us!" began Mordby with a look of relief, and then broke off suddenly, leaving his sentence on a high, unfinished note, staring at his confrère. For a second the glances of the two doctors met like clashing swords.

"Yes," assented Merewether in a quiet, almost dreamy voice. "It is an alibi for all of us . . . except myself."

"Ah!" said Laurence, who had come to a halt in his restless prowling and stood looking up at the wall, "that's where the knife came from. I thought I'd seen that steel inlay on the handle before somewhere. See, Christmas. You can see the shape on the wall where it used to hang. Looks as if the murderer knew his way about here . . . or else the murder was unpremeditated."

Mordby and Merewether looked around to where he pointed and saw a faint outline like the ghost of a long straight knife where the hanging weapon had kept the light from the cream wall-paper. Christmas, however, did not turn. Both he and Sir Marion Steen were leaning out of the window, as though trying to distinguish some object in the fog. And even as Laurence uttered his name, John put a leg over the sill, heaved himself out, clung for a moment and vanished. They heard a scraping and slithering sound, the scratch of his shoes on some out-house roof, and then a thud as he landed in the passage below.

Merewether remained where he was, but Laurence and Mordby rushed to the window.

"There's somebody down there," said Steen, making room for them at the sill.

They could see the outline of the scullery roof below them, and the high wall at the other side of the passage and one . . . two dim figures moving in the fog below. There was a muffled gasp of terror, a cry, a scuffle, a sound of blows. A man's uncultivated voice with a note of anger blended with fear cried raucously:

"Let *go*, blast you! Oo-ooh! Let go! You're breaking my arm!"

And they heard John Christmas reply firmly:

"Now then, my man. Come along and give an account of yourself!"

Whimpering and protesting, the one dark figure was

hauled by the other up the passage-way from the road towards the back entrance to the building.

" Good for John," murmured Laurence approvingly. " But I hardly think he's got the right man. He'd be the other side of London by now."

" Not necessarily," replied Mordby, with a return of his old pomposity now that there seemed a prospect of the mystery being quickly cleared up. " The more cunning type would try to disarm suspicion by remaining in apparent ignorance close to the premises."

And he glanced at Merewether, who was sitting in an arm-chair by the writing table as if wrapped in thought.

A moment later John Christmas pushed his captive into the room; a slight, fine-featured young man with a weak, sullen face and ruffled fair hair that stood up in a cock's comb over his high, narrow forehead. Old Greenaway, Newtree's servant, followed them in and stood by the doorway wringing his hands and almost whimpering with distress.

" It's only my son, sir," he kept saying plaintively. " My son who valets—used to valet Mr. Frew, sir. He's been out all the evening at his mother's. Haven't you, Ernie? "

But John's captive made no reply. His weak blue eyes seemed to bulge at the sight of his master's body and he backed away, struggling violently in John's none-too-gentle hands.

" He's dead! " he cried hoarsely, struggling to turn away, yet looking with horrified fascination at the bulky body in the chair. " Dead! Who done it? "

There was a pause while he gave a gasp and seemed slowly to collect his thoughts. Then turning towards his father he flung out his hands with a curiously dramatic gesture, and cried in a broken voice:

" I never did it, Dad! By God I didn't! "

He looked wildly round and suddenly his face twitched and he burst into tears.

" The manic-depressive type," murmured Dr. Mordby, fingering his clean-shaven chin, to Laurence. " I should place very little credence in anything he may say."

" Oh, come! " said John not unkindly. " Pull your socks up. The police'll be here in a moment."

" The police! " whimpered the young man. " For me? I swear I never done it, sir! However black it may look against me, I never done it! Upon my oath, sir! "

" If you didn't do it, there's nothing to worry about," replied Christmas. " Don't make a show of yourself, and answer any questions sensibly, and you'll be all right."

As he spoke there came a loud, authoritative knocking on the entrance door below. Old Greenaway started, and went out of the room to perform his duties, but before he reached the stairs the sound of voices and heavy footsteps could be heard, and Serafine came up followed by the police-sergeant and two constables.

As they came in, ponderous and self-possessed, the mental atmosphere seemed to become in a moment a little clearer and steadier. The cool breath of the enduring workaday world seemed to blow lightly through the turgid atmosphere of horror and unreality. The sergeant examined the body with grave and stolid interest and made a few laconic, keen inquiries.

" Well, sir," he said at last to Laurence, " it's a case for the Yard, and if you'll allow me I'll get on the phone."

The valet, who had become very still at the entrance of the police, drew a sobbing breath as the officer lifted the receiver, and seemed to shrink together as if he wished to shrivel and vanish away from those alert, kindly, official eyes.

CHAPTER IV

INSPECTOR HEMBROW

"AND now, Sir Marion," said Detective-Inspector Hembrow, "will you please describe the man you met in Greentree Road?"

"Certainly, so far as I can. . . ."

Sir Marion cleared his throat and looked thoughtfully at the Inspector, as though seeking to conjure up in front of that officer's fresh, firm-lipped face the dim features he had seen for a moment in the fog. They were sitting in the tiny dining-room that led off Gordon Frew's beautiful studio, one on each side of the lacquered table. Here Inspector Hembrow was conducting his inquiries, interviewing the members of Newtree's party one by one. He had his note-book open on the table before him. Sir Marion sat back in his chair, placed his finger-tips lightly together and began rather uncertainly:

"I'm afraid I didn't notice him much in detail. But he was a smallish man, about my own height, but rather stouter, I should say. He had a dark skin——"

"How dark? Do you mean like an Indian's?"

"No. Like a dark European skin. Brownish. Sallow. He was wearing a dark overcoat, buttoned up close to the neck in an unusual way. And a fez."

"Gloves?"

"I didn't notice. He seemed to be a man of between

forty and fifty. He had a greyish dark moustache, and, I think, a slight cast in his eye—his left eye. And a gold tooth, the upper row, I fancy."

"Did he speak to you, Sir Marion?"

"Yes. As far as I remember, his words were: 'To Golders Green, please, how may I go?'"

"And?"

"I told him to take a No. 2 bus. The buses were running slowly, because of the fog, but there wasn't much disorganization. He bowed and smiled and walked on towards Wellington Road."

"H'm," said the Inspector thoughtfully. "And what time was this, Sir Marion?"

There was a pause, while Steen considered this point.

"I should say," he replied at length, "within a minute or two of ten past eight. The clock in Newtree's lobby pointed to the half-hour as I came in, and I should allow twenty minutes to walk from the point at which I met him to here."

"Can you tell me the exact point in Greentree Road where you met this man, Sir Marion?"

"Yes. It was just this side of Shipman's Mews."

"Thank you, Sir Marion. Your description tallies exactly with Dr. Merewether's, except for one point. You are more observant than the doctor. He didn't notice the cast in the eye."

Sir Marion smiled thoughtfully.

"I wouldn't swear to it myself, Inspector. It was just an impression—something oblique about the glance of the eye."

"Thank you, Sir Marion," said the Inspector smilingly, and bowed the great financier out.

" This looks as if it might be an interesting case," said Christmas, as Hembrow shut the door behind Sir Marion. At his own request and Hembrow's indulgence, he was acting in the capacity of an unofficial assistant to the Inspector, who was a friend of his. The two had been friends since three or four years before, when Hembrow had been sent to investigate a daring and well-planned robbery from the safes at the Christmas Stores. Christmas, who had then had a lazy, dilettante interest in criminal investigation, had in fact helped the Inspector a good deal, and Hembrow had never forgotten that had it not been for one or two inspirations of John's all his patient and thorough investigations might have ended lamentably in a blind alley. John's arbitrary, amateur and sweeping methods of deduction had amused Hembrow at first, but in the end he had found himself in debt to them; and the friendship had persisted and been cemented a year later during the course of the extraordinary affair known as the Museum murder, which had opened with the discovery in the early hours of the morning of a well-known journalist lying dead under a table in the British Museum reading-room. Hembrow's unravelling of this affair had been a masterpiece of skilfully-collected and co-ordinated evidence, which had gained him much kudos with his superiors. But it had been Christmas who had first detected the forged post-mark which had formed the nucleus of the whole intricate web; and Hembrow had accordingly come to have a certain respect for the abilities of his amateur assistant, although he was never tired of reminding him that to jump to the right conclusion was a very different thing from proving its rightness.

" Seems to be quite straightforward at present," he said now, with a smile. " But one never knows. I think

I'll take a statement from the servant next. . . . He's got something to hide, I fancy."

Old Greenaway came into the room looking pale and harassed, and at the Inspector's invitation sat down submissively with an air of abandoning himself to fate.

"Now, Mr. Greenaway," said Hembrow briskly, "will you tell us what you know of this affair, please?"

The old man hesitated, with a strained, puzzled look on his face. It was plain he did not know where to begin. Finally, moistening his lips, he stammered:

"Well, sir, I was in Mr. Newtree's pantry getting a tray of glasses together when I heard a noise—hammering and banging on the landing, sir. So I went up to see what was wrong."

"Did you know that Mr. Newtree and his guests had gone up to see Mr. Frew?"

"Yes, sir. And when I heard the hammering I guessed they was trying to break into the flat, sir. And at once I thought of the Oriental gentleman. . . ."

Hembrow said impassively:

"Oh. The Oriental gentleman. What Oriental gentleman?"

"The Oriental gentleman as came this evening to see Mr. Frew, sir."

"Did you see this gentleman?"

"Yes, sir," replied the old servant, with more assurance than he had yet shown, speaking, in fact, quite eagerly. "I'd just been in to Mr. Newtree's studio with some logs, sir, and was going out with the scuttle when I met him in the hall doorway, sir."

"What doorway?"

"The front door of the building, sir. I was going to the outhouse with the scuttle to fetch some more coal."

" What time was this? "

" I couldn't say to the minute, sir, but round about half-past seven. And at five minutes to eight by the kitchen clock I heard footsteps coming down which I took to be the same gentleman leaving, sir."

" You didn't see him leaving? "

" No, sir."

" Well, Mr. Greenaway, please describe in as much detail as possible the man you met in the front doorway."

" It was a short, dark gentleman, sir," began Greenaway eagerly, " just an inch or so shorter than what I am. He looked like a Turkish gentleman to me. He had a queer red hat like Turks wear in pictures, and a black overcoat done up to the neck. He was a stoutish gentleman, sir, with a little greyish-black moustache, and a gold filling in one of his front teeth, sir."

" Did he speak to you? "

" No, sir."

" How did you notice the gold filling, then? "

" He smiled at me, sir, and bowed, and stood back, like, in the doorway."

" Any other peculiarities? I mean did you notice a mole, say, or a scar, or a squint, or anything of that kind? "

Greenaway paused, then:

" No, sir," he said rather regretfully, as if he would dearly have loved to embroider his description. " But I thought at the time he looked—well, sinister-like, sir, for all he smiled so friendly."

Hembrow caught John's eye and gave a fleeting smile. He was used to this sort of wisdom after the event.

" Mr. Frew have any other visitors this evening, so far as you know? "

" There was the young woman, sir," said Greenaway, with an indescribable note of hostility in his voice. " But she didn't stay long."

" Young woman? Did you see her? "

" Yes, sir. It was Miss Shirley, the model who poses for Mr. Frew, and sometimes for Mr. Newtree, sir. She came soon after the Oriental gentleman. I met her in the hall as I came back with the coal. And again when she came down after a few moments. . . ."

" Did she speak to you? Come, Mr. Greenaway, you must remember that! What did she say? "

Greenaway looked unhappy. Two faint patches of red appeared in his thin cheeks, and he fidgeted restlessly in his chair.

" I—nothing important, sir."

" That's for me to judge. Come, come. Don't waste my time."

The old man cleared his throat and mumbled unwillingly:

" Well, we aren't too friendly, sir, her and me, owing to the way she's treated my boy. She said as she came down the stairs: ' Hullo, Daddy! How's your blue-eyed boy? Give him my love, but not my address.' "

" And you replied? "

" I didn't say anything, sir," Greenaway answered with some dignity, " not wishing to start her being loud and abusive outside Mr. Newtree's door, sir."

" Very discreet of you, Greenaway. Does Mr. Frew usually do his painting in the evening by artificial light? "

" I couldn't say, sir."

" I was only thinking Miss Shirley couldn't have been coming for a sitting so late in the evening."

Greenaway looked stiffly into space.

" I couldn't say, sir. But I was glad when she broke off with my boy. She—she's not a good girl, sir." He added: " And Mr. Newtree says she's not a good model, either. He only had her the twice when his usual model had the flu. And he said—well, he expressed himself strongly, sir."

" Oh? " murmured Hembrow encouragingly.

" He said," went on Greenaway, obviously glad to relieve his feelings and express his opinion of Miss Shirley thus vicariously, " he said: ' A whole damn wasted morning! If that damn girl's a professional model I'll eat all the Chinese white.' "

Hembrow laughed and was silent for a moment, playing with his pencil. Then with an abstracted frown he asked casually:

" And now, Mr. Greenaway, do you mind telling me when your son last threatened to murder his employer? "

Christmas gave a start of surprise, and glanced up in time to see all expression fade from Greenaway's face. For a second the old man stared blankly, open-lipped, dark-eyed, at his interrogator. Only for a second. Then a look of fear and agony swept over his face, and he pushed his chair back and impulsively half-rose to his feet, opening and shutting his white lips and fascinatedly staring at Hembrow's face as a bird is said to stare hypnotized at a snake. His throat moved convulsively as though he were trying to swallow something.

" Sir—sir——" he stammered piteously at last, and looked wildly round as though for some way of escape.

" Come, come," said Hembrow gently. " Don't be so alarmed, Mr. Greenaway. I may tell you for your comfort that the people who threaten murder are not often the ones that commit it. Your son did threaten to murder his employer, then?"

"Oh, sir!" cried Greenaway pitifully, with a contorted face. "He wouldn't hurt a soul, my son wouldn't! Why, the very sight of blood turns him queer, always has, if it's only a cut finger! Oh, sir! You're not going to take poor Ernest? It'd break his mother's heart to hear such a thing had even been thought of him! Why——"

"Sit down, Mr. Greenaway," said the Inspector quietly, "and answer my questions properly. It's the best thing you can do for your son."

The old man subsided limply into a chair.

"You know, sir," he said in a broken voice, looking helplessly from Hembrow to Christmas, "how wild young men talk when they're crossed in love. It used to fret me to hear him, but there, I thought, all smoke and no fire . . . that's always been the way with my boy."

"Your son and Miss Shirley were friends, then, at one time?"

"They were keeping comp'ny, sir, until about two months ago. We were expecting as my boy was going to settle down at last, though we could have wished it'd been with a different girl. We never liked the girl, Pandora as she called herself, my wife and me didn't. We saw as she was the flashy kind as never makes a good wife, sir. Still, we didn't do nothing to stop the affair, and 'twouldn't have been no good if we had, sir, Ernie being head over ears in love. Ernie was always one to go to extremes—not," added the old man fearfully, "in what he does, but in what he feels, sir. Then two months ago she gave him the chuck, and he was fairly heart-broken, threatening suicide and that. And then when he found—

when he guessed—when she kept coming to Mr. Frew's studio, sir, he took it into his head as there was something wrong, and he got desperate with jealousy and that, sir. I kept advising him to leave and take another place and forget the girl, sir. But he didn't seem as if he could keep away from where she was . . . and . . . and . . . Oh, sir! If everybody as ever threatened to do a murder were to do it, sir, the world'd be full of corpses, pretty near!"

Hembrow smiled as he dismissed him, and his smile seemed to put a little heart into the old servant. He lingered in the doorway a moment, looking wistfully at Hembrow as if he would give ten years of his life to be able to read his thoughts. Then he went slowly out with a bent head.

Ernest Greenaway was the last on the Inspector's list. He looked pale and sullen and sank heavily down into the chair like a lifeless thing, and remained looking stonily at the carpet. Christmas looked keenly at him, noting the slack lips, the narrow forehead, the coxcombry of his clothes. Here was an emotional young weakling, degenerate both in physique and character from old Greenaway's simple, sturdy, self-respecting type.

"You are Ernest Greenaway?" asked Hembrow briskly.

"Yes."

"You were valet to Mr. Frew?"

"Yes."

"For how long?"

"Since last January."

"Ten months. Did you come to Mr. Frew through an agency or on a personal recommendation?"

"My father got me the job."

"Mr. Frew had not been here long when you entered his service?"

"A week or two."

"Were you in the deceased's confidence at all?"

An ugly look came into the young man's face. His chin came a little forward and the corners of his slack mouth drew down. He continued to look obstinately at the floor.

"No, I wasn't."

"Did he treat you well? Give you a fairly easy time?"

"Yes."

"Did he entertain here much?"

"No. Not at all."

"No callers at all?"

"Oh, callers!" muttered the young man. "Yes. Queer birds, some of them."

"Queer birds!" echoed Hembrow meditatively. "Now what do you mean by queer birds?"

The young man shrugged his slight shoulders, then replied with a sort of self-conscious rudeness:

"Oh, greasy old Ikes and second-hand dealers. The place is full of their junk."

"Mr. Frew was a connoisseur?"

"Thought he was, I suppose," muttered the young man.

"Some of the things in his collection are of great value, no doubt?"

Greenaway hesitated, with a spiteful look on his weak face, as if his instinct was to depreciate the value of anything connected with his late master. Then he shrugged indifferently.

"I dare say."

"Are they catalogued?"

"Couldn't say, I'm sure."

" What time did you leave the flat this evening? "

" About seven."

" Was it your regular evening off? "

" No. My mother hasn't been well, and Mr. Frew said I could go and see her and spend the evening."

" Where does your mother live? "

" In Church Street, off the Edgware Road."

" And you went straight there? "

Greenaway shifted his position slightly, and a hunted look appeared on his moody features.

" N-no. No, I didn't."

" Where did you go? "

The valet's eyes flickered from one side of the room to the other. He licked his lips.

" Just hung about."

Hembrow raised his eyebrows.

" Hung about this building, do you mean? "

" Yes," mumbled the other, swallowing a lump in his throat.

" For how long? "

" 'Bout three-quarters of an hour."

" You hung about the house on an evening like this for three-quarters of an hour? Why? "

" Do'know," said the valet with the baffled, dispirited air of one who will not tell the truth and has not the wit to think of a plausible lie.

" During the time you were hanging about the house did you see anybody enter it? "

" Dozens."

" Dozens? Come, answer me properly, Mr. Greenaway! How many? "

" Well," said the young man sulkily, " there was Mr. Christmas first and two ladies with him. And then a stoutish chap in a top hat and cloak—Dr. Mordby, I think he calls himself. And then my father carrying a bucket of wood. And then a queer bird in a fez."

"That all?"

A curious stubborn and desperate look came into the valet's light eyes. He mumbled:

"Yes."

"Are you sure, Mr. Greenaway?"

"Yes."

"And did you see any of them come out again?"

"No—only my father. He came out for a scuttle of coal and went in again."

"Where did you go when you had finished hanging about here?"

"Went down the road and turned into Greentree Road and walked up and down."

"Really, Mr. Greenaway, a most extraordinary way of spending an evening in unwholesome weather like this! Why did you not go to your mother's?"

The lad looked flickeringly round the room, keeping his eyes lowered, as though hoping to find some convenient lie written miraculously on the carpet. At last he said heavily:

"Do'know. Didn't feel like it."

"And while you were walking up and down the road did you pass anybody on the pavement?"

"No. Saw one or two people on the opposite side of the road, but it was too foggy to see who they were."

"And how long did you go on walking up and down?"

"Oh, Lord!" muttered the young man, licking his dry lips, "I don't know! I didn't look at my watch. If I'd known I was going to be asked questions, p'r'aps I should have done. Can't a person do what he likes on his evening off? "

His voice rose on a rather hysterical note. Hembrow went on calmly :

" Well. What did you do afterwards? "

" Went for a walk."

" Where? "

" Up towards Hampstead, I think."

" You *think!* Come, Mr. Greenaway! "

" It was foggy," said the young man with a sort of weary obstinacy. " I was thinking. I didn't notice where I was going. I know I turned north out of Greentree Road, but I don't know where I went after that. Then I came back to come in at about half-past nine, and Mr. Christmas jumped on me and tried to kill me in the passage."

" Oh," said the Inspector thoughtfully. " Just one more thing. The man in the fez whom you saw going in at the front door. Had he ever visited Mr. Frew before as far as you know? "

" Don't think so. I didn't see him much in the fog. Only when he pushed open the door and the light fell on his face. But I don't recollect ever seeing him before."

There was a pause while Hembrow looked through his notes, and Greenaway watched him with a furtive, sullen look on his worn young face.

" Will you answer me a question? " asked John Christmas, leaning forward. " Did you ask your employer for permission to go out this evening? "

The young man flushed unaccountably and looked at John with suspicious, narrow eyes.

" No, sir, I didn't," he replied surlily. " I didn't

know I was to have the evening off till about a quarter to seven, when the master called me in and said he wouldn't be wanting me this evening, and I could go and see how my ma was."

" Do you know whether your master was expecting any visitors this evening? "

Greenaway answered with a sort of savage brusqueness :

" No, I don't."

" Had he a telephone call or a telegram before he gave you permission to go out? "

" Not that I know of," answered the valet a little less inimically. He added : " The evening post came in about a quarter to seven. I'd just taken him his letters when he called me back and told me I could go out."

" Do you remember," asked John, " how many letters there were? "

" Yes," said the young man sulkily, " there were three. One of them was a bill or something in a halfpenny envelope, and then there was a type-written envelope with a crest on the back and the College of Arms, or something, written on it. And there was a letter in a little grey envelope. But you won't find that, because Mr. Frew was just tearing it in bits and throwing it in the fire when he called me in."

" Thank you," said Christmas, looking interrogatively at the Inspector, who nodded to Greenaway to go.

" That was a good point, Mr. Christmas," said Hembrow approvingly, shutting his note-book. " Looks as if the deceased was expecting one of his visitors, anyhow —probably the girl. Though it seems queer, if he was expecting her, that she should only stay a few minutes, as according to old Greenaway's evidence she did. That young man seems to have kept an observant eye on his master's correspondence, by the way, which may be useful to us, but isn't altogether to his own credit."

"Natural, though, in the circumstances."

"You mean——"

"That Miss Pandora Shirley probably corresponded with Frew occasionally, although, as Newtree tells me, she lives quite close by in Greentree Road. The vagaries of Miss Shirley, in fact, may account quite satisfactorily for young Greenaway's nocturnal wanderings and all the rest of his rather fishy story. I wonder, by the way, on which side of the road she lives?"

"Her address," said Hembrow, turning over the leaves of his note-book, "is No. 14 Greentree Road."

"No. 14," repeated Christmas thoughtfully. "Yes, the even numbers are on the north side of the road, and it was on the north side that young Greenaway walked up and down for a period of time he didn't seem able to specify."

"Come, Mr. Christmas," protested Hembrow good-humouredly, slipping his note-book into his pocket and rising to his feet. "We have only young Greenaway's own word for it that he did anything of the kind. In my opinion—however, it's too early yet to have an opinion, and far too early to state one, even to an old friend like yourself, Mr. Christmas!"

CHAPTER V

WHEN DOCTORS DISAGREE

"THE other gentlemen and the ladies have gone home, I see," observed Hembrow approvingly, as he and Christmas re-entered the studio. "Glad they had so much sense. Generally at times like these everybody in the place wants to hang around and behave like Sherlock Holmes."

Laurence, who was bending over the writing-table looking through a pocket magnifying-glass at some sheets of paper lying there, looked up at this remark with a rather abashed smile. He murmured:

"Yes, it's queer the fascination these things have for ordinary peaceable folk like me. I suppose Mordby would say it was the primitive blood-lust finding an outlet."

He had had, in fact, great difficulty in persuading Serafine to go home, and only the piteous protests of Imogen Wimpole, who was beginning to fear the effect on her health and beauty of all this excitement, had at last driven the younger lady forth in search of a taxi. Mordby had offered to escort them with alacrity. He preferred, apparently, to study the psychology of murder from text-books rather than at first hand, and seemed possessed with the plain, respectable man's earnest determination not to get mixed up in anything unpleasant. He had taken it for granted that Sir Marion Steen would accompany them, and Sir Marion, although it seemed to Laurence that he would have preferred to stay and watch the police investigations, had offered no objection. Mordby had shepherded him out with the air of a champion bearing off a trophy.

" Taken those photographs? " asked Hembrow of his assistant, who was packing away a large camera. " Good. You might photograph the room as well from every possible angle. I have an idea, Mr. Christmas, we shall find robbery mixed up in this."

Laurence Newtree looked thoughtfully around the walls which had almost the appearance of a museum, so draped they were with embroidered hangings and rugs, so hung with queer weapons, masks and mirrors.

" It all looks much as usual," he murmured. " If it was a burglary, the thief has left a great deal of valuable stuff behind him. That missal, for instance, must be worth several hundred pounds. . . ."

" That could easily be explained," said Hembrow. " Either the thief was after one particular object of great value and preferred to lessen the risk by leaving all the lesser treasures behind, or he was after money and did not know the value of all this stuff."

" If we can find out what has been stolen, then," said Laurence, " we shall have some idea of the kind of man the murderer was."

Inspector Hembrow, who was engaged in dusting a fine yellow powder over the handle of the dagger that had killed Gordon Frew, smiled a little at Newtree's eager tone. He blew the surplus powder gently away and examined the weapon intently through a magnifying-glass. After a moment he gave an exclamation of disgust.

" Gloves," he uttered shortly. " The murderer knew

his business. Wait a bit! That's queer! There are no marks on the handle, but a very distinct thumb-mark on the blade, about two inches down—and a finger-print to correspond on the other side."

Holding the weapon carefully by the ornate inlaid handle, he showed his discovery to John, who had been watching him with much attention. Plainly printed in the fine powder were the intricate loops and spirals that show on the skin of a thumb or finger.

"I'm afraid these won't help us to the murderer, Mr. Christmas. There are only the two—thumb and the side of a forefinger, and they're placed in such a way as to suggest that the person they belong to was holding the dagger-point towards himself."

"It would certainly be quite impossible to stab a man with a knife held in such a way," agreed John. "The thumb-print runs at a slight slant towards the handle."

"Probably they were made at some time when the weapon was taken down and dusted," commented the detective. He compared them rapidly with a set of the dead man's finger-prints which had been taken by his assistant soon after their arrival.

"Thought so," he commented, laying the knife down. "They're the deceased's own thumb-prints. Well, that doesn't get us much farther. Except that as the murderer evidently took the precaution of wearing gloves, it's fairly safe to assume that this was a premeditated crime. . . . There's no need for you to wait any longer, Sergeant," added Hembrow to the local man who had been first on the spot. "Get your men to remove the body to the mortuary. You can go, too, Collings, if you've got those photographs."

Laurence gave a sigh of relief when the door had finally

closed behind the three officers and the arm-chair by the desk stood empty. The dark, oppressive atmosphere seemed to lift a little now that the blank white face of the murdered man no longer dumbly accused the unknown. He watched with interest Hembrow's methodical examination of the papers on the desk, and was surprised on glancing at Christmas to see that he did not appear equally interested. The eccentric young man had taken a silver pencil-case from his pocket and was holding it out gravely between his finger and thumb.

"What on earth are you doing, John?" asked Laurence, absentmindedly taking the pencil thus held out towards him, divided between his interest in the detective's quick, methodical procedure with the papers and his surprise at his friend's peculiar behaviour.

John's grave face relaxed. He smiled.

"Just thinking," he replied. "Thinking that if one were dusting an edged weapon or otherwise fingering it one would naturally take it by the handle, not by the blade, which is extremely sharp."

"I suppose one would," assented Newtree, "unless, of course, one wanted to examine the handle. . . . What am I to do with this pencil you've given me, I'd like to know?"

"Give it back again," said John with a smile, holding out his hand. "Thank you for taking it from me so meekly."

He put it back in his pocket and seemed to forget about it, strolling over to where the Divisional-Surgeon, a small Scotsman of brisk and cheerful aspect, was packing his bag preparatory to departure.

"Plain case, isn't it, Doctor?"

"Of murder? Oh, yes! But——" He hesitated

and looked apologetically through his glasses at Merewether, who was sitting near the writing-table and watching Hembrow with a stoical and indifferent air. Then, addressing the Inspector in a brisk, official tone he went on: " It is my duty to state that had it not been for the fact that Dr. Merewether saw the deceased alive soon after nine o'clock, I should have put his death at least an hour earlier than that."

All eyes turned instinctively to Merewether, the Inspector's in a brief, keen glance.

" Putting aside for the moment Dr. Merewether's evidence on that point. Would it occur to you on examining the body that there was a possibility of death having taken place between nine and half-past? "

" N-no. Frankly, it would not," replied the police-surgeon uncomfortably, with another rather deprecating glance at his silent colleague.

" Do you find anything positively incompatible with death having taken place after nine? "

" Well . . . yes. Yes," said the little doctor, gathering courage, " I do. When I first examined the body at a quarter-past ten the blood had already clotted considerably in the neighbourhood of the wound—very much more so than I should have expected to find it had the death taken place only an hour before. The small drops of blood which had fallen upon the parquet floor were completely dried. I should have thought it impossible that they should have dried within an hour. However——"

" Now, Dr. Merewether," said Hembrow in a kind but business-like tone. " A good deal hangs on this. Can you swear that the man who opened the door to you at nine o'clock was the deceased himself? You thought it was at the time. But think. Don't answer in a hurry. Try to revisualize the man as he opened the door. Are you positive of his identity?"

"Absolutely."

"Could it not have been a brother or somebody bearing a strong resemblance to the deceased? Or somebody impersonating him?"

"The man who opened the door to me at nine o'clock," said Merewether with a sort of weary firmness, "was Gordon Frew, and no one else."

"You were well acquainted with his appearance?" persisted Hembrow.

"Yes. As I have told you already, Inspector, I attended him last April during a prolonged attack of influenza. I assure you I am not mistaken. The man I saw was Gordon Frew. I would swear to it anywhere, at any time, in any court——"

His voice rose queerly, and he broke off abruptly, as if he were afraid he was about to lose control of himself. This sudden ascent into rhetoric was so unlike the Merewether he knew that Laurence looked at him in amazement. Merewether looked back at him and round at the other faces with a queer, defiant smile. There was a pause.

"Well," said the police-surgeon amiably at last, "I'll be getting back, Hembrow. Can I give anybody a lift?"

"If I may," said Merewether, regaining his urbanity with a visible effort and looking questioningly at Hembrow, "I will accompany you. If there is nothing more I can do, Inspector?"

"That's all right, Doctor," replied Hembrow, looking stolidly, but, as Christmas knew, very observantly, at the pale, set face. "There's nothing more."

He glanced at John with a slight lift of his eyebrows as the two medicoes left the room.

"Seems a bit rattled, for a medical man," he observed, resuming his examination of the papers on the desk. "They're not usually so put out by a little matter of a murder or so. Friend of the deceased?"

"No, I don't think so," replied Laurence, looking as puzzled as he felt. "Apart from having attended him professionally and meeting him once or twice at my place, I don't think he knew him at all."

"Oh, well!" said the Inspector in a casual tone. "Perhaps he was annoyed at our man seeming to question his evidence. . . . Hullo! Mr. Frew seems to have been writing a book." He lifted the top page of a pile of manuscript lying face downwards in a shallow basket. "This sheet, which seems to be the last, is numbered eighty-seven, and the one underneath it is number eighty-six."

He took up the pile of manuscript and flicked it through.

"'People and Places,'" he read from the neatly-written title-page. "'A Record of an Adventurous Career.' Seems to be a sort of book of reminiscences. Everybody writes them nowadays."

"If they're true reminiscences, they ought to be very interesting," observed Laurence. "Gordon Frew had an eventful life, according to his own account."

"Unfortunately," said Christmas, who had been raking carefully among the ashes and cooling cinders in the fire-place, "the capacity to live an eventful life and the ability to write about it don't often go together. Gordon Frew's book on Persia was really one of the dullest works I have ever run across. And I see," added Christmas, glancing at a letter which lay in the basket from which Hembrow had removed the manuscript, "that even to produce that masterpiece he had to have a good deal of assistance."

Hembrow picked up the letter and read it through, then handed it to Laurence. It was a note written on the cheapest block paper but in a good clear hand to remind Mr. Frew, after many compliments and apologies, that he owed the writer the sum of twenty pounds in consideration of the manuscript "The Soul of Persia" re-cast, re-written, and duly delivered to Mr. Frew.

"*I am sorry to trouble you with this small matter so soon after the delivery of the manuscript,*" *the letter ended,* "*but the fact is that I am rather pressed at the moment, and the money would be most acceptable to pay one or two creditors who are becoming rather troublesome. With all best wishes for the success of the book, believe me,*

"*Yours very truly,*

"GILBERT COLD."

"Poor devil!" said Christmas, making a note of the address. "Some mute, inglorious Milton making a poor living by licking into shape the effusions of the illiterate rich!"

"Hardly likely to know anything about the murderer, is he?" remarked Newtree.

"No. But having for his sins read through one of Frew's own original untouched compositions, he may know something quite interesting about the murdered. And the more one knows of a man, the more one knows of his murderer."

Hembrow laughed.

"At your old theories, Mr. Christmas!" he observed good-humouredly. "I believe you'd hang a man because you thought he was the sort of man who'd be likely to murder the sort of man you took the victim to be!"

"I shouldn't be quite so arbitrary as to hang him," said John gravely. "But I should inquire very closely into his history."

"Well, it's early to say," remarked Hembrow cheerfully. "But my feeling at present is that we shan't have far to look for the murderer."

"And mine," said Christmas, looking thoughtfully at a scrap of charred paper he held in his hand, "is that we shan't have to look too near."

Hembrow smiled indulgently.

"Ah, you don't like the obvious thing, do you, Mr. Christmas! When you've had as much experience of this game as I have, you'll know that when the obvious means and the obvious motive stare one in the face, the obvious man's probably the murderer. Life isn't so much like plays and novels as you clever gentlemen think."

"Is the motive so obvious?" asked Christmas dreamily.

"Robbery and a woman," replied Hembrow succinctly. "Motive of ninety-five per cent. of the murders that get themselves committed, one or other of them. Here we have certainly one, and possibly the other as well."

"And yet, you know, young Greenaway's story rings so true. His behaviour, as recorded by himself, seems so natural."

The Inspector stared at his friend, then laughed.

"You're joking, aren't you, Mr. Christmas? If you think it natural for a servant who's been given an unexpected evening off to spend half of it hanging around his master's front door and the other half of it walking up and down in a thick fog—well, I don't, Mr. Christmas!"

"But consider the circumstances, Hembrow, and the state of mind of the man we have to deal with. Young Greenaway is obviously a weak emotional character of the type easily thrown off its balance by an unhappy love affair."

"Exactly," interpolated the Inspector grimly.

"But one moment, Hembrow. Now consider his evidence. He is given an unexpected evening off. What are his natural suspicions in the circumstances? That Frew expects a visit from Pandora Shirley. Instead of going home or otherwise amusing himself, he, in his own words, hung about the house for three-quarters of an hour. Why? To watch for the arrival of Pandora Shirley. After three-quarters of an hour, in other words at about a quarter to eight, he left Madox Court and walked up and down Greentree Road. According to old Greenaway's evidence, Miss Shirley left the building at about a quarter to eight. Isn't it fairly obvious that the young man watched her in, watched her out, followed her home and walked up and down the road she lived in to make sure she did not go out again?"

"You're forgetting, Mr. Christmas, that by his own account Ernest Greenaway did not wait to see Shirley enter the building. The last person he saw enter the court was the man in the fez."

"But my dear Hembrow," protested John gently, "do remember that a murder has been committed, and that I am presuming young Greenaway knows nothing about it. For all he knew, Pandora Shirley might herself have been the murderess. His suppression of the fact that he had seen her enter Madox Court was a laudable, if not very well-considered, attempt to shield her."

Hembrow looked thoughtfully at his friend for a moment.

"Well," he said at length non-committally, "if Greenaway's story is true, it oughtn't to be difficult to get corroboration of it. There's a taxi-rank in Greentree Road, and one or two of the drivers will probably be able to tell us whether they saw a man walking up and down between eight and nine o'clock. . . . Is that a piece of the letter that was burnt you've got there, Mr. Christmas? "

"The only piece, unfortunately, that remains," said Christmas, handing the Inspector a small torn fragment of greyish paper, slightly charred at one edge. "But it's not uninteresting. The complete letter would have told us quite a lot, I fancy, if Frew hadn't so inconsiderately burnt it."

"Queer writing," commented Hembrow, and indeed the hand, though small and fairly legible, was peculiarly loose, straggly and ill-formed. "Looks as if it had been written in a hurry. Let's see what we can make of it."

The fragment measured about a square inch and a half, and appeared to have been torn from the middle of the page, showing torn edges all round. On one side were the words, or parts of words: "or God's sa," and underneath "tolerable posi." On the other side, more informatively, the words "bout eight o'cl," and, on the second line, clear and distinct, three complete words: "risk. The fog. '

"This is certainly tantalizing," commented Hembrow, studying the broken words with knitted brows. "It's fairly obvious, of course, that the first line represents 'For God's sake,' but the 'tolerable' something doesn't convey much."

"You notice, though," said John, "that the 't' of 'tolerable,' starts with a long up-stroke. Very few English people decorate their 't's' like that. It looks to me as if the 't' were not at the beginning of the word, but somewhere in the middle. As if the whole word, in fact, were not 'tolerable,' but 'intolerable.' And the next word, I take it, will be 'position.' 'For God's sake let us end this intolerable position,' is the sentence that comes naturally into one's mind."

"Yes," assented the Inspector. "You're probably right there, Mr. Christmas. And the back of the paper would give one the impression that something was going to happen at eight o'clock that would involve risk, and that the fog—by the way, at what time did this fog come on?"

"Soon after three," replied Laurence promptly. "At ten past three I had to turn on the light. I looked at my watch because I was surprised it was getting dark so early. And then I saw it was a fog coming up."

"H'm," said Hembrow. "In that case the letter must have been posted fairly near at hand—or else the writer had the gift of prophecy, and I don't think we need trouble ourselves with that supposition!"

He laid the scrap of paper carefully in his pocket-book and put it away for later reference, and returned to his methodical search through the papers in the drawers of the dead man's desk.

"Deceased," he observed conversationally, "seems to have made a habit of burning his letters. It's a funny thing, but I haven't found a single personal letter of any kind among all this stuff. Files and files of receipts and bills and press-cuttings, all very orderly. But not a line in the way of a private letter. Plenty of cards for picture-shows and catalogues of exhibitions, but nothing that really throws much light on the dead man's affairs."

"There's a good deal to throw light on the dead man's character," observed John, "which is the next best thing. This book of press-cuttings, for instance, so beautifully bound in morocco. He was a vain man."

"Dash it, John," said Newtree, looking a little pained.

" You can't call a man vain just because he keeps press-cuttings about himself. Lots of people do. I do it myself, in fact."

John smiled.

" But just have a look through these press-cuttings, Laurence, and you'll see what I mean. What's the first thing that strikes you about them? "

" That there aren't very many," said Laurence promptly.

" And the second? "

" That they're mostly from provincial papers, and all appreciative—gushing would be a better word."

" Yet Frew's book on Persia had a good many reviews from London papers, and was not at all well received on the whole. It's obvious that he discarded all the more unsympathetic criticisms and kept only those which pleased his vanity. In other words, that he was a vain man."

" And much good may that conclusion do you, Mr. Christmas," said Hembrow with a smile, as he whipped open a secret drawer and took from it a cheque-book and several small piles of used cheques neatly banded with india-rubber.

John returned his friend's smile and went on blandly to Newtree:

" In fact, I should say that our late friend was a pretty considerable poseur. He posed as a writer, but he did not write his own books. He posed as a painter, but whether he could paint or not you know better than I."

" Well," said Laurence slowly, " he had a good feeling for colour, of course—but——"

" Exactly. He posed as a connoisseur, but——" John looked slowly around the richly-hung and decorated room. " Doesn't it strike you that there's something rather curious about this collection? "

" Well," said Laurence again, " some of the things are very beautiful, and some are obviously valuable, but of course one can see that they're not very well arranged. In fact, they're in an awful muddle."

" Just so. They suggest an ignorant indiscriminate collector rather than a connoisseur. They're not only badly arranged, but some of them are trash. Those cast, and badly-cast, bronze altar candlesticks, for instance, which have certainly never been near an altar. There's a whole library of books on art in this bookcase, but——" and John rapidly took out three or four volumes and glanced through them, " most of the books are uncut. What do you make of that, Laurence? "

" I suppose, that he hadn't had time to read them."

" A man may buy a few books that he hasn't time to read," said John, continuing to take volumes from the shelves, open them, run through the pages with his thumb and put them back, " but he doesn't buy hundreds and not have time to read one. Inclination was lacking, I think, rather than time."

" I don't see why anybody should buy all these books—jolly expensive, some of them—if he didn't intend to read them," said Laurence, looking with rather an envious eye at the well-stocked shelves.

" Oh, well! " said John lightly, closing the glass doors and brushing the dust from his fingers. " They look nice in the shelves, don't they? " He stood back with his head on one side and contemplated the rich and attractive array. " And remember, Laurence, that Frew was a vain man."

So saying, he left Laurence looking covetously at vellum and gilding, and went over to the writing-table, where Hembrow was looking through the counter-foils of the dead man's cheque-book. He had begun to examine with great care a large piece of white blotting-paper which had lain under the dead man's body, when Hembrow exclaimed in a puzzled tone:

"This is queer! May 1, Emily Rudgwick, ten pounds; June 1, Emily Rudgwick, ten pounds; July 1, Emily Rudgwick, ten pounds. And so on up to November 1. A monthly allowance, apparently. Starting on May 1 this year."

"Some poor relation or other dependent, perhaps. Why is it queer, Hembrow?"

"The queer thing," answered Hembrow slowly, "is the name. Emily Rudgwick. I came across an Emily Rudgwick about ten years ago, when I was first promoted. I've good cause to remember her, too, for when I arrested her she gave me a black eye, which did her more harm in the end than it did me. Blackmail's quite serious enough in itself without having a charge of assaulting the police added on to it." Hembrow smiled, and then looked grave as he resumed: "I wonder if it is the same woman. She's a notorious fence, and as clever as they make them. This little allowance of ten pounds a month certainly needs looking into."

Christmas, who had been listening attentively, asked:

"Did you find the other letters that were delivered here this evening, Inspector? There was a receipt, according to young Greenaway, and an official letter from the College of Arms."

Hembrow shook his head.

"I'm afraid the letter went into the fire with the other one, Mr. Christmas. There's not a sign of it. The half-penny envelope is here, with its contents, but it's only a bookseller's receipt, and of no interest to us."

Christmas took the thin envelope the Inspector handed him and drew out a slip of paper headed with the name and address of a bookseller in Charing Cross Road.

"Now what in the world," he asked, "did the late Mr. Frew want Fraser's 'Law of Libel and Slander' for? Was he going to pose as a lawyer, as well as a connoisseur of the arts? A queer addition to that library of illustrated books! Just have a look in the shelves, Laurence, and see if it's actually there."

"Yes," said Laurence after a moment, pulling a discreet and sober volume out from among its magnificent neighbours. "Here it is. And, I say, John, every page is cut, so you can't say old Frew didn't read any of his books."

"So here," commented John slowly, "we have a connoisseur who left the Life of Benvenuto Cellini uncut on his shelves while he devoured in a few days the whole of a volume on the laws of libel. This is a queer case, Laurence. And the queerest thing in it is the character of the dead man."

He returned to the contemplation of the piece of blotting-paper, raising his head after a moment to remark:

"I wish very much that we knew what had happened to that communication from the College of Arms."

"I'm afraid there's not very much doubt what has happened to it, Mr. Christmas. It was obviously a habit of the deceased to burn his correspondence."

"And yet," said John, "even a man who habitually burns his letters does not as a rule burn them until he has answered them."

"This particular letter may not have required an answer," Hembrow pointed out.

"And yet it has been answered," said Christmas gently. "And I should also like very much to know what has happened to the answer. For although the late Mr. Frew may have burnt the letters he received, he certainly did not make a habit of burning the letters he wrote. . . . See, Inspector. The ink on this blotting-paper is quite fresh. I have not yet made the test myself, but I think if you use a mirror you will find that this patch of writing in the corner represents an envelope addressed to the College of Arms in Queen Victoria Street. And I read these rather more blurred lines lower down as 'Dear Sir, in answer to your communication I have to say that my desire is——' There the letter breaks off. The rest was either not blotted, or not written at all. The latter, probably. Frew had a pen in his hand when we found him dead."

"There is nothing to show that these lines were written to-night," objected Hembrow. "There is no date that I can see, and ink will retain this fresh look for several days. It is more probable, I think, that this letter was written a day or two ago, and that the communication Mr. Frew received from the Herald's Office to-night was in answer to it."

"They must have been carrying on quite a correspondence, in that case," said John lightly. "However, a few inquiries will soon settle the point, and we need not trouble our heads about it at the moment."

Newtree, however, who had been listening attentively to this conversation, said musingly:

"I wonder what he wanted with the Herald's Office, anyhow."

Hembrow laughed.

"A pedigree, I expect, Mr. Newtree, or a coat-of-arms, or something of that kind. Well, he'll get on quite well without them now, poor chap."

CHAPTER VI

CONFABULATION

THE next morning John Christmas was sitting alone in the small library-sitting-room of his flat in Great Russell Street when Inspector Hembrow was announced. He had not slept, but had sat up the rest of the night thinking over the strange pattern of events and persons which lay like a spider's web around the bulky, gorgeously clad body of Gordon Frew sitting dead in his Aladdin's cave of treasures. Above all, the queer personality of the dead man, as revealed in his belongings, intrigued and fascinated John. He had a strong persuasion, as yet without foundation in reason, that it was in this personality that the key to the riddle would be found.

Hembrow looked heavy-eyed and sallow, as though he had slept but little, but his smile and tone were as brisk and cheerful as always.

" You've not been to bed, Mr. Christmas."

" Wonderful! " murmured John with mock solemnity. " How do you do it, Sherlock? "

The Inspector smiled.

" I notice that although you have changed your coat, sir, you are still wearing an evening shirt and waistcoat."

" Marvellous how the trained eye observes these tiny details," sighed John. " Have a drink, Inspector. What are you doing in this part of the world? "

" Following up a clue to last night's business, but it

came to nothing. So as I was passing your door I thought I'd drop in and tell you of one or two new facts that have come to light."

John's tired face lit up.

"Oh? That's interesting, Inspector. What's the news?"

Hembrow lit a cigarette and blew out a thoughtful stream of smoke.

"Well, in the first place I have gone systematically through Mr. Frew's collection, comparing it with the catalogue, and I find——"

The Inspector paused dramatically.

"Well?" asked Christmas. "What? Don't keep me in suspense, Hembrow. And don't tell me that it is robbery, after all! I felt strongly last night that this was one of those murders in which the motive must be looked for in the hidden recesses of the soul, so to speak. If it turns out to be a mere primitive robbery I shall be bitterly disappointed."

"I find," repeated the Inspector impressively, having waited for his friend to finish, "that there is not a single item missing from the large collection."

Christmas brightened up and leant eagerly over the table.

"Not robbery, then! I must say I'm glad. There's something so crude about a mere murder for gain that it needs very unusual circumstances to rouse one's interest in it. There remains the other usual crude motive to dispose of, and we may find ourselves up against something really interesting."

"Personally I would rather find myself up against the murderer, as soon and as close as possible," replied Hembrow with a wry grin. "But I must say this case looks less simple to me now than it did last night. To begin with, idiotic as young Greenaway's story sounded, it is apparently true."

Christmas smiled.

" The idiotic has a way of being true. After all, Inspector, ' life is a tale told by an idiot. . . .' You know the quotation, I expect."

" Yes," replied Hembrow stolidly. " But I don't think much of it. There's such a thing as cause and effect."

" Remarkable discovery," murmured Christmas. " So there is. Where would Scotland Yard be if there weren't? Echo answers, Where? "

" I was going to say," resumed Hembrow, disregarding this problem, " that I've collected evidence from two of the cabman on the taxi-rank in Greentree Road corroborating Greenaway's account of his own movements between a quarter to eight and half-past last night."

He took out his note-book and turned the pages.

" Andrew Milton, licensed hackney-cab driver, of 7 Cauldon Street, N.W.8, deposes that he was in and about the shelter in Greentree Road between the hours of seven-forty-five and eight-thirty last night, and that during that time he saw a man walking up and down the north side of the road. The first time he saw him was a little after eight, when he was walking down towards the Finchley Road about ten yards behind a woman, who was hurrying and who turned in at the gate of No. 14, a house let off in flats which stands some thirty yards away from the cab-rank. Several times during the next half-hour Milton saw the man walk slowly up and down. He pointed the man out to another driver, James Hemington, who also makes a statement to the same effect, and further adds that he had a fare at about eight-forty-five, and that as he drove off the rank he noticed the man turn north into Grove End Road and walk off. This supports Greenaway's statement that before coming home at nine-thirty he walked up Hampstead way."

Hembrow closed his note-book with a sigh. It was plain that he was sorry to see his prospect of an immediate arrest vanish away.

"I told you so, if you'll allow me to make that time-honoured remark," said Christmas. "Life *is* a tale told by, about and for idiots, and the conclusions drawn by an idiot often hit the mark when those of a man of sense (yourself, Inspector) fly wide. I thought so silly a story must be true. Have you never, in your extreme youth, Hembrow, walked up and down past a lady's house, gazing sentimentally at a light in a bedroom window which afterwards turned out to be her aunt's? I have."

"No," replied Hembrow stolidly. "Before we were married I used to go and see Mary every Sunday for tea and supper. But I never felt any call to walk up and down first. Why should I?"

"Why, indeed? Well, that disposes of young Greenaway and his misplaced affections. Is there any news of the gentleman in the fez whom everybody seems to have seen and nobody seems to have known?"

"No, there isn't," replied Hembrow with a frown. "And although you'd think a person like that would be easy enough to find, it doesn't look as if it's going to be easy to trace him. When I saw the name Fuzuli in Mr. Frew's catalogue under an address in Theobald's Road I thought I was on the track. But I've been down there this morning—came straight from there, in fact—and it doesn't help us. Mr. Fuzuli does not answer in the least to the description of the man who went to see the deceased last evening, and has had no dealings with Mr. Frew since last July. I've got a man making a list of all the Turkish curio and carpet-dealers in London. But there must be hundreds! "

" Facts not generally known," murmured John sententiously. " The Turkish carpet-dealers in London, if laid down end to end, would carpet the road from London to Edinburgh and interfere a good deal with the traffic."

" The only useful clue to the identity of the stranger," went on Hembrow, taking no notice of this frivolous interruption, " besides the description of his appearance, of course, is that he asked both Sir Marion Steen and Dr. Merewether the way to Golders Green. As it was late in the evening at the time, it is probable, though not by any means certain, that he lived there. And I have an assistant going through the directories of that district. The fact that he wore a fez should make him easier to trace."

" You mean, a fez impresses itself upon the jaded eyes of a bus conductor, for instance, where a face, however noble, would pass unnoticed. Quite true. We must hunt out the conductors of all the Golders Green buses that passed the end of Greentree Road between a quarter past eight and half-past or so. There can't have been many."

" There weren't," said Hembrow gloomily. " There were only two. And neither of the conductors has any memory of seeing a man in a fez among their passengers. In fact, they both swore that no such person boarded their buses at Greentree Road or anywhere else."

" I say, you have been busy, Hembrow," said John

admiringly. " Have you crowded anything else into your morning of glorious life? "

" Went to interview Shirley," said Hembrow. " But I found her out, and the caretaker at the flats had no idea where she was likely to be. It appears she lives alone. I shall go back this evening, when I was told I should probably find her in."

" May I come with you, Inspector? I should like to see the lovely Pandora."

" Lovely or not," said Hembrow grimly, " I should like to know why she paid that flying visit to Madox Court last night."

" The queer thing about this case so far," said Christmas thoughtfully, " is that all these mysterious visitors were well out of the way before the murder took place. Pandora Shirley left the court at ten minutes to eight and the Oriental gentleman, as old Greenaway calls him, met Steen and Merewether in Greentree Road soon after eight o'clock. Yet Gordon Frew was alive at nine, when Merewether went up to his flat. Of course our mysterious Oriental may have returned, and so, for that matter, may Miss Shirley, but——"

" Mr. Christmas," interrupted Hembrow slowly, " would you mind telling me what you know of Dr. Merewether? "

Christmas looked at his friend's face and was surprised at the gravity he saw there.

" Merewether? " he repeated vaguely. " Why—but surely you can't imagine that Merewether——"

" Well, Mr. Christmas," said Hembrow heavily, " it's a very queer thing that Dr. Merewether should be so positive he saw the deceased alive at nine o'clock. Because our doctor, Dr. Hallet, who examined the corpse, has told me that there's no manner of doubt at all that the deceased died before nine o'clock, and no manner of doubt at all that Dr. Merewether was either mistaken or lying."

Christmas said nothing for a moment. He seemed to see again the sweat upon Merewether's forehead, the shaking of his hands, as he stood upright after laying the corpse back in its chair. He wished that this memory would not insist upon obtruding itself between him and the protest Hembrow's suggestion forced out of him.

" If that is so, it is a queer thing, certainly," he agreed. " But not so queer a thing as the suggestion that Merewether could have had anything to do with the crime, Inspector. Why, the thing's fantastic to anyone who knows him! "

" Have you known him long, Mr. Christmas? "

" I first met him at Newtree's studio about eighteen months ago. He's a friend of Newtree's rather than mine. That is to say, although he is a friend of mine, he is not the sort of man with whom one quickly grows intimate."

" No? " commented Hembrow impassively.

" I'll tell you all I know, of course, which isn't much. He has a practice—not too flourishing—in Swiss Cottage somewhere, and has had it about four years, I believe. He's unmarried, and lives with his only sister. He's thirty-seven, and I believe he took his degree at University College. He attended Gordon Frew during an attack of influenza and bronchitis last April, but otherwise I don't think he knew the man at all. Frew wanted a doctor, and not having been long in England hadn't got one, and Newtree put him on to Merewether. It was purely by chance that Merewether was called in, and the two men were certainly strangers then. . . ."

Hembrow, who had been listening with attention, nodded gravely.

" And is that all you can tell me, Mr. Christmas? I thought from the way you spoke up for him that the doctor was a friend of yours."

" Well, so he is," replied Christmas rather testily, " but one doesn't know the past history of all one's friends. And one doesn't have to know Merewether very intimately to know that he's the last man in the world to be mixed up in anything shady."

Hembrow eyed him gloomily.

" It's a pity you feel that way about it, Mr. Christmas, if I may say so. It doesn't do to feel personal about these things. One has to have an open mind at this game."

" But, Hembrow," objected John, " what possible reason could there be for Merewether to lie about having seen Frew alive at nine o'clock? For if your man is right, Frew died about eight o'clock, and in that case it can't have been Merewether who killed him. For Merewether came to Madox Court with Sir Marion Steen at about half-past eight, and went straight into Newtree's flat. And even conceiving it possible that he had paid an earlier, secret visit to the Court, what reason can he have had for wishing to make us believe that Frew was alive at nine o'clock? The murder had to be discovered soon, in any case. And being a doctor he would surely have known that his statement would be contradicted. The whole thing seems so purposeless! "

Hembrow shrugged his shoulders.

" Our business at present is to find out facts, not invent theories," he reminded John. " But of course there are plenty of theories to fit the fact that Dr. Merewether was lying. There's the theory of his being an accessory, for instance. But, as I say, our business at present is with facts. And whatever the reason may be, the fact seems to be that Dr. Merewether was lying." Hembrow looked up keenly at John's troubled face. " Didn't you think yourself, Mr. Christmas, that he was a bit excited last night, for a medical man? Ah, I can see you did! "

There was a pause, and then the Inspector added gravely:

" And there's another thing, Mr. Christmas. What makes you think Dr. Merewether had never met the deceased before Mr. Newtree introduced them last April? "

" As a matter of fact," responded Christmas, " Merewether told me so himself, one day when I met him at Newtree's after he had been in to see Frew."

" Well," said Hembrow, " it's a funny thing, Mr. Christmas, but I've just seen a copy of the deceased's will. It's a queer will altogether, and the queerest thing in it is the clause which makes Dr. Merewether the residuary legatee."

" What? " asked John, hardly able to believe his ears.

" Yes," said the Inspector, unmoved. " There are one or two legacies of bronzes and so on to museums and national collections. But the most important clause reads: ' I leave the remainder of my possessions to my medical adviser, Dr. George Merewether, who so unselfishly refrained from turning my serious illness this April into a fatal one.' "

There was a silence, then:

" Good Lord! " ejaculated John. " What an extraordinary way of putting it! "

" Yes," agreed Hembrow calmly. " Especially if he'd

never seen Dr. Merewether before Mr. Newtree called him in."

Christmas said nothing for a moment. Once again the memory of Merewether's tortured face swam before his eyes, coming between him and the faith which his liking for the man prompted.

"Well," he said at last with a sigh, "the will, at any rate, is a fact which must be accepted. Did the lawyers have anything to say about it?"

"Frew didn't have a lawyer, in the ordinary way. It seems he just drew up the will himself, and took it to a firm in Bedford Row to know whether it would stand, and having been told that it was perfectly legal, though rather unusual in wording, signed it there and then. The lawyer never saw him before or since, and knows nothing about him."

"The queer thing is," remarked Christmas thoughtfully, "that nobody seems to know anything about him. Had he *no* relations or intimate friends?"

"He had a father and a mother and a sister and a brother," replied Hembrow. "I found the records in Somerset House all right, so we know that the name he went under was his own, which is something. He was born in a village in Northumberland in 1871. His father and mother are both dead, and his sister is married——"

John interrupted.

"As we're dealing only with proved facts, Inspector, may I say that I don't see that the records at Somerset House can be said to prove that Gordon Frew went under his own name? All they prove is that a man named Gordon Frew existed. A quibble, I know, but I can't resist the *tu quoque*."

Hembrow smiled.

" You are quite right, Mr. Christmas. But the records taken in conjunction with one or two other facts that have come to my knowledge prove the identity pretty conclusively. You'll see that presently. I've got a visit to pay now to an antique-dealer in West Kensington, and if you care to come with me, I shall be very pleased to have your company."

CHAPTER VII

HENNEKER MEWS

"NOT in a very prosperous way of business, it seems," commented Inspector Hembrow, as he and Christmas walked along a street in West Kensington that became grimier, shabbier and more depressing at every step.

" Well, it isn't exactly Bond Street, certainly," murmured Christmas, glancing up at the tall, narrow houses with their bleared windows and dirty lace curtains that hid from the eye but not from the imagination a host of pitiful squalid lives. " I wonder what sort of antiques get sold in a place like this? And who buys them? But perhaps before we get to Henneker Mews things will have brightened up a bit and taken unto themselves another coat or so of paint."

" Here we are," said Hembrow, coming to a stop at a side crossing, and looking up at the name Henneker Mews fastened to the grimy wall of a corner shop. " And there is the place we're looking for."

He pointed across the road to where a little way down an indiscriminate collection of second-hand furniture was standing outside a low shop front, and a pile of dirty volumes on a table bore out the claim of the shop-keeper painted above his window: " LIONEL STEEN, Antique Dealer. Books Bought and Sold."

" Hullo! " said John, studying this announcement. " Do you think this is one of Sir Marion's financial ventures, Hembrow? "

The Inspector laughed.

" I shouldn't think so, Mr. Christmas. They say everything Sir Marion touches turns into gold. And I shouldn't think there was much of that commodity lying round here. Steen's a fairly ordinary name, though Sir Marion's certainly not an ordinary man."

Henneker Mews was a small cul-de-sac of mean houses that seemed to have gathered together in furtive conclave round three sides of a rectangle. One or two grubby children played in the middle of the road that never felt the wheels of traffic, and a little girl walked slowly along the pavement dragging a stick across the iron paling of the leafless gardens.

Hembrow and Christmas crossed the road and made their way to the second-hand shop, eyeing the commonplace battered furniture and the muddled windows with some interest.

" I suppose," said John, " that once in a blue moon some article of value may pass through a place like this on its way to a collector's rooms." He looked critically at the heterogeneous collection of jetsam in the window.

Hembrow smiled grimly.

" Quite often, I should say, Mr. Christmas. But they don't go into the window."

A small bowed man with a mild and careworn face was coming diffidently towards the door, threading the piled up articles inside the shop with an ease born of long practice. Squeezing himself between an immense mahogany chest of drawers and a table piled with the chipped remains of an important-looking dinner service, he arrived in the doorway and, looking anxiously at the two men, asked sadly:

"Is there anything I can show you, gentlemen?"

"Mr. Lionel Steen?" asked Hembrow.

The little man bowed. He had sad brown eyes rather like those of a timid monkey under the arched furrows on his high bald forehead.

"Was it this table you were looking at, gentlemen? I can let you have it for fifteen shillings."

It was plain to understand why Mr. Lionel Steen, Antique Dealer, had not prospered in his interesting business. He looked sadly at the table in question as though he regretted its existence, and there was a note of apology in his gentle voice.

"It's a nice table," he added on a dubious note.

"I am Inspector Hembrow of Scotland Yard," said Hembrow mildly, "and I should like a word with you, Mr. Steen."

The little dealer blinked mournfully up at the stalwart detective. Christmas thought that his lips twitched sharply under his ragged grey moustache.

"Certainly, sir. Will you please to step this way?"

They made their way into the dark interior of the shop where the damp and musty smell of rotting wood and long undisturbed dust strove with the sharp tang of some highly flavoured dish cooking in the back room. Mr. Steen led them through into the kitchen, where a tall, untidy, black-browed woman was manipulating a frying-pan over a small gas stove.

"My wife," he remarked. "Emily, my dear, this is Inspector Hembrow come to see us."

Having thus, as it were, cast Hembrow upon the mercy

of his better half, he drifted away to an obscure corner of the ill-lit room and stood scratching his chin and gazing pensively at the three others with his melancholy, mildly-astonished eyes.

Christmas, closely watching the woman's face, saw every line in it slacken and then draw tight at Hembrow's name. She blinked and thoughtfully prodded at the fish in the pan before she said quietly at last:

" Good morning, sir," and waited for him to state his business.

" We have met before, Mrs. Steen," said Inspector Hembrow amiably.

Mrs. Steen turned her head and gave him a long, considering stare.

" Not to my knowledge, sir."

" It was a good many years ago," said the detective, waiving the matter. " And has nothing to do with my visit this morning. You have had business dealings, I understand, with a certain Mr. Gordon Frew, of 5 Madox Court, St. John's Wood."

" Yes," replied Mrs. Steen with a look of mild surprise. " Mr. Frew bought one or two little things from us in September, if I remember rightly. And we have orders to let him know if anything interesting in the way of small curios comes into our hands. It doesn't often happen," she added with perfect good humour, " as I suppose you can judge by the look of our windows."

Hembrow hid his surprise at her use of the present tense, and asked:

" I should like you to tell me how you first met Mr. Frew, and all you know of him, Mrs. Steen."

The woman carefully turned the fish in the pan, and the fat caught fire and blazed up, giving off an acrid blue smoke. When she had blown it out she replied thoughtfully:

" He first came to the shop some time in March, I think. We had a place off Westbourne Grove then. It was just before we moved. He came in to ask about a little Chinese bowl we had in the window. I forget whether he bought it. Do you remember, Alfred? "

" Yes," said her husband mournfully. " We were just going to pack it up for him when he found it had been mended with soft paste, and brought his price down from two pounds ten to seven and six."

" And since then you have had frequent dealings with him?"

" Occasional."

" When did you last see him, Mrs. Steen? "

The woman shot a glance at him sideways from under her strong black lashes, and paused. With her extreme composure she seemed to John like a voyager determined at all costs to keep his head while walking along a path beset with invisible dangers. She replied steadily at last:

" Oh, five or six weeks ago, I should say. He used to look in occasionally when he was in the district. He took rather a fancy to Alfred, I think."

Alfred's eyebrows went up a fraction at this remark, and the hand scratching at his stubbly chin paused for a moment while he gazed at his wife with a sad, wondering admiration.

" And that's all you know of Mr. Gordon Frew? " asked Hembrow affably.

The woman lifted her fish carefully on to a plate and put it in the oven, then turned and looked squarely at the detective.

"That's all," she answered with an air of surprise. "Why, Inspector?"

"I thought," said Hembrow suavely, "that you might be able to explain why the counterfoils of Mr. Frew's cheque-book show that he sent a cheque for ten pounds on the first of every month to Emily Rudgwick. That is your name, is it not?"

The woman's composure deserted her at last. Her eyes widened and her lips fell apart. She said nothing. It was plain that she was flabbergasted beyond the power of uttering even inarticulate words. A chair creaked violently at the far end of the room as her husband suddenly sat down. She glanced at her husband and back at Hembrow, and moistened her lips.

"Steen, I take it," went on Hembrow, "is a name used for purely business purposes."

"Well," said the woman defiantly, as if glad of this diversion from the matter of the cheque-book, "there's nothing very peculiar about taking a fancy name for a business, is there?"

Even in her obviously genuine fright and anger her voice retained its cultured accent, which contrasted curiously with her dirty, slatternly appearance and circumstances and placed her in a class apart from her little Cockney husband.

"Not in the least," agreed Hembrow amicably. "But there is something peculiar about a woman who professes to know nothing about her own brother."

Of the three listeners Christmas was not the least surprised. He glanced incredulously at Hembrow, and then at the tall, slatternly woman with her square, high-coloured face and black brows that met over her nose and large-boned, masculine figure, and he knew why it was that her appearance had been faintly, teasingly familiar to him.

She had just that cold glance, that polite and yet inimical composure, that hard swagger that had made Gordon Frew a striking, if not exactly a lovable personality.

She drew in her breath quickly, opened her lips as if to let out a flood of abuse, then suddenly closed them again, and smiled, tight-lipped and hard-eyed. Slowly she undid the strings of her apron, took it off, and sitting down in a creaking wicker chair, folded her hands on her large knees and asked quietly:

"Well? What's the game?"

"You are Emily Rudgwick, formerly Emily Frew, are you not?" asked Hembrow sternly.

"I don't deny it."

"The sister of Gordon Frew?"

"Gordon Frew is my brother, though until he walked into the shop at Westbourne Grove last March I didn't know he was alive, not having seen him for thirty years."

"Mrs. Rudgwick," said the Inspector slowly, "have you not seen a morning paper?"

The woman looked up curiously at his tone.

"Not yet," she answered. "And not likely to, unless a customer leaves one in the shop. Why? What's up?" she added, and slowly rose to her feet.

"Gordon Frew was murdered yesterday evening in his studio in Madox Court," said Hembrow quietly, and narrowly watched her face.

She went pale and stared at him. Her lips fell apart. From the corner of the room came a faint high exclamation:

"Murd—— Oh, my God!"

There was a silence. Slowly the colour came back to Emily Rudgwick's florid face. She said stoically:

"That means no ten pounds a month for us, Alfred, in future."

The more susceptible Alfred repeated:

"Oh, my God! Murdered! Oh, my God!" and subsided into quietness.

"Well," said his strange wife, "I didn't murder him, gentlemen. Neither did Alfred. And if you think I'm taking the matter lightly, just remember that I'd forgotten I ever had a brother till he turned up last March. I was glad to see him, he looked so prosperous. But I couldn't be expected to feel sisterly towards him. I never could make out," she added dreamily, "what he wanted with us. If I'd been in his shoes I'd have steered clear of my poor, disreputable relations."

"He may have thought it his duty to provide for you," remarked Hembrow tentatively.

The woman shrugged her shoulders.

"Perhaps," she said with a cynical smile. "I was always expecting him to give me some dirty job to do. But he never did, though the cheque came regularly every month. We shall miss it."

"Were there no conditions attached to your receiving the allowance?"

"Only that we were never to let anybody know that he was my brother, and were never to try to see him at his own address. I didn't mind. I'm not proud. Neither's Alfred."

"You say you had not seen your brother for thirty years?"

"Not seen him nor heard of him. Thought he was dead, or settled down to be a true-blue American, like my other brother."

"Your other brother?"

"My elder brother James. He went to America when I was quite a girl. Went for his health, so to speak, having emptied the till at the shop where he worked. And a year or two afterwards Gordon went after him. Felt lonely without someone to quarrel with, I suppose. And till last spring I never heard of either of them again, and never expected to."

"At what date was this, Mrs. Rudgwick?"

"Well, let me see. I was a girl of twenty-two when my eldest brother went, and now I'm fifty-four, and my second brother, Gordon, who was a couple of years younger than me, he went two years later, when I was twenty-four and he was twenty-two. Just thirty years ago, in fact."

"What made them go, Mrs. Rudgwick, can you tell me? Did they go to join friends, or had they jobs waiting for them?"

The woman laughed.

"Not they. My eldest brother, James, he went because he thought the air'd be healthier for him, I should imagine. And after a year or two he wrote home to say he was doing well, so Gordon went to see if he couldn't do better. They were always trying to go one better than each other. I never knew two brothers dislike one another so much. And they both had ideas above their station."

Hembrow looked at his informant curiously.

"If it's not too personal a question, Mrs. Rudgwick, could you give me an idea of what the station was?"

She laughed again, good-naturedly.

"Lord, I don't mind! I never did see any sense in making oneself out to be better than one was. Well, you see, Mr. Hembrow, it was this way. My great-grandfather belonged to a good family that had a title somewhere in it, and a coat-of-arms, and all that. But he was one of the younger branches, as they say, and a very long way off the title, and a longer way still, if possible, off the money. It was just something for him to boast about. He had no money. He was an artist by profession. His son, my grandfather, was an out-and-out rotter. And by the time it came to my father, our branch of the family had sunk a bit low in the world. My father taught at the village school in Arrodale. He was quite contented. But my brothers were different. You never saw two young men so full of swank, with so little to swank about. . . . Not that they weren't clever. They were both that, in a way. But they hadn't had any proper education, and though they thought so much of themselves, they weren't really fit for anything better than the jobs they got. James went to work in a draper's shop in the big town near Arrodale, and Gordon became a bank clerk. Gordon made a great fuss and pretended he wanted to be an artist. But of course he didn't really, he only wanted to have an easy, gentlemanly job and a lot of money. And after James had sulked and sworn over the draper's shop for two or three years, he grabbed all the loose cash he could find lying about, and bolted. The draper was a friend of my dad's and a good sort, otherwise it would have been a matter for the police, and Master James would have found himself in prison. They let him go, and we had a letter a year after saying he had fallen on his feet, and since then I've not heard of him. Somebody's strangled him by now, I should think. Superior blighter, I never could stand him. Gordon wasn't such a bad sort, as a boy, though you couldn't trust him a yard. . . . Oh, Lord! It's funny! "

" Funny? "

" Funny how brothers and sisters live when they're kids, like a lot of young puppies fighting and scrambling togethe , and then thirty years afterwards it's 'Yes, sir,' and 'No, sir,' and 'Anything you like, sir,' as long as you're rich and I'm poor."

"I should always call a customer sir," spoke up her husband with a sort of quavering dignity, as if he suspected a taunt in her words. "Brother-in-law or no brother-in-law, I should always call a customer sir. I should think it only proper."

"Am I to understand, Mrs. Rudgwick, that you know nothing about your brother's private affairs since thirty years ago?"

Emily Rudgwick's bold, florid face relaxed suddenly into a wide, candid smile, not unattractive, though it disclosed a great gap in her front teeth.

"You can search me, Inspector. I'm glad to say I know nothing. Though I can guess a good deal. I asked my brother Gordon how he'd managed to make so much money. And he said he'd made one or two lucky investments, and grinned. I bet I can make a rough guess at the sort of investments they were!"

"You don't seem," remarked Christmas gently, speaking for the first time, "to have a very good opinion of your brother's character, Mrs. Rudgwick."

This queer, strong, sardonic personality intrigued John no less than the family resemblance he perceived between her and her dead brother, whose uncompromising cynical humour had at times attracted and repelled him. Emily Rudgwick turned her hard, dark eyes on him and considered him lazily, as if she wondered what he were doing in this galley.

"Ah!" she uttered, with a negligent gesture of her large hand. "Honesty doesn't seem to be in the blood, does it?" She glanced at Hembrow with a sardonic smile.

" Wasn't he my brother, wasn't he my own flesh and blood? Aren't there a thousand things I can remember about him when we were both children? He went away, and I didn't see him for thirty years. But was he any less my brother when he came back? Do you think I didn't know the kind of man he was? Do you think I couldn't feel? Pah! He was like my twin when we were children, we were so alike. Do you think I couldn't feel the likeness when we met again, that I shouldn't have known if he'd been altered into a different, honest man? I know my guesses are no use to you, Mr. Hembrow. What you want is facts. And I can't give you any. And I can tell you it's good to be talking to a detective without having to think whether one's yarn sounds plausible or not. It's restful, it's a change. It's nice to know that however hard you try you won't be able to mix me up in this thing."

" Emily! " remonstrated her husband in tones of sorrowful surprise.

" Ah, what's the good of putting on side in front of a tec? " she threw over her shoulder at him scornfully. " He knows as well as you do we've both seen the inside of quod."

" Mrs. Rudgwick," began Hembrow, " you're a very intelligent woman——"

" I am," she put in simply. " But I don't make the best use of my gifts. That's because I drink. I'm not drunk now. But very often I am. Aren't I, Alfred? "

" I was wondering whether you could help me," went on Hembrow. " I expect you know a great many second-hand dealers——"

" If you mean fences, say fences, Mr. Hembrow. We shan't feel insulted."

" Would you tell me whether this description conveys

anything to you? A man of about fifty, olive-skinned, small grizzled moustache, height about five foot six, gold filling in front tooth, slight cast in left eye, wears a fez——"

"A what?"

"A fez."

"Oh, I know." She looked thoughtfully up at Hembrow and then at Christmas. "No, none whatever. Except that the age and the height are just the same as Alfred's."

"Here, don't say things like that, Emily!" cried her husband with a note almost of physical pain in his voice. "I don't like it!"

"Oh, don't be a silly fool!" she replied good-humouredly. "No, I don't know anybody like that. Most of my friends wouldn't care to make themselves quite so conspicuous as that. But surely it's not difficult for a clever tec like you to lay your hand on a man with all those peculiarities! Why, if he lived in these parts he wouldn't be able to go down the street without a crowd following him. They'd expect him to stop at a corner and start to do conjuring tricks!"

"Well, he did one conjuring trick last night, Mrs. Rudgwick. The Vanishing Turk. There's one more little thing I should like to know. What made you change the name on your shop front to Lionel Steen?"

"We were tired of the name we traded under before," replied the woman innocently. "It's just as well to have a change of name occasionally." She grinned.

"Any special reason for the name of Lionel Steen?"

The woman looked puzzled.

"Well, we had to call ourselves something. I always liked the name Lionel. And Steen—— I suppose we saw it in the paper and thought it went well. I don't know."

" Yes, that was it," spoke up her husband quaveringly. " We got it out of the paper. Mr. Frew gave us a little money to start the new shop with when we moved, and he says: ' You'll want a new name with a new start, and what name shall we choose? ' I couldn't think of anything, so he says: ' We'll open the newspaper at page five, and the first surname on the page'll do, so long as it's not too long.' So we agreed, and Steen was the first name on page five. I remember it was all about some new Homes of Rest that a gentleman named Sir Marion Steen was having built near Regent's Park. Don't you remember, Emily? "

" I do," she agreed carelessly, " now you mention it."

" I remember, because I thought Steen sounded too German, or too Jewish, I don't know which. But Mr. Frew he said that was all to the good for an antique-dealer, and he bought us in some stock, and we started off in style. But we couldn't keep it up," added the little man regretfully.

" I never could make out what brother Gordon was driving at," said Mrs. Rudgwick pensively. " I'd give a lot to know."

" Driving at? " encouraged Hembrow. " I suppose he wanted to give you a chance to—settle down, shall we say? I suppose he felt it his business to help his sister."

Mrs. Rudgwick gave him an amused glance.

" Not he. I don't say that there aren't plenty of people in the world soft enough to do as you say. I only say my brother Gordon wasn't one of them. And I shall wonder to my dying day what he was up to."

There was a pause. The woman, with her large red

hands clasped round her knees, gazed pensively at the gas oven. One might have imagined her lost in memories of her own childhood and the brother once so live and familiar a figure, now so far removed from her sphere and so strangely dead. But if Christmas felt disposed to credit her with these reveries, Hembrow had no such illusions. And when he said:

"Well, Mrs. Rudgwick, all good things come to an end," she took him up quickly with a laugh.

"You mean my ten pounds a month," she said. "Not my brother Gordon, I presume. For he wasn't a good thing, and I've no doubt there are more people glad of his death than sorry, though I'm not one of them."

Hembrow took up his walking-stick and prepared to go.

"I'll say good morning to you, Mrs. Rudgwick."

But the woman's husband hovered round the door, detaining them.

"You don't think——?" he stammered, peering up at Hembrow with his anxious monkey's eyes. "You aren't thinking we had a hand in it, Inspector? It makes me come over bad to think of such a thing! Murder! There's something about the word that—that——"

He swallowed and looked piteously from Hembrow to Christmas.

"Oh, stow it, Alfred!" said his wife, with something between a laugh and a yawn. "They've only got to look at you to see you haven't the guts to kill a mouse! But to save you trouble, Inspector, I may as well say that yesterday evening we spent at my husband's mother's, it being her eightieth birthday. We got there at six and stayed till after twelve. She lives at 7 Harple Buildings, Fentiwell Road, Battersea. There were fifteen at the party, some relations, and some outsiders, and if you can get round the alibi, you're welcome to hang us both. Good morning, gentlemen."

The cold clear air of the November morning struck gratefully on John's cheeks after the close, oily atmosphere of the Rudgwick's kitchen.

"What an amazing woman," remarked Christmas after they had walked a few yards in silence. "I don't think I should care to be an enemy of hers. How did you know her name, Inspector? You surprised me more than you did her, even."

Hembrow frowned.

"Nothing in that, Mr. Christmas. I recognized the name Emily Rudgwick when I saw it on the counterfoils, and I had a look at her record when I got back to the Yard. And I found that there was an Emily Rudgwick who'd done time for blackmail who went under the name of Emily Frew sometimes. Then when I looked up the births at Somerset House, and found a Gordon Frew with a sister Emily, I put two and two together. . . . Yes, she's a queer woman, but not at all a pleasant one, Mr. Christmas. I should say she hasn't so much as the germ of a scruple in her whole make-up."

"I wonder," remarked Christmas thoughtfully, after a little while, "whether she's right in thinking Frew had some queer motive for looking her up and allowancing her?"

"Remains to be seen," replied Hembrow. "But she's the type of woman who'd never credit the existence of a decent motive for a decent action. Rather a disappointing interview, on the whole. She hadn't much to tell us."

"Oh, I don't know!" demurred John. "She's given a very good idea of the kind of man Gordon Frew was, which is always useful. She's explained a lot that puzzled me about Frew's studio last night. He *was* a poseur. I can understand now why he didn't write the books he published or read the books he bought."

"Oh, I dare say," said Hembrow negligently, "that that's all very interesting to a gentleman like you who makes a hobby, as one might say, of curious characters. But it isn't likely to help us find the murderer. People don't get murdered just for not reading their own books, nor for not writing them, if it comes to that."

"No," agreed John with a laugh. "More people deserve murdering for writing books than for not writing them." He stopped suddenly and looked at his friend with an expression of excitement. "And, by the way, Hembrow, Frew *was* writing a book. There was part of the manuscript on his table."

Hembrow laughed.

"Nobody'd murder him for writing that, Mr. Christmas. I had to read it through, for my sins. Anything more uninteresting I've never come across."

"But still," murmured John, speaking to himself, "there was a book on the laws of libel tucked away in those wonderful book-shelves, and every page had been read."

CHAPTER VIII

OBSTINACY OF A CROSSING-SWEEPER

JOHN CHRISTMAS strolled along Greentree Road, enjoying the clear November sunshine which, in spite of the sharp tang in the air, gave a delusive look of early springtime to the lopped elms and leafless ash-trees in the pleasant brick-walled gardens of the old informal houses. He glanced up as he passed No. 14, a tall, square, stuccoed mansion that stood up above the heads of the other low, rambling, creeper-grown buildings with their pleasant reminiscences of the time when St. John's Wood was a quiet suburb, before the canker of flat-building had begun to invade its green dreamy roads and gardens. The tranquil blue sky looked as if it could never have been obscured by an evil yellow fog, just as the gay and brisk demeanour of the few people John passed on the pavement seemed blandly to disclaim all knowledge of the existence of such a thing as murder. Yet less than twenty-four hours before this road had been like one of the dark labyrinths of Hades, and less than fifty yards away a man had died with a knife in his back.

He turned into Madox Court and found it bathed in sunshine, with a holly-tree covered with scarlet berries that told of the approach of Christmas and the season of good-will. Admiring its festive effect over his shoulder as he entered the building he knocked heavily up against a man emerging from the front door.

"I beg your pard—— Why, how d'you do, Sir Marion? I hope I haven't injured you in any way. I was lost in thought, as they say, and forgot to blow my horn coming round the corner."

"How are you, John?" asked the great financier, taking his hand with his customary quick, nervous grip, and smiling his diffident, pleasant smile. "I hope you slept last night. I must confess that I didn't."

"Neither did I. Poor Newtree's party turned out to be more exciting than he intended it to be. But this extraordinarily lovely day had almost entirely blown the cobwebs away for me."

Sir Marion glanced across the court to the tall holly-tree that made so brave a show with its glossy leaves and vermilion berries against the pale blue sky. His refined, gentle face took on an expression of extreme sadness.

"A heavenly day," he agreed, "in the truest sense of the word. It makes last night seem like a queer nightmare. The sunshine deludes one for a while into thinking with Pangloss that all is for the best in the best of all possible worlds. And then the memory of last night comes back, and one knows—well, that it isn't." He sighed, and then his sudden, attractive smile flashed back. "Are you hot on the trail? I understand that the detection of crime is one of your many hobbies. A gruesome one, in my opinion. It wouldn't be to my taste."

Christmas smiled.

"I was just thinking that you must be emulating Sherlock Holmes, Sir Marion. You are so early on the scene of the crime."

"Heaven forbid that I should help to bring a man to be hanged," said Sir Marion quietly, and Christmas remembered suddenly that the great philanthropist was a fierce opponent of capital punishment, and had written and lectured a good deal on the subject.

"I am afraid it was only idle curiosity that brought me here this morning. I have been disturbing Mr. Newtree at his work. And now I'm disturbing you at yours. But take an old man's advice, John. Leave this kind of thing to the police. I'm a sentimental old fogey, I suppose, but I don't like to see a young man using his talents in such a direction. Who touches pitch—eh? However, good luck to your hunting, my boy, if you are quite determined to teach Scotland Yard its business!"

And with a smile of friendly malice Sir Marion nodded and walked on towards the gate. John raised his hat and watched the debonair little figure turn out into the road.

"Rum cove, Sir Marion," he meditated, "but one can't help rather liking him. I wonder where he keeps his go-getting machinery, as the Americans would call it. It certainly doesn't show on the surface. The iron hand in the velvet glove, I suppose."

Having thus satisfactorily compressed the complex character of the suave little millionaire into a platitude, John dismissed him from his mind and rang the bell of Newtree's front door.

He found Laurence sitting in his shirt-sleeves at his drawing-table, surrounded by a small, untidy army of little bottles containing ink, body-colour, paste and other materials of the artist's curious trade. His hair was standing on end and his cigarette was firmly fixed to his lower lip, sure signs that he was in the throes of composition. He looked up as Christmas entered the room and said briefly:

" Go away," and continued to repeat absentmindedly: " Go away, go away, go away," at intervals while John calmly laid down his hat and stick, chose a comfortable chair and lit a cigarette.

" Dash it," said Newtree suddenly in tones of indignation, " did you or did you not hear me telling you to go away, John? "

" I heard."

" People seem to think a wretched artist has nothing to do but receive callers. People seem to think he does his work, if any, in bed or in his bath. People seem to think that he has all day to sit and listen to their ridiculous troubles. People seem to think——"

" D'you mean to say I'm interrupting you, Laurence? " asked Christmas in injured surprise. " I'm only sitting and thinking. I haven't said a word since I came in."

" You'll soon start," replied Laurence gloomily. " They all do. First Mordby, and then old Steen—they've both been here sitting and thinking nineteen to the dozen. I had to be polite to Steen because he's a millionaire and buys pictures. But I'm dashed," said Laurence with sudden ferocity, " if I see any reason for being polite to you."

Christmas looked reproachful but said nothing.

" Here was I trying to think of a subject for the *Comet* cartoon, and there was he blithering away as if there wasn't such a thing as work in the world. People seem to think daily papers can come out once a week. I'm putting him in my cartoon as a revenge. He'll probably be pleased, though, and come again when I'm working out the next one to tell me how jolly it was of me. So do for goodness' sake leave off talking a minute, John, and let me hear myself think."

He flounced back to his bristol-board, and the scratching of his pen was the only sound to be heard in the studio for a minute of two. After a moment he turned a worried eye over his shoulder and asked:

" Whatever's the matter with you, John? You're sitting there like a blessed mute at a funeral. Come and have a look."

John strolled over and stood at the back of his friend's chair. A colossal Sir Marion in the traditional robes of the necromancer straddled a wooded valley, and with a magician's wand dripping sovereigns drew a charmed circle from hill to hill.

" You know he's just presented a thousand acres of the Haysling Valley in Gloucestershire to the National Trust? "

" Yes. Jolly good."

" Do you mean my cartoon or the presentation? "

" Both," replied Christmas dreamily, studying the drawing with a fascinated expression. " It's an awfully good caricature, though you've made him look rather predatory for a fairy godfather."

" Have I? Well, if people come and jabber at one for an hour when one's got work to do they can't expect to be flattered."

" My dear Laurence, you gave all your guests such a thrilling experience last night that you must expect them all to come and pay duty calls. You'd better put your work away and come out with me now, or you'll have to spend the afternoon entertaining Merewether, Imogen Wimpole and Serafine."

" Your Serafine terrifies me," said Newtree gloomily.

" Then you'll probably end up by marrying her."

" Thanks. I'd rather marry Lucrezia Borgia."

" Well, you can't," said Christmas reasonably. " She's dead. So get your coat and come along."

As if cowed by his friend's terrible prognostication, Laurence meekly got his coat and followed John out into the street, and it was not until they had turned into Greentree Road that he stopped and asked:

" Where are we going? "

" We are going to call on Mr. Gilbert Cold, of 9a Camperdown Terrace, W.9," replied Christmas calmly, taking his friend's arm firmly to make sure he should not slip back to his studio.

" Gilbert Cold," repeated Laurence, who had an excellent memory. " Who—— Oh, yes, that's the chap who wrote poor Frew's books for him."

" The same. I am Sherlock Holmes. You are Doctor Watson."

Laurence shook his head.

" I'll be Watson for this afternoon, but let it be understood that I'm not going to make a habit of it. I've got a great deal more work to do than that obliging gentleman had."

Camperdown Terrace proved to be a row of shabby but dignified Victorian stucco houses fronting an exact copy of itself across a quiet backwater near the Edgware Road. Once solid and prosperous family residences, the large basement houses had passed from gentility to shabby-gentility, and had a look now of awaiting the house-breaker's hammer and the rising of a phœnix, in the shape of a large red-brick block of flats, from their quiet ashes. Many of them, in fact, had anticipated the future by turning themselves into self-contained maisonettes, as the rows of door bells at some of the porched and pillared doors testified. No. 9 was one of these.

Christmas rang the bell of 9a, and they waited some time in the little lobby before they heard a footstep inside the flat. Then the door was opened suddenly and noisily, and Christmas, who had subconsciously expected to see a small, timid, scholarly figure, could hardly repress a start as he found himself looking up into the scowling, square, rather fine face of a broad, burly man two or three inches taller than himself. The unexpectedly commanding presence of Mr. Gilbert Cold, combined with his extraordinarily unfriendly frown, took the wind out of John's sails for the moment, and the other spoke first.

" Well? Well? " he rapped out impatiently, his deep-set dark eyes glancing swiftly from one to the other of his callers.

" Mr. Gilbert Cold? "

" Yes. What can I do for you? "

But though he still spoke brusquely his frown had relaxed a little, as though he found the appearance of his visitors more to his taste than he anticipated.

" My name is Christmas," said John with a smile. " And this is my friend Laurence Newtree."

Mr. Cold's dark, sallow face cleared. He smiled.

" I know the name well. In fact, I take the *Comet* every morning principally on account of Mr. Newtree's brilliant cartoons. Is it the same Mr. Newtree? "

Newtree smiled uncomfortably, blushed and glanced reproachfully at John. The stream of self-expression which had flowed so fast and turgidly alone in his studio with John, was dried up within him. He hated talking to strangers, and hated himself for hating it. He cleared his throat and made a benevolent, inarticulate sound.

"I wonder whether I might have a word or two with you, Mr. Cold?" said Christmas, who had planned his line of attack in the omnibus. "I do hope we are not interrupting your work?"

"Come in, come in," said the large man genially, and led them through a narrow, dark passage into a very large, untidy, shabby room where an enormous cut-glass chandelier glittered mournfully over a horse-hair couch, a large table littered with books and papers, two or three worn arm-chairs and an inadequate gas-stove. From the appearance of the couch, on which lay a disarranged rug, several cushions and a magazine of the more lurid type, John guessed that they had disturbed Mr. Cold's siesta rather than his labours.

"The fact is," said John with effrontery, "I am thinking of writing a life of Dante Gabriel Rossetti, and I understand that you knew the family well at one time. I was wondering whether you would think it presumptuous if——"

Mr. Cold, who had looked perfectly blank at John's opening sentence, now pursed his thick but well-cut lips and shook his head slowly from side to side.

"I am afraid you have been misinformed. I can't claim to have been personally acquainted with any members of that distinguished family, although I am second to none in my admiration of their genius."

Having delivered himself of this sonorous period, Mr. Cold sat down carefully on the creaking sofa and surreptitiously pushed the rather gaudy magazine under a cushion.

"I have met a great many interesting people in my

time," he went on, " but the Rossettis are not among them. Dante Gabriel, of course, was a leetle before my time."

His manner seemed to indicate that, had it not been for this unfortunate fact, he would have been able to oblige his inquirer with as many personal reminiscences as he could desire.

" Now I wonder who can have so misinformed you, Mr. Christmas? "

He spoke to Christmas, but he looked most of the time at Newtree, and it was plain that Christmas's proposed work did not interest him half as much as Laurence's accomplished fame. Christmas, recognizing in Mr. Cold the more amiable type of snob, was glad that he had brought his friend along with him as bait, and thought that he would have little trouble in hooking the fish he wanted.

" Well, as a matter of fact," said Christmas slowly, " it was a mutual friend of ours whom I am afraid it will be painful for us both to mention, as he died so short a while ago as last night in rather horrible circumstances."

Mr. Cold turned sharply from a scrutiny of Newtree which that gentleman was beginning to find embarrassing.

" Not poor Gordon Frew? " he exclaimed. " Yes? I see by your face that it was. Oh, what a terrible thing that is, Mr. Christmas! I don't know that I have ever had a more unpleasant shock than when I opened my *Comet* this morning. These terrible things happen every day, and yet it is so rare that one has it brought home to one like this. Was poor Frew a friend of yours also, Mr. Newtree? "

" M'm," said Newtree, rather inadequately, he feared. He added: " He had the flat above mine." In response to a glance of encouragement from Christmas he went on unwillingly: "He was a—a nice chap. Did you know him long?"

"Some time, some time," replied Mr. Cold vaguely. "I had the pleasure of helping him with some of his literary work. He had a great deal of material, and not much—ah! time for putting it together. I can hardly believe that he is dead—and in such a way. Only a few weeks ago I saw him, looking the picture of health and prosperity. I suppose robbery was the motive?"

"I—I suppose so," agreed Newtree. "He had a lot of valuable things."

"Ah, worldly possessions are not always a blessing," murmured the writer philosophically. "I have always thought so. I prefer a simple way of living myself, as you can see. Though, as a matter of fact, even the simplest way of living doesn't exempt one from the attentions of burglars, apparently. You may hardly believe it, Mr. Newtree, but this humble flat of mine was broken into last night."

"Really?" said Newtree, glancing at John for guidance. "Did the thieves take anything?"

"Not a thing," replied Mr. Cold blandly. "In fact, I should not have known of their visit if it had not been for the chaos in which I found this room when I got down this morning—or I should say, got up, for I sleep in a very pleasant room in the basement, looking on to the garden. Every drawer and cupboard in the room was pulled open and the contents hauled out on to the floor. But I have not so far found that anything is missing."

"Didn't you hear anything of the thieves?" asked John.

"Not a sound. He, or they, must have come in

through this window—not a very difficult feat, as the catch is broken. I fancy they must have mistaken this house for another in which they knew there was something worth their while. For certainly there's nothing here worth stealing except a few first editions and autograph letters, which do not appeal to the taste of Mr. Bill Sykes."

"Have you notified the police?"

"Not yet. I suppose I ought to, as a good citizen. But personally I don't feel inclined to bother. I am not at all a nervous person, though I must say I could hardly eat my breakfast after reading my paper this morning."

"Did you know Frew well?" asked Christmas sympathetically.

"Oh, very," replied the other in a rather vague tone, and then more definitely: "He was writing a second book, I believe, which I was to have had the pleasure of revising for him. A book of memoirs, I believe, which would have been interesting. He was a much travelled man."

"So I gathered," said Laurence, once again in response to a sign from John. "Rather a mysterious fellow. I saw quite a lot of him, but I'm as much in the dark as to his origin as I was when he first came to Madox Court."

"He rather liked to be thought a man of mystery, I imagine," agreed Cold. "It was a—an amiable affectation of his. I, too, knew very little about him, although he reposed a good deal of trust in me."

"With his literary work, I suppose," murmured Laurence.

"Not only that," replied the other, and he hesitated a moment. Then his vanity conquered his caution and he went on: "It seems now, poor fellow, almost as though he had a presentiment of his coming death. . . . It was two or three months ago. I had called on Frew in connection with some small matter in his work, and he was looking through his drawers to find some papers I required. All of a sudden he tossed across the room to me a large envelope done up with tape and sealing-wax. 'By the way,' he said, 'would you take charge of that for me, Gilbert?' (It was a pleasant habit of his to call all his friends by their Christian names, you remember.) I looked at the envelope and saw that it was addressed ready for posting. I naturally asked him what it was and whether it contained anything valuable. He replied that it contained family letters and papers, and that in the event of his death I was to put it in the post immediately. Of course I pooh-poohed the notion that he was likely to die before I did. He laughed, and said that he certainly didn't anticipate dying for several years, but all the same I should oblige him very much by taking charge of the packet. He added that it had no interest but for himself and the person to whom it was addressed —a Mrs. Emily Rud——" Suddenly Mr. Cold's caution seemed to return to him. He coughed, cleared his throat, and finished: "I was rather touched at his confidence in me, as he had only known me for three or four months."

"You must have had an anxious moment when you saw that you had been visited by burglars. I imagine they would take an unhealthy interest in a package tied and sealed."

"Not at all," replied their host blandly. "I had the package quite safe with me in my bedroom. Under my mattress, in fact, where I keep most of the small things I value. It is now in the post, and will reach its destination some time this evening, I imagine, if it has not already done so."

"A queer request," said Christmas in a casual tone, but inwardly much excited. "I don't think I should have cared to undertake such a responsibility."

"Yes," agreed Cold. "I don't to this day understand why he didn't leave the package with his lawyer in the obvious way. And I was certainly in two minds about accepting the responsibility at first. But when he assured me there was nothing of value in it, I thought I might as well humour his caprice—his rather flattering caprice."

The big man stretched his long legs and sighed philosophically.

"I little knew the responsibility would be mine for so short a time," he added. "And even now I find it hard to believe that so rich and live a personality is wiped out. He warmed both hands before the fires of life," he continued to misquote impressively, edging his feet a little nearer to the gas-stove's weak yellow flames. "It sank, and he was——"

"Yes," said John, firmly stemming the flow of a very inapplicable quotation which was leading them away from a more interesting subject. "These wealthy bachelors are often as incalculable and capricious in their doings as prima donnas. It comes of——"

"*But,*" interrupted Mr. Cold, and paused heavily, rubbing his imperfectly-shaven chin, and gazing meditatively at his boots. He paused so long that Christmas, fearing that he was about to take up the thread of his interrupted quotation or find a new one, repeated firmly:

"It comes of not——"

"*But*," said his host mildly, "our poor friend Frew was not a bachelor. I've met his wife."

With enormous self-control John managed to repress a start and an exclamation. This was an unexpected bombshell.

"Yes," went on their host complacently, and he seemed to grow visibly larger with the importance his superior knowledge gave him, "he was a Benedick, all right. Or he said so, and I can't conceive why he should, if it weren't true. Did not Mrs. Frew live at Madox Court, then?"

"Certainly not," replied Newtree. "Frew never so much as mentioned her to me, or to any of us. He lived alone, with a valet. We all took him to be a bachelor."

"Queer," commented Mr. Cold dreamily. "But he was a queer fellow altogether. And his death is as queer as everything else about him."

John stood on the hearth-rug and looked narrowly at the big, lethargic man, wondering how to force him to be more explicit without arousing his suspicions. He was disposed to take everything Mr. Cold said with a healthy salting of scepticism, recognizing the man as one of those romantically-minded beings to whom the line between fact and conjecture is always a little blurred and who will make very positive statements on very flimsy evidence. Laurence came opportunely and unconsciously to the rescue.

"Very queer," he murmured, "that the widow hasn't been in evidence at all, after last night's happenings. Isn't it possible you are mistaken, Mr. Cold? I am sure that not even Frew's valet knew he was married. And they say valets know everything about their masters."

"Mistaken?" echoed Cold. "My dear Mr. Newtree,

certainly not. It was about a month ago that I met poor Frew quite by chance in a Soho café. Naturally I went over to his table to speak to him. He had a lady with him, and introduced me to her, saying that she was his wife. I cannot imagine why he should say so if it were not true. There is nothing criminal, or even unconventional, about sitting in a café with a lady who is not your wife. The lady did not seem to see anything strange in the introduction, either, though she was not exactly responsive to the few remarks I addressed to her. She hardly spoke, and seemed either very reserved or very shy. She looked ill," added Cold meditatively, "but she was a very beautiful young woman, in the petite, perfectly finished style."

He seemed a little disappointed when they rose to go, and pressed them to stay and have some tea, but finally accompanied them to the hall door, expressing his hope of seeing Laurence again.

"Do you know," he added, with a sudden rather engaging burst of frankness, "when I saw you both coming up the steps, I thought you were come to seize some furniture I bought some time ago and haven't paid for yet. They generally hunt in couples, you know. But I don't suppose you've had my experience of their ways."

"Oh, yes, I have," replied Laurence. "I once had a drawing-table pinched from under my pen, as it were, in my young days."

Gilbert Cold gave his great booming laugh.

"I'm hopeless at domestic finance, I'm afraid. And I haven't got anybody to look after it for me. As a matter of fact," he added candidly, "I never have any money. The fact is, I'm abominably lazy. It's ruined my life. That's why I write other people's books instead of my own.

But I don't mind. I enjoy my ruined life! Eh? Ha, ha, ha!"

His laughter followed them down the unwhitened crumbling steps, and he waved a large hand to them as they turned out at the creaking gate.

"Rather a nice chap, that," commented Laurence as they went towards their bus. It was his invariable comment on all the people he met; and it was true that, confronted with Laurence's simple, diffident amiability, even the surliest misanthropist showed his more genial side.

"He certainly finished better than he began," agreed Christmas. "I thought he was a sham at first. But I've noticed people generally present you with the truth sooner or later, Laurence. You're so infernally amiable."

"Amiable? Me?" stuttered Laurence indignantly, and for several yards his gentle, mildly-surprised face wore a meretricious scowl, as if to give the lie to such an accusation.

"I would give a good deal to know," murmured John, "what is in the packet that Mr. Gilbert Cold has just posted to a notoriously shady character. There's a word that's been buzzing in my head all day, and the word's blackmail. Is there such a thing as vicarious blackmail? Too risky, perhaps. But blackmail from the grave? Why not? A dead man can't be prosecuted. A dead man can't go in fear of his life."

"What *are* you talking about?"

"I say, why not?" repeated Christmas thoughtfully. "It argues hatred on a grand scale, of course. Most people are content to let their antipathies die with them. Did Frew hate anybody, do you happen to know, Laurence?"

"I should say not. He was one of those queer cusses who don't give a damn for anybody either way, but make themselves agreeable all round just out of habit. He'd have been just as ready to see a man hanged as stand him a drink. There was something—well, what I call mediæval about him."

"There's something mediæval about hatred," murmured John dreamily. "At least, it's not a modern thing. We get annoyed, irritated, bored. We don't *hate*. Leave me alone a bit, old chap. I want to think."

He thought so long and so deeply that Laurence had to rouse him when they arrived at the end of Greentree Road, and drag him from the bus. They walked up the quiet street in silence. The sunshine had vanished with the approach of evening, and there was a sharp chill in the still air. The women they passed on the pavement wore their furs muffled close around their necks, and the crossing-sweeper who exhibited a broom and a wooden leg at the corner of Shipman's Mews was blowing on his purple hands.

"Good evening, sir," he cried in a hoarse but genial voice as they passed. In his younger days before he lost his leg and had his outline blurred by a too sedentary life, he had been an artist's model, and now subsisted very comfortably on the small sums contributed by passers-by in this small artist's colony. He had humour and a genial philosophy, assets even greater than his connection with art.

Laurence's hand dived automatically into his trouser-pocket.

"Dreadful doings up at your place last night, sir," remarked the crossing-sweeper conversationally, looking politely away while Laurence examined his small change and found that he had nothing between a halfpenny and a florin. "Thank *you*, sir." Unbuttoning his ragged coat he produced a small black purse into which he stowed the florin, replacing it carefully in some mysterious hiding-place among the multitudinous ragged garments that were part of his stock-in-trade. " Did you hear anything of the murder? But there, o' course you did, for I see your name in the paper, Mr. Newtree? It didn't 'alf give me a queer turn when I see it were Mr. Frew as 'ad gone like that. I s'pose there'll be a ninquest, sir? "

" I suppose so."

" He was a queer gentleman, Mr. Frew was. One day he give me half a sovereign, an' the next day he said I was a parasite, and did I know there was laws against begging. But I didn't mind. I could see as he didn't mean it, but just wanted to be thought a peculiar gentleman. And sure enough two days after he called me an old scoundrel, just as you might yourself, sir, and give me half a dollar. And now to think the poor gentleman'll never come walking down this road again! Used to walk as if he owned the street and half London into the bargain, too, poor gentleman. My sight's not much good nowadays, but I always knoo who it was as soon as he turned the corner. Ah, well! It just shows as riches isn't always a blessing."

" I suppose," said Christmas, " you weren't on your beat at the time the thing happened? "

" Well, as it 'appened, I was, sir. See, I live 'ere." He jerked his head back towards the small grey houses and stables of the mews. " And on a foggy night like last night I often stays on me beat a bit longer to see if I can earn a bit 'elping people to find their way, sir. Lot o' people about last night, too, considerin' what the weather was like. One queer customer didn't arf give me a turn."

" Oh," murmured Christmas, producing half-a-crown. " How was that? "

" I was sittin' at the corner 'ere, sir, a little after eight it was, cos I'd just 'eard it strike and was wondering whether I wouldn't pack up me traps and 'ook it. Thinkin' about the 'ot tea my old woman ud have ready for me, I was, when all of a sudden somebody comes round the corner and bolts into the mews like as if the police was after him. 'E stands just in 'ere a bit and looks around as if 'e didn't know what to do next, and I sees 'e's a kind of a foreigner in a red 'at, but quite a gentleman, sir, and good for a tanner, sir, I thought, though I was mistaken, as it turned out. So I hollers out: ' Can I direct you, sir? ' Blowed if 'e didn't let out a kind of grunt as if 'e'd been landed in the wind, an' jump round as if somebody'd thrown a knife at 'is back. Then 'e comes a bit closer, as jumpy an' nervy as you please, an' stares at me as if I was a ghost. An' 'e ses: ' Tell me how far to Primrose 'Ill, please, tell me what way . . .' speaking like a Frenchman, sir, or some other furriner, which I can't do meself. So I tells him, friendly-like, not forgetting to 'old out me hand a bit, suggestive-like. An' off 'e bolts in the opposite direction to what I've told 'im without givin' me so much as a copper. I've noticed before furriners are apt to be disappointin', sir. Thank *you,* sir."

" He went off in the opposite direction to what you'd told him," repeated John thoughtfully. " And he asked the way to—where, did you say? "

" Primrose 'Ill, sir."

" Primrose Hill. Are you sure he asked you the way to Primrose Hill? "

" Course I'm sure, sir."

"I mean to say, it couldn't have been Shootup Hill, or Haverstock Hill, or a hill that lies in this direction? Or Kilburn Lane, or Golders Green, or——"

The crossing-sweeper looked up at John with an injured expression on his dirty, amiable face.

"'Ere, sir, I asks yer! Why should it a been any o' them? Primrose 'Ill 'e asked me for, and why not? Plenty o' people does live round Primrose 'Ill. I mean to say, there ain't anything peculiar about wantin' to get to Primrose 'Ill, is there?"

"Oh, no! Only his going off in the wrong direction after asking you seems a bit queer."

"Ha!" ejaculated his ragged friend sardonically. "You wouldn't think it queer if you'd directed as many people as I 'ave, sir. Often as not they does go off in just the road you've wasted your breath tellin' 'em not to. Before you'd bin in my place a week, sir, you'd begin to find out that arf the population of London is as scatter-brained as rabbits, sir. As for the foreign gentlemen, 'e asked me the way to Primrose 'Ill as if 'is life depended on 'is gettin' there, but did 'e listen while I was tellin' 'im? Not 'e! 'Thank you, thank you,' 'e ses, an' off 'e bolts 'fore I'd got farther than the third turnin' on the left, an' didn't leave so much as a copper be'ind 'im, sir."

"Suppose," said John slowly, "I were to tell you that five minutes before he met you this same man asked somebody else the way to Golders Green, what would you think?"

"Think?" echoed the old man with a hoarse chuckle. "I should think the place 'e really wanted was Anwell. Tell yer the truth, the thought did cross my mind last night, 'e stared at me so queer for a moment."

" Was there anything else queer about him? "

" Well, 'e was a darkish-coloured gentleman, an' wore a red 'at. Looked as if 'e might be carrying somethin' under 'is coat, too, way 'e kept 'is arm to 'is side. But I dunno."

" Nothing else queer? " asked John, abstractedly turning over a little pile of sweepings with his walking-stick as though he hoped to find a clue to the mystery buried in it. " No scar, or squint, or——"

" Not as I noticed, sir. But it wasn't a night for noticing. You won't find any buried treasures in that little 'eap of leaves, sir," added the old man with a grin. " I always picks up the cigarette-ends before I sweeps."

John came to himself with a smile.

" I should imagine that the soil of Greentree Road isn't very rich in ore," he said chaffingly, " though I dare say you manage to scrape a living out of it, eh? "

" Well, sir," replied the old man with a humorous glance at Newtree, " the soil ain't so bad. Artists are very generous gentlemen, sir. And talkin' of the soil, I found a bit of gold in my sweepings this morning."

He dived once again into his hidden pouch and held out a horny palm with a small, glittering object lying in it. Picking it up Christmas saw that it was a small piece of yellow metal, slightly roughened at the edges as if it had been broken from some larger object. Examining it closely, he saw that it was engraved all over one side with a tiny pattern.

" Looks like a piece out of the back of one of those little lockets our grandmothers used to preserve the hair of the dear departed in," he observed. " Where did you find it? "

" Picked it out of the sweepings this morning, sir,"

replied the old man. " Didn't notice it till I'd swept it up. You can have it, sir," he added generously, " as you seem to have taken a fancy to it; it's only brass I fancy. And even if it's gold there ain't enough of it to be any use."

" Thank you," said Christmas, rewarding him suitably for the gift. " I'll keep it. It may be interesting."

They left him stowing away his coins with the rest of his fast-accumulating store, and walked along in silence towards Madox Court. Laurence waited for John to comment on what they had just been told, but John did not seem communicative. He twirled his stick and hummed a tune and walked very fast. Just as they were turning in at the Court the nursery tune he was humming resolved itself into words.

" And he asked me the way to Primrose 'Ill, to Primrose 'Ill, to Primrose 'Ill, he asked me the way to Primrose 'Ill on a Christmas day in the—dash it, Laurence. Why Primrose Hill? "

CHAPTER IX

A COFFIN FOR ONE

"DON'T waste much money on electric light and caretakers, do they?" remarked Inspector Hembrow, as he and Christmas toiled up the narrow, dim-lit, uncarpeted stairs to Pandora Shirley's flat. The long, narrow, flat-converted house in which she lived looked well enough from the outside, but the entrance hall and stairway had the indescribably gloomy, forlorn, slightly dirty appearance of a place which it is everybody's, and therefore nobody's, business to keep presentable. Up from the basement, where the caretaker lived, drifted a thin, permeating suggestion of damp and closed windows and stale food.

However, the knocker on Miss Shirley's door glittered self-respectingly under the inadequate light on the landing, and the door-paint was fresh and green, and the door-mat had the word "WELCOME" printed on it in large, black letters. Hembrow smiled grimly as he noticed this.

"I don't think the lady'll feel so hospitable as her door-mat," he remarked. "If I'm not mistaken she doesn't feel too friendly towards the police. I've been looking her up, and I find her record includes shop-lifting and obtaining money on false pretences."

He knocked as he spoke, and the door was opened with extreme celerity by a golden-haired young woman wearing the crimson doublet of a mediæval page. Her long slim legs were encased in parti-coloured tights of green and black, and as if living up to her clothes she stood jauntily with her feet planted apart and one large, capable hand resting on her hip. As she saw that Hembrow was not alone her eyebrows shot up under her thick, straight, golden fringe.

"Good evening, Inspector," she said demurely, and with the sound of her voice, nasal, harsh and with the indescribable drawl of the would-be refined, the illusion created by her appearance broke and vanished. It was not a figure from some old tapestry come alive, but a well-set-up, coarse-featured little Cockney dressed to go to a ball. The room into which she led them would have effectually destroyed the illusion, anyway. Miss Shirley's notion of domestic beauty and comfort seemed to comprise little but rose-coloured lamp-shades, gilded mirrors and cushions of rainbow hues. The place reeked with scent and cigarette smoke with a soft, persistent undertone of fried food.

"You must excuse my clothes," said Miss Shirley, hoisting herself gracefully on to the top of a small grand piano, where she sat swinging her legs and smoking. "I'm going to the Albert Hall. An artist friend lent me these clothes." She contemplated her shapely legs complacently. "Do I look nice in them, do you think?"

She asked the question in a naïve, child-like tone that seemed devoid of all coquetry, and gazed earnestly at Christmas. Most rare in a grown woman, she had eyes of a true, clear blue, making no concessions to grey or green. Their effect was quite dazzling, used thus in a wide, earnest stare. John made the appropriate reply, but Hembrow cut his compliment short.

" Miss Shirley," he said abruptly, " you know, I think, what it is I have called here about? "

She blew out a cloud of smoke and looked at him through it.

" Well," she said gently at last, " I can guess. It's about poor Mr. Frew. Won't you sit down, Mr. Hembrow? And—and you? "

She looked shyly at John from under her thick, light lashes. It was plain that, though she had no illusions about Hembrow, she regarded John as a possible victim to her blue eyes. Sitting down obediently on a black divan littered with multi-coloured cushions, he saw plainly enough her coarse lips, her low forehead, pointed jaw and large ugly hands, yet had to admit her grace and bold boyish charm. He profoundly pitied the weak, romantic Greenaway, caught in the stream of a vitality such as this.

She fidgeted with a ring on her finger and murmured:

" I'll tell you anything, Inspector. I don't know anything really. I——"

" Just answer my questions, please, Miss Shirley, and try to be as accurate as you can. At what time were you in Madox Court last night? "

" I left here at about twenty minutes past seven. It was twenty to eight when I got there, I suppose. One couldn't walk fast in the fog."

" Did Mr. Frew expect you? "

" No. I wanted to see him about the ball at the Albert Hall to-night. I'd asked him to take me, you see, and he said he wouldn't. But I thought if I gave him a last chance, he might—well, he might alter his mind."

" Did you see anybody in the courtyard or in the entrance hall? "

A faint flush appeared in Pandora's cheeks. She said resolutely:

" Yes, I did. I saw Ernest Greenaway in the courtyard."

" Did he speak to you? "

" No. I don't think he knew I saw him. He was standing beside the clump of bushes near the doorway. It was very foggy. I didn't know he was there until I nearly touched him going past. I was frightened."

" Did you say anything? "

" No, I kind of gasped, because I was startled, and then I saw who it was and hurried in."

" You saw who it was and hurried in," repeated Hembrow thoughtfully. " Why, Miss Shirley? I understand that you and Greenaway are old acquaintances."

The colour deepened in Miss Shirley's cheeks.

" We—we quarrelled," she said at last. " He was jealous of all my other friends. I'm frightened of him. He has such an awful temper. Often he's threatened to do me in, and himself afterwards. I don't suppose he meant it. But you never know with that sulky kind of man."

" I see. And after you were in the building? "

" I met Father Greenaway in the hall. We didn't speak. We're not on speaking terms, owing to this row with Ernest. I went up to the flat."

" And how long did you stay in Mr. Frew's flat? "

" How long? " echoed the girl. " Why, I didn't go into the flat at all! "

She spoke with a defiant air, as if she expected to be disbelieved, but Hembrow was unmoved.

" How was that? "

"I knocked on the door, and Mr. Frew called out to me to go away. He said he was busy and he'd ring up in the morning. I felt a bit annoyed at being spoken to like that, so I didn't say any more."

"It was unusual, then, for Mr. Frew to shout through the door instead of opening it?"

"Well, he never did it to me before. I wouldn't have stood it." She tossed her head indignantly, and then as if suddenly regaining her sense of humour, smiled at herself and reaching a long arm across the piano, took another cigarette and lit it from the stump of the last.

"And you went away directly?"

"Yes." Then she hesitated. "Well, almost directly. My—my shoelace had come undone, and I stopped to do it up."

"Didn't know ladies ever wore lace shoes in these days," remarked Hembrow casually.

She looked at him meditatively through the smoke, and then suddenly laughed.

"Oh, all right! Have it your own way! I stopped to listen at the key-hole, not to tie my shoe-lace."

"Why?" asked Hembrow sharply. "Did you suspect that there was something wrong?"

The girl laughed, rather harshly.

"Not in the way you mean. Just thought I'd like to know who it was that Gordon didn't want me to meet."

"And did you find out?"

"I found out it wasn't a woman. D'you know," she went on meditatively, "I've always fancied Frew had a wife knocking about somewhere, for all he made himself out to be a bachelor. I once picked up a book to look at in his studio, and it had one of these little pictures inside the cover that people stick in books to show who they belong to. 'Ex Libris Phyllis Frew,' it said. *I* asked him straight out if it was his wife."

"And he denied it?"

"No, he didn't!" She smiled reminiscently. "He said it was like my blasted impudence to inquire into his private affairs, and he'd thank me not to paw his books about without his permission. He wasn't a bit upset, really, though. He grinned. He was like that. The worse language he used, the more amiable he spoke. When he was really angry, he didn't say anything."

Hembrow made a careful note of this little reminiscence.

"And now, Miss Shirley, will you please tell me what you heard while you were—tying up your shoe-lace?"

Miss Shirley laughed.

"Oh, let's call a spade a spade!" Then a puzzled look came into her blue eyes. "It's difficult," she murmured. "I didn't really hear much, and nothing that seems to make sense. You see, when I found that it was a man I didn't stop to listen much."

"Did you recognize the voice?"

"No."

"Would you recognize it if you heard it again?"

"Lord, no, I shouldn't think so! It was just an ordinary voice, a nice voice, a gentleman's voice, I should think, not loud or—or anything. Not so loud as Mr. Frew's. I don't think I heard anything it said. Just a buzz."

"Did you hear anything that Mr. Frew said?"

"Well . . . I heard him laugh out loud, very jolly, like he always did when he was suddenly amused. And I heard him say: 'You've mistaken the date, old man!' And then the other man spoke, for quite a long while, but I couldn't catch what he was saying."

" Could you tell from the sound of his voice whether he was angry or amused? "

" Oh, I don't think he was angry! Unless he was like Mr. Frew, and spoke gently when he was annoyed. And then I heard Mr. Frew laugh again, and he said—he said——"

" Well? "

The girl looked uncomfortable.

" It sounds so silly, and you'll think I'm making it up. But I did really hear it, I can swear."

She looked appealingly at Christmas, as if imploring him, at least, to believe her.

" Well? " said Hembrow patiently. " You heard him say? "

" Well," said Pandora, dropping her voice artistically to a mysterious whisper, " he said something I couldn't hear at first, and then he raised his voice, and I heard him say quite clear: ' A coffin for one! ' "

She looked from Hembrow to Christmas with large round eyes, evidently much intrigued by what she had overheard and anxious to see what impression it made on them.

" When I heard poor Gordon'd been killed, I thought of it at once," she murmured. " It seemed so—well, as if he knew what was going to happen."

Christmas wondered for a moment whether the love of sensation had not, after the event, created these sinister words out of some quite ordinary half-heard sentence. Then he dismissed the idea. Pandora Shirley, whatever her faults might be, seemed to him an eminently clear-headed young woman.

" Yes," she went on, " that's what I heard. A coffin for one! He said it out loud with a kind of ring, and laughed. And then the other man said something, and I heard Gordon say: ' Oh, have it your own way, but I thought it'd save argument! ' "

" And then? " asked Hembrow.

The girl looked at him, rather disappointed at his stolid reception of her report.

" Well, then I came away," she replied in a rather injured voice. " I went downstairs. I met Ernest's father in the hall, and we—we just passed the time of day."

" You said," interrupted Hembrow stolidly, reading from his notes, " ' Hullo, Daddy! How's your blue-eyed boy? Give him my love, but not my address.' "

The girl giggled, swinging her long legs to and fro.

" Doesn't it sound silly when you read it out like that! Yes, that's what I said. It got my goat the way he looked at me as if he was trying not to see me! "

" Doesn't Ernest Greenaway know your address? "

The girl looked troubled and defiant. She frowned, and her blue eyes seemed to go black under the heavy fringe that covered her eyebrows.

" Yes, of course he does. That was just a joke, a manner of speaking. I wish to goodness he didn't know it! "

She stared broodingly across the room, her face set in sullen lines that robbed it of all charm. Then she stirred suddenly, shrugged her shoulders and smiled.

" Well, what's the use of worrying? " she demanded of the world in general. " A short life and a gay one, eh? " She looked mischievously at John, slipped down from the piano and walked restlessly over to the hearth.

" I have a few more questions to ask you, Miss

Shirley," said Hembrow. " What did you do when you left the building? "

" Went straight home like a good girl and spent the evening altering this dress to fit me," she replied promptly. " If you don't believe me, ask Maidie Hally who lives in the top flat. She was here helping me all the evening."

Inspector Hembrow used his note-book for a few moments while the girl waited, facing him defiantly. Then he shut the book deliberately and remarked:

" How is it, Miss Shirley, that though you never entered Mr. Frew's flat last night, this handkerchief of yours was found in the dining-room? "

The girl looked blank for a moment, then flushed up.

" It isn't mine! " she said immediately, without looking at it. " Or if it is I must have left it there the day before."

" It was crumpled into a ball, and quite damp when I found it. You had been crying, had you not, Miss Shirley? "

" I tell you it isn't mine! " cried the girl indignantly. " Crying! I haven't cried for ten years. I didn't cry when I heard about Gordon this morning, and he was a good friend to me! What d'you take me for? I tell you I didn't so much as put my nose inside the door last night! "

" No need to be so indignant," said Hembrow calmly. " Take a look at the handkerchief, Miss Shirley. P is your initial, is it not? "

" Yes." Still hot-eyed and angry, she scrutinized the small square of cambric. " It isn't mine," she said, but with less assurance. " At least——"

" Well? "

" Oh, how should I know! I've got dozens and dozens of handkerchiefs! People keep giving them to me! I—I don't know whether it's mine or not! But I didn't leave it there! I swear I didn't! You can't mix me up in this! I swear——"

She looked wildly round, and suddenly to his immense embarrassment Christmas found her clinging to his hand and sobbing.

" I—I liked Gordon," she sobbed incoherently. " I didn't want him to die! I—I liked him, I tell you! "

As suddenly as she had begun to weep she left off, and releasing John's hand, got up from her knees and dried her tears.

" Has it got my laundry-mark? " she asked, fairly composedly, but with a catch in her breath. " It's F27 in ink."

" There's no laundry-mark," replied Hembrow. " But it appears to be a new handkerchief."

" I did have a dozen new hankies given me about a fortnight ago," said the girl unsteadily. " I don't know. It may be mine. . . ."

She went to the mirror over the mantelpiece and began to repair the damage her tears had done to the rouge and powder on her face.

" I wasn't there, Mr. Hembrow," she said at length. " That's all I can say. I wish I had been. I wouldn't have thought twice about knifing anyone who tried to do poor old Gordon any harm. . . ." Her eyes began to fill again, but she blinked away the tears and smiled determinedly. " But what's done's done, and watering people's graves don't bring them to life again." She stood a moment hand on hip looking at the carpet, then roused herself and shrugged her shoulders. " Well," she said cheerfully, " we've all got to die some day. What difference does it make? "

" Thank you, Miss Shirley," said Hembrow, rising. " That's all I want to know for the present. We'll wish you good evening."

She preceded them slowly to the door, and paused with her hand on the knob.

" Mr. Hembrow," she said slowly. " There's something—perhaps I ought to tell you——"

" What? "

She moistened her lips and spoke in a lowered voice.

" Ernest," she said. " Ernest Greenaway. He was jealous. He hated Gordon. Often he swore he'd do him in. And him hanging about in the courtyard last night, in the fog. It seems queer, doesn't it? "

" Thank you for telling me," said Hembrow stolidly.

She looked disappointed at his cool reception of her news.

" Well," she said uncertainly, " I suppose you know all that already." Her large eyes searched his impassive face for the information she wanted. " He terrifies me," she said sullenly. " Always threatening and hanging about. Men like him aren't safe. One never knows what they'll take it into their silly heads to do."

It was plain that Miss Shirley would not have been sorry to see her former betrothed convicted of murder and comfortably removed from her sphere.

Hembrow said indifferently:

" If he's been threatening you, you can have him bound over."

" Fat lot of good that'd do," muttered Pandora sulkily. " Oh, well! I can look after myself, I suppose. Good-bye."

She smiled sadly at John, ignoring the heartless Hembrow, and standing in the doorway watched them descend the gloomy stairs. In the hall they passed a tall, florid man in a cloak and opera-hat who had just come in—Pandora's escort to the ball, no doubt.

John Christmas offered to accompany Hembrow back to Scotland Yard, and in the taxi he told him of the interview he had had with Gilbert Cold, and the queer story of the sealed envelope left in that gentleman's care and sent to Mrs. Rudgwick. Hembrow listened carefully, and when John came to the story of the apparently purposeless burglary at Camperdown Terrace, the bright snap of his deepset eyes and the abruptness of his voice showed his excitement. He leant immediately out of the window and gave the driver instructions to drive him to 9 Camperdown Terrace.

"This is a clue that must be followed up immediately," he said. "For it certainly looks as if somebody else besides Mrs. Rudgwick had an interest in that sealed envelope. And if we can lay our hands on the burglar we shall probably find ourselves not far from the murderer. I meant to go home and work out a little problem that has occurred to me, but it looks as if I shall be out late to-night, after all."

"Wish I could come with you," said John regretfully. "But I promised to spend the evening with some friends. I wonder if Serafine would let me off."

"Is that the Miss Wimpole who was at Madox Court last night? I heard you call her Serafine. If so, you might be better employed if you kept your promise than if you came with me."

"Good Lord!" exclaimed John with a laugh. "You're not beginning to suspect Miss Wimpole, are you?"

" Oh, no," said the Inspector, smiling. " But there's sure to be a good deal of talk about the murder during the evening, and you might find an idea present itself to you, especially if some of the guests of last night are there."

" Newtree will be," said John meditatively, " and Sir Marion Steen, and Mordby, no doubt. Yes, perhaps you're right, Hembrow. I expect they'll each have a different theory about the criminal, each one more far-fetched than the last. By the way, Hembrow, Miss Shirley's evidence seemed to corroborate what Gilbert Cold said about Frew having been a married man. Queer, if he has a wife, that she hasn't put in an appearance. But of course she may be abroad, or even dead."

" Possibly," said Hembrow quietly, " but I don't think so. And I think we may find that her silence is not so queer after all. I may as well tell you, Mr. Christmas, that I have positive proof that there was a woman in the deceased's flat last night before he died."

" This is something new, Inspector! What's led you to that conclusion? "

" Well," explained Hembrow, " to begin with, there's this handkerchief, marked with a P——"

" But," interrupted John in some surprise, " is there any reason to think it isn't Pandora Shirley's? She admitted herself that it might be hers."

" But she denied having entered the flat last night. When I found this handkerchief, on first entering the dining-room, it was soaking wet, as if somebody had been crying into it quite lately. Now I wouldn't trust too much to Miss Shirley's truthfulness, and she may have been lying when she said she never entered the flat. But we have a witness to the fact that she was only in Madox Court about ten minutes altogether, and also to the fact that she was quite cheerful both when she entered and when she left. It's rather too much to believe that the girl burst into tears, cried long enough to soak a handkerchief, recovered her good spirits completely and removed every trace of tears in ten minutes. But the handkerchief, of course, is not proof in itself."

" Go on, Hembrow," said John as the Inspector paused. " Don't keep me in suspense. This is extremely interesting, though it looks as if it were going to complicate matters considerably."

" I don't know about that, Mr. Christmas. Rather the reverse, I fancy. Early this morning I examined the earth and gravel round the block of buildings in Madox Court. I found a woman's foot-prints in the passage that runs along the back of the flats—where you had your little tussle with young Greenaway. They were made by a thin, high-heeled pair of shoes, size four, and they led only one way, towards the road. There are no women servants employed in the block, and no women living there. Pandora Shirley takes size six in shoes. The foot-prints did not lead all the way from the back door to the road, but started suddenly in the middle of the passage, as if their owner had dropped out of heaven. And," said Hembrow impressively, taking out a pocket-book, " I found this clinging to the corrugated iron of the outhouse roof under Mr. Frew's studio window."

Carefully Hembrow removed from the book a small shred of fuchsia-coloured silk. Christmas stared at it, fascinated. As he looked at the grimly-incriminating slip of silk he seemed to see the phantom of a small pale woman in a brilliant fuchsia gown; and for a moment his instinctive pity for any woman tied against her will to a man like Gordon Frew protested against the ruthless work he was engaged upon. Then his interest in the case as a case reasserted itself.

"Have you followed up this clue at all, Inspector? Did anybody see the woman, I wonder, in Hurst Road or elsewhere?"

Hembrow shook his head.

"So far, all the inquiries we've made have drawn blank. She seems to have simply vanished into the fog. The murderer, whoever he or she may be, has a lot to thank that fog for. So far all we know is that a small woman wearing a red dress, scarf or shawl climbed out of Frew's studio window last night and escaped along the passage-way into the street. I shall lose no time in following up her trail, but meanwhile I think this burglary at Camperdown Terrace calls for more immediate attention. Why didn't the fool of a man call in the police this morning? Probably every clue to the identity of the burglar is destroyed by now!"

"She must have been a very athletic woman," said John thoughtfully, "and a brave one, too, to drop from the window on to that outhouse roof. It's a wonder she didn't break her neck, especially if she was a short woman, as her size in shoes seems to indicate. Why, it was quite a feat for me! I shouldn't have cared to do it in cold blood, and I stand six foot two. When I was hanging on to the sill by my finger-nails my toes were still inches off the roof, and it's a sloping one. I don't see how she could have done it. Even if she managed not to injure herself, the drop on to that galvanized iron must have made the devil of a noise! Yet nobody heard anything."

Hembrow looked at his friend with a sidelong, rather sorry look.

"I think I've got the explanation of that, Mr. Christmas, though I'm afraid it's one you won't like. I'll keep it to myself for the present. . . . This the place? H'm! Certainly doesn't look very enticing to an ordinary thief! Do you want the taxi, Mr. Christmas? I shan't keep it."

John wished his friend good luck, and sat watching in the taxi until the door of 9a opened and closed behind Inspector Hembrow. Then he gave the driver Serafine's address and drove off. He wished very much that he could go home to his flat and think over the events of the day in solitude. He felt not at all in the mood for light conversation.

CHAPTER X

A PARTY AT SERAFINE'S

THERE was the usual lively crowd at Serafine's little house on Hampstead Heath, the usual roar of conversation on the usual subjects. Laurence Newtree, persuaded much against his will by John, was there, and Simon Mordby and little Sir Marion Steen. Imogen Wimpole, implored by Serafine not to turn the evening into a post-mortem by recounting the previous night's adventures, was mystifying her guests by hints and veiled allusions to terrible experiences which had robbed her of her night's sleep and made her really unfit to perform the duties of a hostess properly. She looked, however, her usual beautiful, large, eupeptic self. Serafine, John thought, seemed to have suffered most from the shock. For one so energetic, she seemed a little lifeless and absent-minded, rousing herself occasionally to her usual argumentative brilliance and then dropping back into platitudes or silence. She looked pale and careworn and confided to John that she wished very much her guests would all go.

"My dear, what's the matter with you? I thought you were your happiest in a crowd?"

"So I am, as a rule. I don't know. I feel morbid."

"Last night?"

"I suppose so. But it's worse than that. I feel as if I were waiting for something too horrible to happen."

John smiled.

" Don't tell me you're the criminal."

" I couldn't feel more jumpy if I were," said Serafine with a tired grin. " Here's that fool Mordby. Stay and keep him off me, for heaven's sake! "

" Ah, Christmas! " Mordby came up behind John with his soft, secretive tread and took his hand in a soft, boneless clasp. " Why, you're looking worn-out, man! " He dropped his voice. " How do you find the trail? "

" Distinctly long and winding," replied John flippantly, wishing the doctor would not stare gravely and intently into his eyes as if he were reading the symptoms of a serious complex, inhibition or what-not. However, it was no use wishing, for that wide, vague yet earnest stare was part of Mordby's stock-in-trade. Patients like Imogen Wimpole liked to think that those wide grey eyes could see into their inmost souls and save them the trouble of explaining themselves. Privately, John diagnosed myopia and guessed that even the earthly garment of the soul was more than a little blurred to that searching gaze.

" I understand," went on the psychologist in confidentially lowered tones, " that the detection of crime is a hobby of yours. I also find crime and the criminal a most interesting study, though I prefer to study them from the arm-chair, as they say, rather than at first hand Now——" He moved a little closer to John, and John, who heartily and instinctively disliked him, had to repress a discourteous impulse to move abruptly back, " I wonder —have you formed any theory as to the murderer? "

Christmas smiled at this bald question.

" A hundred," he replied amiably. " All equally interesting, all equally unlikely to coincide with the facts."

" Ah! " said Mordby, shaking his large head. " Of course you won't tell me. But I ventured to wonder whether I mightn't be of some service to you, in a purely unofficial way. I suppose I may say, without vanity, that I know as much about abnormal psychology as any man in England. And I've often thought that such a knowledge, helping one as it does to recognize the potential murderer practically at sight, would be invaluable to a student of crime, like yourself."

"The difficulty is," said Christmas gravely, "that, to quote your own words, Dr. Mordby, we are all potential murderers."

"Yes, yes," said the doctor eagerly. "That is so. But only the student of psychology can gauge the—ah! breaking-point of a given individual with anything like accuracy. I suppose this is hardly the time and place to discuss such a matter. . . ." He looked regretfully towards the door as if he would have liked to lead John off to some more private place. "But I hope to have an opportunity of a talk with you soon. I may say that I have formed a certain opinion, and I shall be interested to see whether events bear me out."

"Indeed!" Serafine, who had so far made a silent third in the group, suddenly joined in. A little surprised at her incisive tone, John glanced at her and saw that her cheeks were flushed and her eyes unusually hard and bright. "Won't you give us your opinion, Dr. Mordby, and let us share the interest?"

Mordby put his head on one side and disclosed a row of even white teeth and one gold one in a whimsical, consciously charming smile.

"I hardly feel that such a gruesome subject of discussion is appropriate to these charming surroundings."

"What does it matter?" said Serafine, still in that hard, light tone. "It isn't a personal affair. The murderer, whoever he may be, isn't a friend of ours. Why not discuss him?"

She laughed. John, who knew her so well, could not understand her in this mood.

"I hope you don't think I did it, Dr. Mordby," she went on flippantly. "In that case, I would much rather you kept your theory to yourself. I don't want to have John sleuthing me all over London. It would quite spoil our old friendship."

"My dear Miss Wimpole," replied Mordby, smiling, "as I told you last night, your potentiality for murder, or in fact any violent act, is extremely low. I can hardly imagine the circumstances in which so well co-ordinated a mind as yours would reach breaking-point."

He gave a quaint, pompous little bow to lend his words the air of a soothing compliment. Serafine took no notice. Her set, hard smile did not leave her lips.

"Won't you give us the benefit of your theory?" she persisted with a tactless obstinacy and disregard for the amenities of conversation that was most unusual in her. "If I ask you to, Dr. Mordby? I've been doing a little theorizing myself, and I should like to see if your theory fits in anywhere with mine."

The intense seriousness which John divined beneath her flippant manner puzzled him beyond words. He moved a little closer to her, half with an instinctive impulse to protect, half with a vague desire to remind her by a look or touch that this was not the time for dragging out of Mordby his possibly absurd but probably obnoxious theories. She took no notice of him at all, still looking inquiringly at the doctor, who seemed rather pleased than otherwise at this interest in his ideas coming from such an unlikely quarter. He knew well, since it was part of his business and the secret of his success to be sensitive to such things, that Serafine disliked and distrusted him, and he returned her dislike in full measure.

" Well," he replied at length, " I will reply by asking you a question, Miss Wimpole. Did you notice yesterday evening that a certain member of the party took out his handkerchief to wipe his forehead, glanced at it and suddenly thrust it back again into his pocket? I did. And I also noticed that the handkerchief was stained with blood."

John started and looked at Mordby with real interest, wondering how far his observation could be depended on. He knew that the doctor had mentioned no such incident to Hembrow the evening before. Serafine changed countenance slightly, and there was a just perceptible pause before she said lightly:

" Indeed? Bloodstains always sound terribly incriminating, don't they? But after all it's quite a common thing for a man to cut his finger."

" Not during an evening party, Miss Wimpole."

" Before he sets out for his party."

" He would take a clean handkerchief before setting out."

" I suppose we had better not ask who the blood-stained gentleman was? "

" I would rather not tell you, Miss Wimpole."

" Then I shall take it that he was a friend of mine. But the only friends of mine at Mr. Newtree's last night were John, Sir Marion and—yourself, Dr. Mordby. Mr. Newtree and Dr. Merewether I had not met before. It was not yourself, or you would hardly be taking me into your confidence. It was not John, or you would hardly mention it in his presence. Am I to understand that you think Sir Marion Steen——"

"Certainly not!" said Mordby very hastily and in a shocked tone, glancing uncomfortably over his shoulder as if he feared the millionaire might have overheard this preposterous suggestion.

With each word uttered these exchanges seemed to John to take on more and more the character of a duel, and Dr. Mordby's last sentence was uttered in an almost openly inimical tone. John, standing by and listening, felt extremely uncomfortable. His civilized soul was shocked at Serafine's persistence in such a conversation, and he determined to tell her so at the first opportunity. He could not imagine what demon had taken possession of his urbane and amiable friend.

"Not Sir Marion?" murmured Serafine, still with that glassy smile. "Well, I hardly thought it could have been, but a long acquaintance with detective fiction has led me to believe that the blood-stained handkerchief always belongs to the most unlikely man." Suddenly she laughed, a laugh that was nearly, but not quite, natural and set John's teeth on edge. "But really, is that all you have to tell us, Dr. Mordby? You make me feel quite nervous, and I shall be very careful about my handkerchiefs in future. For I've often managed to get blood-stains on my handkerchief, but I've never yet committed a murder."

John, fearing a recommencement of the verbal duel, was about to break in and change the subject completely, when Imogen Wimpole, with an earnest and portentous expression on her smooth fair face, came up and laid a hand on his arm.

"John," she said impressively, "I've been talking to Mrs. De Valley—you know, the medium. And I do so want you to meet her. She says it's not at all impossible to get into touch with poor Mr. Frew before he passes too far on, and find out that way who did—you know. (Serafine says I'm not to talk about it, though I'm sure I can't think of anything else to talk about, after last night.) Mrs. De Valley says it's often been done, when people have—have died suddenly, with marvellous results. And if anybody could do it, she could. She really is marvellous! She gets the most amazing results at all her séances."

"Oh, auntie!" laughed Serafine, who seemed to have completely recovered her composure. "You're not proposing to turn this party into a séance, are you?"

Her aunt looked at her reproachfully.

"Serafine doesn't believe in it," she said sadly to John. "But she's such a dreadful materialist. She doesn't believe in anything incredible. I tell her she doesn't realize what she misses. Don't you agree with me, Dr. Mordby?"

Dr. Mordby turned the full battery of his gold and ivory smile upon his former patient.

"I should not say that Miss Wimpole is lacking in faith," he replied silkily, and it seemed to John that there was an underlying note of satire in his voice. "And as for spiritualism, I'm afraid you must expect a certain scepticism in a man of my profession. The whole matter is so easily explained on psychological grounds that——"

"Oh, I believe in psychology!" protested Mrs. Wimpole with delightful comprehensiveness. "And I believe in spiritualism too! I don't see why one shouldn't believe in both, or in everything, for that matter! It makes life so much more interesting."

Serafine and John exchanged smiles, and Dr. Mordby murmured soothingly:

" It does, it does, it certainly does."

" Come along, auntie," said Serafine, slipping her hand through the older woman's arm. " Introduce me to your Mrs. De Valley. Tell her I'm a sheep to be gathered into the fold. I'll promise to behave myself. John and Dr. Mordby are in the thick of a terribly absorbing conversation."

The two ladies drifted away, and John, with a smile at Mordby, murmured:

" Are we? "

Once again he found himself wondering what Serafine was after. Did she wish him to pump Mordby further as to his theory of the crime? Personally he did not see that anything was to be gained by it. It had always been obvious that Mordby disliked George Merewether, and it was natural that he should joyfully put the worst construction upon such a matter as that of the blood-stained handkerchief. But could it be possible that Mordby's patronizing dislike of the other doctor was based upon something more tangible than the natural antipathy of one type for another? Could it be possible that Mordby had some ulterior motive in wishing to force suspicion upon the man he disliked? Was Serafine groping towards some discovery which might straighten out the threads of this mystery?

Simon Mordby answered blandly:

" We did begin one, but we were abruptly and charmingly interrupted."

" It is early days as yet," said John conversationally, hoping to draw the doctor out, " but this murder looks as if it were going to be the most puzzling mystery I have ever run across. Do you remember the British Museum murder? That was a puzzling affair, if you like, but in a different way. In that case suspicion pointed absolutely nowhere. In this case it points in all directions at once."

" Is that so? " murmured Simon Mordby. He went on with an air of diffidence : " Of course I'm not *au fait* with the course of events since last night. But a man of my profession is naturally observant of the demeanour of the people with whom he comes in contact. And I noticed one or two things last night which have caused my thoughts to trend in a direction which makes me feel quite ashamed. And yet——"

He sighed. Merewether's name had not been mentioned, but it was obvious enough of whom Dr. Mordby spoke. John's first impulse was to defend Merewether by assuming perfect ignorance of what Mordby referred to, followed by shocked surprise when Merewether's name was mentioned. But just as he was about to speak he altered his tactics. There was nothing to be gained by such a display of innocence. He could hardly hope even to deceive Mordby by it, for it was obvious that Merewether had placed himself in an equivocal position by his display of agitation, and that anybody investigating the case could not fail to take a good deal of interest in him. John determined to try the effect of a bluff and breezy candour. He had learnt from experience that men of Mordby's type feared and distrusted candour above everything, and were sometimes betrayed by it into quite interesting reactions.

" You've never hit it off very well with Merewether, have you, Dr. Mordby? " he asked with a diffident smile that robbed the blunt question of offence, and waited in silence for the reply.

Mordby shot a quick glance at him. For a moment he seemed uncertain how to answer. Then recovering his poise, he smiled, shook his head, and replied with a composure John could not but admire:

"I have a great respect for Dr. Merewether. He has always seemed to me the perfect type of integrity. We went through the hospitals together, and I think I may say it is not my fault that we have not kept up our old acquaintance. The little rivalries of youth are not always forgotten when one grows older and wiser. I have long ago forgiven Merewether for once having been my rival; or rather I have realized that there is nothing to forgive. But I do not think he has forgiven me."

The doctor rounded off his well-delivered little speech with a sigh. Christmas did not believe a word of it, for he knew Merewether well enough to know that he was the last man in the world to nourish a grievance for fifteen years or so, and the casual insolence with which Mordby treated his less-successful confrère had always been disagreeably noticeable. Still, it was an admirable speech, admirably spoken, and John realized that Mordby was not to be betrayed by bluff candour into any expression of his real feelings.

"Your interests lie so far apart," murmured John thoughtfully, "that I shouldn't have thought there was room for professional rivalry."

"The rivalry was not professional," said Dr. Mordby with ready amiability. "Though at the beginning of my career I did intend to be a surgeon. No. The rivalry was in the realm of—ah! sentiment, my dear Christmas. There was a certain beautiful young lady, a fellow medical student. And although she favoured neither of us, our feelings for one another were none the less bitter." He smiled and sighed, as if both deriding and regretting the stormy days of youth. "She cared for neither of us, and she married neither of us, and for at least twelve years I have not seen nor heard of her. Yet the bitterness remains —on the one side. As for my side, though you may not believe me, I cannot at the moment so much as recall her name! "

Christmas did not believe him. Excellent as the story was up to this point, the last touch, intended as a guarantee of genuineness, betrayed unmistakably the faker's hand. It was artistic; it was altogether too artistic. And as, still with the lingering smile of one who recalls his dead self, the eminent psycho-analyst moved away, John could not tell whether his whole story had been a fabrication or whether it were a skilful interweaving of truth and falsehood. The latter, he was inclined to believe, since the story sounded altogether too romantic and too unlikely for a man of Mordby's intellect to make up on the spur of the moment.

Later in the evening, Imogen Wimpole, mistaking young Conway the engraver for a popular singer who was also present, persuaded him to " sing just one little song before people went away "; and John, who happened to be standing near Dr. Mordby, found further food for thought. With much enthusiasm but little tunefulness young Conway sang a song called " Phyllis is my only Joy." At the opening bars the doctor's slight habitual smile went out like a blown candle. Of course, young Conway's cheerful bawl was enough to cause a change of expression on the face of any lover of music. But there was also the possibility that Simon Mordby remembered the lady's name only too well.

Soon after this most of the guests took their departure, and John to his relief found himself alone in the smoke-laden, disordered room with his hostesses, Newtree and

Sir Marion Steen. Imogen Wimpole yawned delicately and looked at the tiny watch on her plump wrist. The precious hours before midnight, which do so much to restore fatigued beauty, were gone beyond recall.

"Well," she said complacently, "I think it went off very well, Serafine dear, though I never felt less like entertaining people in my life. And now I suppose you're all going to talk about the murder."

"You were a beautiful hostess, Imogen," said her niece. "You did all my work as well as your own. But, darling, you really shouldn't ask people like Peter Conway to sing."

"I know," said Imogen placidly. "I thought he was what's-his-name. But it didn't really matter a bit, because I'd told lots of people what's-his-name was going to sing, and they all said how wonderfully he sang. Luckily, he'd gone home."

"There was one person who wasn't impressed," said John. "And that was Dr. Mordby. When Peter began, he looked as if somebody were treading on his feet."

"Probably somebody was, then," said Mrs. Wimpole tranquilly. "It couldn't have been Peter's singing that made him look like that. Because he's often told me music means absolutely nothing to him at all."

"The man that hath no music in his soul," began Sir Marion, and then, suddenly perceiving that the quotation in the circumstances was an unfortunate one, left it unfinished, and exchanged with Serafine a smile at his own embarrassment.

"Lord!" said Serafine with vigour, when her aunt had wandered away to tell the servants to go to bed. "How I hate that man Mordby!"

She flung her cigarette violently into the fire as though she were flinging a brick-bat at Mordby's head, and shivered, and drew her shawl around her as though she felt cold, although indeed the room was extremely warm.

"What a poisonous tongue!"

Sir Marion and Newtree smiled a little at the lady's violence, and John remarked gently:

"Well, my dear, you certainly encouraged him to use it."

She dropped into a chair and looked broodingly at the fire.

"I know," she said abruptly. "I was a fool, I suppose. But last night in the cab coming home, he kept hinting and skirting round—oh, you know what, John! Of course we all talked about the murder all the way home. And he—oh well, you heard him, Sir Marion!"

She looked appealingly at the philanthropist, who nodded sympathetically.

"And so," went on Serafine, "I wanted to make him come out into the open and say what he thought—or pretended to think, instead of just hinting at it, the old serpent. I thought then we could—oh, stop him somehow! I didn't know he'd seen——" She caught herself up sharply. "I didn't know he was going to say he'd seen so much."

She stopped suddenly on an overwrought, uncertain note. There was a silence.

"Sir Marion," said John slowly, "did you notice anything unusual in the demeanour of any of the people at Newtree's last night?"

Sir Marion looked thoughtfully and pityingly at Serafine. Finally he said diffidently:

"I noticed what I suppose everybody who was present at the dreadful scene must have noticed: that Dr. Merewether was much more cut up at the sight of the murdered man than one expects a doctor to be on such an occasion. But I confess that I have never before seen a medical man confronted with the body of a man who has been murdered. And I did not think much of the matter. I merely thought that doctors were, after all, more subject to human emotion than novels and so on would lead one to suppose."

He placed the tips of his fingers together, studied them thoughtfully for a moment, and then looked interrogatively at John. John was about to speak, but the elder man went on:

"As I told you this morning, John, I have no sympathy at all with the—the impersonal sort of interest you and many others take in cases of this kind. I feel the horror of the thing too much to be able to treat it as a kind of game of chess. Yes, yes," he said with a smile and an upraised hand as John was about to protest, "I know already all that you are about to say. I know that justice must be done. I know that the murderer cannot be allowed to go free. I know that neither you nor anybody else interested in the detection of crime is responsible for our penal laws. I know that you would not hurt a fly. I know, in short, that I am a sentimental old juggins. I am merely stating my personal feelings when I say that I would rather help a murderer to escape than give him up to be hanged. Come," went on Sir Marion in a half-jocular tone that did not disguise his real earnestness, looking with his air of gentle, bird-like intelligence from one to another, "are we not all alike in this? If he were in your power, would any one of you give a murderer directly up to the law without a qualm of conscience? A murderer is not necessarily a monster. I think a learned gentleman told us last night that we are all potential murderers. I do not say that I altogether agree with him. Still, there is undoubtedly some truth in the assertion."

There was silence for a moment or two after Sir Marion's diffident voice had ceased. Then John said gravely:

"You must remember, Sir Marion, that in pursuing the guilty we clear the innocent of suspicion."

"I was coming to that," said the great financier gently, looking from one to another of the little group around the fire. "From what I have heard this evening, I gather that suspicion is falling heavily, in some minds at least, upon an innocent person—a person, rather, whom we all believe to be innocent."

Serafine looked up quickly.

"Then you believe him innocent, Sir Marion?"

"I never met Dr. Merewether before last night," replied Steen levelly. "I know nothing whatever about him. Yet I do believe him innocent. Or rather, shall I say, I believe him to be an upright, honest and courageous man, and I feel that even were he proved guilty of this crime I should not modify my opinion of him. I should feel that he must have had some justification. I will not say that I am utterly convinced he is innocent. But I say that if he is guilty I hope the crime may never be brought home to him. You, I take it," he turned to Serafine, "are completely convinced of his innocence?"

Serafine hesitated, and replied at last huskily:

"I feel as you do, Sir Marion."

But Newtree cried almost scornfully, in tones of the most utter conviction:

"Merewether! Merewether might kill a man, if the man deserved killing, but he's absolutely incapable of stabbing him in the back! If he told me himself he'd done it, I shouldn't believe him!"

Sir Marion went on:

"If there is anything I can ever do to assist our friend, I hope that I may be given the chance to do it. I do not know when I have felt more drawn to a man at a first meeting. I only wish I could produce evidence which would immediately clear him of suspicion. That's beyond my power, alas! But I am a rich man, and I have a certain amount of influence. If there is ever anything I can do, either to help you prove Merewether's innocence, or if the worst happens, to give him a good defence, you have only to call on me, Mr. Newtree. By the way, John, has anything been heard of the mysterious stranger who passed us in Greentree Road? I can't help feeling that a clue to the mystery lies there."

"We haven't found him yet," said John, "but we have found a new witness to his presence in Greentree Road last night, and he becomes even more mysterious. For, according to the crossing-sweeper in Shipman's Mews, he altered his mind soon after leaving you and decided to go to Primrose Hill."

"Primrose Hill! Why, that's in the opposite direction!"

"Quite so. The crossing-sweeper gave it as his opinion that Hanwell was the place he was really bound for."

Sir Marion smiled.

"Let me know how the affair progresses, John. I shan't feel easy in my mind until I know that our friend Merewether is safely out of the wood."

So saying he took his departure, and soon after John and Laurence rose to go.

"John," said Serafine, speaking in a low voice, while

Newtree was making his adieux to Imogen Wimpole, "is there really a possibility that Dr. Merewether will be arrested?"

"Not the slightest, at the moment," replied John with a cheerfulness which he did not altogether feel. "There's really no evidence against him at all, except the one rather serious fact that for some reason known only to himself he chose to say that he had seen Frew alive at a time when the medical evidence proves that he was dead. This is certainly serious, but it does not necessarily go to prove that Merewether killed Frew. Don't worry, Serafine. As Newtree said just now, men like Merewether don't stab their enemies in the back."

"How does he know?" she asked sombrely. "How can anyone tell what another person may be driven to do?"

"Ah, my dear," said Christmas, "you're letting the horrible thing that happened last night get on your nerves. You're building up a tragedy on the strength of Merewether's momentary nervousness. Why, he wasn't the only one. Mordby certainly lost his nerve pretty completely for a moment, and Laurence went the colour of cheese, and I don't think I showed any great sangfroid. Yet we're not all murderers. Any man might seem a little off-colour at being suddenly confronted with what we saw in Frew's rooms last night."

Serafine brushed this well-meant explanation aside.

"Not so much so. Not a doctor, anyhow. Certainly not Dr. Merewether. You can't deceive me, John. You said all that just to cheer me up."

John looked gravely at his old friend, noting how some sudden strain had aged her strong, humorous face, robbed her of the brilliance and animation which gave her such an air of timeless youth, and made her look what she was —a strong and over-energetic woman wearing fine and thin with the approach of middle age.

"Serafine," he said gently, and hesitated. Her keen black eyes, set in bistred rings, held his moodily for a moment. Then she smiled, not very mirthfully, and answered the question he had not asked.

"I'm sure I don't know, John. I mean I don't know why I should take this morbid interest in the affairs of a perfect stranger. I can only say that I do. I—I liked Dr. Merewether. He interested me. He seemed to me to be built on a larger scale than most of us—a tragic scale. I suppose that's why I feel that this particular tragedy may be his tragedy."

She was silent for a moment, her long fingers plucking at the fringe of her shawl. Then suddenly she shrugged her shoulders so that her shawl slipped down over her arm. She smiled straight at John, as if she had determinedly shrugged off trouble with the yellow silk.

"You're dying to point out to me that the murder of one perfect stranger by another perfect stranger needn't rob me of my beauty-sleep," she said. "And although you kindly refrain from doing so, I'll take the idea to heart, all the same."

"I'm not dying to do anything of the kind. Certainly I don't like to see you looking so tired."

"And old—eh, John? Tragedy disagrees with me, I know. I'll try to leave it alone and stick to comedy, which is certainly more in my line. Laugh and the world laughs with you, weep and you weep alone. Upon my soul, John, there was never a truer thing said in worse verse!"

CHAPTER XI

MY DEAR WATSON

"HOW would you like to live in Primrose Hill, Laurence?" asked John Christmas conversationally the next morning, as the two friends took their seats on the top of a bus bound for Highgate. John had made an early raid on Madox Court and firmly detaching Newtree from pencil and paper had lured him out on what he called a tour of detection. The day being fine, with a bright sun and a slight exhilarating frost in the air, Newtree had not been altogether unwilling to come, although he had asked plaintively, with a conscience-stricken glance at his drawing-board, whether John couldn't do his detecting by telephone. On being firmly assured that this was impossible, he had given way to pressure and his own inclinations, and sallied forth with his friend into the sunshine.

"*On* Primrose Hill, I suppose you mean," he replied now, in a slightly carping tone, having just been reminded by the sight of a newsbill at a street corner that he had not yet thought of a subject for the week's political cartoon. "People don't live *in* Primrose Hill."

"Do they live on it?" asked John in the tones of the earnest seeker after information.

"Well—as a matter of fact they don't live on it, either," said Newtree. "You know as well as I do that

Primrose Hill is a sort of mound of earth with grass and trees and a few railings on it. There aren't even any primroses."

"Dash it!" expostulated John gently. "If the inhabitants of the district can't live *in* Primrose Hill or *on* Primrose Hill, where do they live?"

"What does it matter?" asked his friend rather irritably. "They live round it, or near it, or by it or in its neighbourhood, I suppose. They live *in* St. John's Wood or Camden Town."

"Then if a person asked you the way to Primrose Hill you'd think he wanted to climb up it and look at the view?"

"Not necessarily," said Newtree testily. "He might want to go to a house in St. Edmund's Terrace or somewhere and ask for Primrose Hill because it's a good landmark. But look here, John, if you're thinking of inquiring at every house in the neighbourhood of the hill for a cross-eyed gentleman in a fez, I'm not coming with you. Life's not long enough. Besides, you won't find him there."

"Why not? He asked the crossing-sweeper the way to Primrose Hill."

"Obviously he meant to say Golders Green, and made a slip."

"Exactly. He meant to say Golders Green, and he did not mean to say Primrose Hill. But when he lost control of himself for a moment, he said what he did not mean to say. I don't propose to make a house-to-house search in the neighbourhood of Primrose Hill, because, as you say, it would take too long. But I shall certainly not inquire for him in Golders Green, because it is the last place on earth in which I expect to find him."

" I believe you asked me at the beginning of this idiotic conversation how I should like to live roundabout Primrose Hill," said Laurence. " Are you thinking of presenting me with a bijou residence there, or what? Because I'm quite comfortable in Madox Court, thank you, and Primrose Hill doesn't attract me in the least, in spite of the fact that it's near the ancestral home of my friend John."

" Eh? "

" The Zoo."

John expostulated.

" This is not the way that Watson speaks to his friend Holmes."

" Holmes didn't take Watson away from a pile of work just to sit on top of a bus and talk like a house-agent. If this happens often, I probably shall end up in the neighbourhood of Primrose Hill, in the new Steen home."

" Steel? Are they putting up sky-scrapers in that peaceful district? "

" Ass! The Steen Home of Rest for the Incurably Impecunious Aged. The residents are rather annoyed about it, I believe. They think it lowers the tone or something."

" They'll probably have reason to think so when you become an inmate. Gower Street. This is where we hop out."

Laurence rose with a sigh and followed his energetic friend down the street and in at the entrance of the University College grounds.

" Are we going to attend a lecture on medical jurisprudence? "

" No. I'm going to arrange for you to take one or two

lessons in drawing at the Slade School, which I believe has its being somewhere inside this temple of learning. You'd better wait outside like a good boy while I go in and smooth the way with the Professors."

John vanished through the neo-classic portals, and Laurence wandered obediently around the grounds, watching the fat pigeons searching for crumbs in the gravel, and looking with faint envy at the hatless young men and women who passed occasionally in and out of the gates in the pursuit of knowledge. The brilliant sunshine and the sight of youth combined to make him feel pensive, vaguely discontented and rather old. He thought, as is the way with every mortal, no matter what his achievements, at such a moment: Forty, and nothing done! Soon I shall be fifty, sixty, seventy. . . . And his work and life at Madox Court, which at most times seemed all that a man could desire of life, appeared for the moment unadventurous and wearisome in the extreme. He was so wrapped in this contemplative melancholy that he started when John Christmas suddenly appeared beside him.

"I'm sorry I've kept you waiting so long, Laurence, but there were a good many formalities to be gone through. However, I got what I wanted out of them in the end. And now we're going down to the city."

Laurence allowed himself to be escorted back to Tottenham Court Road and into a passing taxi-cab. As they drove along this lively and interesting thoroughfare his spirits revived, and by the time they reached Trafalgar Square his natural interest in the spectacle of bustling, consequential human life had returned and the last leaf of willow had dropped from him.

"What did you find out at University College, John?

I can't imagine that there's anything to be seen there that might throw light on this murder."

John, who was looking rather well-pleased with himself, replied:

"At Serafine's last night Simon Mordby spun me a romantic yarn about one of his early affairs of the heart. I wanted to find out from the registers whether it were true."

"And was it?"

"Part of it, certainly. All of it, very probably."

"Don't be so exasperating, John. I won't be Watson and follow you all over London unless I'm allowed to know what's what and why."

John smiled.

"Well, to go into details, the registers told me that Simon Hetherley Mordby and George Mathew Merewether took the degree of Bachelor of Medicine at University College in the same year. And they told me that two young women bearing the Christian name of Phyllis were medical students at the college at the same time as our two friends."

"Well?"

"Their names were Phyllis Nicholson and Phyllis Hilary Templar," went on John with enjoyment. "Phyllis Templar did not complete the course. Phyllis Nicholson finally took degrees and is now in practice in the West End."

"I hope," said Laurence fervently, "that you don't intend to call on Dr. Nicholson and ask her whether she murdered Gordon Frew. If you do, I am not coming with you."

"How crude you are, my dear Watson," murmured John reprovingly. "Certainly I don't intend to do any such thing. I don't think we need interest ourselves at all in Dr. Phyllis Nicholson. I should prefer to know the subsequent history of Miss Phyllis Templar."

"Well," said Laurence, philosophically, leaning back and lighting a cigarette, "Simon Mordby's love affairs may be very interesting, but I don't see what possible connection they can have with the murder of Gordon Frew. And as it must be at least ten years since he took his degree at University College, the state of his affections at the time can't have much interest for us now."

"He is still a bachelor," murmured John pensively, "and so is Merewether."

"So are you, and so am I. What of it?"

"But Gordon Frew was a married man."

"Well, so are lots of people—poor devils," added Newtree with more convention than conviction.

"Do you believe in love, Laurence?"

Newtree dropped his cigarette, groped for it on the floor of the cab, and having picked it up and burnt his fingers, flung it a quarter smoked through the window. For some obscure reason the question seemed to connect itself with the mood of vague melancholy into which he had fallen watching the students in University College grounds.

"My dear fellow," he protested at last, putting on his pince-nez as if for protection, "are you the editor of a woman's weekly paper? Or am I? And what does the question mean, anyhow? Kindly be more explicit."

"Certainly. Do you believe in a life-long constancy to the object of an early unrequited affection?"

Newtree looked puzzled, but rather relieved.

"Do I believe that such a constancy may exist? Is that what you mean? Well, of course it may, if the attachment is strong enough and the subject sufficiently obstinate. But what *has* Mordby's constancy or otherwise got to do with the matter in hand?"

"I wasn't thinking of Mordby at the moment," answered John gravely. "But this is where I get out, Laurence. I shan't be a minute."

The cab had turned into the courtyard of an imposing building in Queen Victoria Street. Looking curiously at its façade as John stepped out on to the pavement, Laurence read incised on the frontage "College of Arms." The place had a peaceful and timeworn aspect that accorded well with the ancient traditions for which it stood, and Laurence lit a cigarette and settled down to wait in patience until his erratic friend should have finished his business.

It was not long, however, before John emerged with a thoughtful expression on his face, and giving some directions to the driver, got in beside Newtree and sat down with a sigh of satisfaction.

"Where are we going now?" asked Laurence patiently.

"To Scotland Yard."

"And when we get to Scotland Yard," went on the long-suffering Laurence, "how long am I to wait outside?"

"Not at all," replied John with a laugh. "You shall come in with me and see whether Hembrow's got the murderer yet."

"And what did you discover just now at the Herald's Office to make you look as happy as a cat full of cream?"

"Something rather unexpected," replied John quietly. "You may remember, Laurence, that on the night of the murder I commented on the vanity of the late Mr. Frew, as evidenced in his possessions and the use he made of them."

"I remember. And it was pretty obvious when you pointed it out that the man was more than a bit of a poseur. Of course it was always obvious in his painting. But lots of people dabble in paint who've no more gift for it than he had. And somehow it never occurred to me that all his culture was a pose. Am I to understand that there was something sinister about his assumption of tastes and gifts that he did not possess? That he was leading a double life, as they say?"

"No, I don't think so," replied John meditatively. "I haven't found any reason for thinking so; and a double life is neither so easy to lead nor so difficult to detect as the more sensational type of fiction would lead one to suppose. I should say our friend Frew's pose was quite an innocent one, so far as any departure from the truth can be innocent. He desired to be credited with greater talents and more learned and cultured tastes than he actually possessed. But that is a common failing. All of us, except a few simple truthful souls like yourself, Laurence, are tempted to pose as possessing greater knowledge, greater gifts, or wider culture than we actually have. Which is merely a way of saying that vanity is a common human fault. But in some people, and notably in people who have passed their young days in cramping or unappreciative surroundings, this vain desire for approbation, applause, supremacy, becomes a ruling passion. And then it may be dangerous."

"But," protested Laurence, looking rather puzzled, "if Frew's vanity was innocent, it cannot have been dangerous, and you said——"

"When I say that the desire for approbation may become dangerous," said John slowly, "I am not thinking of Frew, but of a possible motive for his murder. And I am taking into consideration three things. The reminiscences that Frew was writing, the book on the libel-laws that he purchased not long before his death, and the sealed envelope which he directed Gilbert Cold to send to a woman who has been convicted of blackmail. Gordon Frew was a vain man, but I do not think that the desire for applause was his ruling passion."

"What then?"

"Another form of vanity, called jealousy."

"You talk," said Newtree curiously, "as if you know already who the murderer is, and all about it."

John laughed.

"I only wish I did! My dear chap, if I were to meet the murderer face to face this minute I shouldn't know him from Adam. At present I am just blocking in the composition of the picture, to use a phrase you will readily appreciate. I have no idea yet how the details will turn out. I am afraid my methods are not what Hembrow would call sound. The sound detective collects facts and deduces his theory from them. I prefer to create a theory out of the broad characteristics of the case, and then test the facts to see if they support my theory. If they don't, of course the theory falls to the ground; and if no other rises from the ruins to take its place, I have to give the affair up as hopeless."

"You haven't told me yet what it was you discovered at the College of Arms," Laurence reminded him.

"Something rather curious," replied John with a smile. "You remember, Laurence, that on the evening he was killed Frew received a communication from the College of Arms? And that the blotting-paper on his desk showed the beginning of a letter addressed to that body, and apparently in answer to one he had just received? And that the letter itself was nowhere to be found?"

"I remember," said Laurence. "But, as Hembrow pointed out at the time, there was nothing to show that the letter had not been written and posted a day or two before."

"I visited the College of Arms just now expressly to clear up that point," replied Christmas. "And I think it is cleared up pretty conclusively. The letter we found on the blotting-paper began, if you remember: Dear Sir, in answer to your communication—— Did it not?"

"Certainly."

"But I have just learnt that only one communication was addressed to Gordon Frew from the Herald's Office, and that was the communication he received on the night he died. So I think we may conclude that Gordon Frew's letter was also written on that night."

"Yes," agreed Laurence. "And in that case it looks as though the murderer had made away with the letter, though it's not easy to see why. What was the business between Frew and the Herald's Office, by the way?"

"Ah, that is the curious thing! Given a man of Frew's character, and given the fact that although he had been born in fairly humble circumstances, he belonged to one of the younger branches of a good family—what business would you suppose he would have with the Herald's College?"

"Why," said Laurence at once, "I should suppose that he was thinking of trying to establish his descent and his right to a coat-of-arms, or something of that kind."

"Of course," agreed John, "that is the obvious conclusion, and the one I came to myself. But it is not the correct one. Our friend Frew was thinking of changing his name."

"Changing his name!" echoed Laurence, looking the

picture of astonishment. " That doesn't sound much like a man who was proud of his blue blood! What was he going to change it to, and why? "

" If we knew the answer to the first question, we might make a guess at the answer to the second," said John. " Unfortunately, we don't. A few days ago a letter from Gordon Frew was received at the Herald's Office, stating that he wished to change his name and asking for information as to the formalities to be gone through. The information was posted to him on the morning of November 24, and, of course, nothing further has been heard from him."

" But what an extraordinary thing! " said Laurence. " Did he give any reason for the wish? "

" None. But here we are at the Yard. We'll pay off the taxi and go and see if Hembrow has any news for us."

" Good morning, gentlemen," said Hembrow cheerfully as John and Laurence entered the room. " I've been expecting to see you along this morning, Mr. Christmas! And I fancy I've got some news for you."

" About the burglary at Camperdown Terrace? "

" That, and some other news which doesn't bear so directly on the crime, but is a good deal more startling."

" You haven't arrested the burglar? "

Hembrow smiled.

" Not yet. But I picked up one or two good clues on the spot, which is more than I expected from a twenty-four hour old job. Foot-prints all over the place. No finger-prints. The burglar had taken the precaution of wearing gloves. The press has given such a lot of publicity one way and another to the finger-print system that even amateur cracksmen take that precaution nowadays. But they're not so careful about their feet.

The man had evidently dropped over the garden wall at the back—the foot-prints were quite clear in the soft earth of the flower-bed. I've sent a man up to photograph them."

"Anything else?"

"A pair of surgical forceps inside a drawer of the chest-of-drawers," said Hembrow cheerfully. "They had evidently been used to pick the lock and dropped inside the drawer and forgotten. Gloves! Gloves won't help a man much if he goes and makes an elementary mistake like that! And the stump of a hand-made cigarette rolled with a dark smoking-mixture and an A.G. paper lying close to the wall where the man got over. It was fairly plain what he was after, too. Every drawer in the place had been opened and every packet of papers sorted out. It was lucky for us that Mr. Cold didn't lock the envelope in a cabinet in the ordinary way."

"You haven't got possession of the envelope yet, I suppose?"

Hembrow shook his head.

"It's my idea that if we hang fire a bit the gentleman may give himself away by making an attempt on the Rudgwick's place, having failed to get what he wanted from Camperdown Terrace. I put a man on to watch the place last night, but so far the mouse hasn't walked into the trap."

"And have you any idea of who the man is, Inspector?" asked Laurence with interest.

Hembrow shook his head.

"Bit early to say yet, Mr. Newtree," he said affably, and John guessed that, early or not, the Inspector had formed his own opinion, but preferred, in Newtree's presence, to keep it to himself.

"I've got a piece of news for you, Inspector," he said, and proceeded to recount his interview with the clerk at the College of Arms. Hembrow listened with a good deal of interest, but not much surprise, John noted.

"So he was going to change his name, was he?" commented the detective, when John had finished. "Well, it wouldn't have been for the first time, though as far as I know he'd never gone to the length of taking legal steps about it before. I had an eye-opener this morning when I received the answer to a cable I sent yesterday to the New York headquarters."

"This sounds very interesting, Hembrow," said John, listening with close attention. "Go on. You're not going to tell us that the late Gordon Frew was a swell cracksman, or something of that kind, are you?"

"You're not far off it, Mr. Christmas," said Hembrow with the satisfaction of one who sees the mine he has laid exploding neatly under his victims' feet. "I thought it'd come as a surprise to you gentlemen, as it did to me."

"Well?" asked Newtree breathlessly.

Hembrow smiled at his eagerness.

"Well, after hearing what Mrs. Rudgwick had to say yesterday about her brothers who emigrated to America, I thought it'd be worth while to cable an inquiry, just on the off-chance that her idea of the deceased's character might prove to be correct. I certainly didn't expect quite so much as I got. It appears that Gordon Frew was one of the names, and thought to be the real name, of an Englishman calling himself Herbert Heath who did penal servitude twenty-five years ago for one of the biggest swindles that ever nearly succeeded. It was before my time, of course, but apparently it made a good deal of stir at the time. He was associated with two other men:

Henry Winter, who was thought to be the leading spirit in the enterprise, and Michael Templar, an older man and a copper-plate engraver by profession. Winter managed to escape, and it is thought that he committed suicide. A body thought to be his was found drowned in a canal soon after the gaff was blown. Herbert Heath, or Gordon Frew, made a desperate attempt to get away, but was overtaken and arrested, and did five years in prison. Michael Templar was convicted of forgery, and did ten years. Although there was a feeling at the time that Templar was merely a tool in the hands of Winter and Heath, it was impossible to prove forgery against Heath. There seems little doubt that it is the same man. The ages coincide exactly, and the appearance of the deceased, allowing for twenty-five years having passed, agrees with the description cabled by the New York police."

Hembrow sat back in his chair with a well-satisfied air, and looked from Laurence's interested face to John's.

"Well, I'm blowed!" said Laurence at last. "So he did lead a double life after all!"

"Not necessarily," rejoined Christmas. "He led two lives, but there is no evidence that he led them simultaneously. Have there been any subsequent convictions against Heath, or Frew, Inspector?"

"None. He left the country soon after his release from prison. It is thought that he went to Russia."

"And what happened to the other two men?"

"Henry Winter was presumed drowned, and Michael Templar, having shortened his period of imprisonment by his exemplary conduct, left the country with the avowed intention of settling in France. He seems to have been rather a different type of man from the two others. He had a good many friends waiting to help him when he came out of prison; and while he was serving his time a cousin of his had died and left him a considerable fortune. It is thought that he is still living in the south of France under an assumed name."

"I suppose," said John thoughtfully, "that you haven't got a description of Henry Winter and Michael Templar?"

"No," said Hembrow, looking rather surprised. "I can't imagine that it's necessary to have one, Mr. Christmas. Winter is dead, and it's pretty plain, I think, that the other man had nothing to do with this affair. My own view is that the past history of the deceased, though it certainly comes as a bit of a surprise, has no bearing on his death. By the way, Mr. Christmas, a witness has come forward who deposes to having seen a woman wearing a red shawl under her coat pass into the entrance of Madox Court just before eight o'clock on the night of the crime."

Hembrow took a paper from his desk.

"This is a voluntary statement made by Mrs. Helen Smith, the caretaker at Ransom House, which, as of course you know, is the new block of flats they've put up in Hurst Road not far from Madox Court." Hembrow cleared his throat and in his most expressionless official voice began to read Mrs. Smith's statement.

"'I am a caretaker at Ransom House, and live on the premises. On the evening of November 24 I went out to post some letters in the pillar-box which stands at the corner of Hurst Road and Greentree Road. As I approached Madox Court on my return journey I passed a young woman who was walking quickly down towards Greentree Road, and about ten yards behind her I passed a young man, who was walking slowly.'"

Hembrow glanced up from his paper.

" That will have been Pandora Shirley and young Greenaway," he interpolated, and went on:

" ' As I passed the entrance to Madox Court I saw a lady approaching from the other direction. She was walking rather slowly. As we passed I saw her fairly plainly under a street-lamp, and although it was very foggy at the time I could see that she was fairly young and that she was wearing a fur coat and a red scarf round her neck, and that she was hatless. Her hair was dark, and she was small and slight in build. As we passed she looked at me as if she was rather startled. I looked back when I had gone on a yard or two and saw her turn in at the entrance to the courtyard at Madox Court. I know by sight all the inhabitants of Madox Court, and she was not one of them. The time was about five minutes to eight.' "

Hembrow laid the paper down with a satisfied air.

" I think," he said, " that this information is worth more to us than the cable from the New York headquarters, though it is not so startling. The letter that Gordon Frew received on the night of his death mentioned the hour of eight o'clock, if you remember. I think we may conclude that the letter contained a proposal to visit Frew at eight o'clock that evening, and that it was written by the woman with the red shawl."

" Yes," agreed John slowly and thoughtfully. " And that Frew gave his servant leave to go out for the evening because he did not wish the woman's presence in his flat to become known. Or it is possible that the woman herself did not wish it. You remember that the fragment of a letter which we found in the fireplace contained the words ' risk ' and ' fog.' It is possible that they referred to the fact that there was less risk of being seen in the fog, or something of that kind. By the way, Inspector, if she entered Madox Court a moment or so after Shirley had left she must have entered Frew's flat a few moments before the man in the fez left it. I wish we could find that elusive gentleman."

"Yes," agreed Hembrow. "He might be a valuable witness. But I shall see you at the inquest to-morrow, Mr. Christmas, and possibly by then we shall be a good deal nearer to the solution of the mystery."

CHAPTER XII

MR. LASCARIDES

AT the inquest held the following morning only formal evidence was taken, and the matter was adjourned for a fortnight.

" And I think we shall have our man safely under lock and key before then, Mr. Christmas," said Hembrow cheerfully as they walked down Baker Street after leaving the court. " Matters are going nicely—very nicely, so far."

He spoke with a good deal of satisfaction, and whistled to himself as they walked along. Hembrow's idea of the identity of " our man " was fairly plain to John. Dr. Merewether had given his evidence at the inquest with composure, it was true, but with the sort of cold and steely composure of self-restraint : or of a liar determined to stick to his lie though he knows that it is not believed. In the two days that had passed since the murder he seemed to have aged ten years. John seemed to hear again the cool, sceptical voice of the Coroner :

" Did you know the deceased well ? "

" I had attended him professionally."

" And are you certain that the man who opened the door to you at nine o'clock on the evening of the death *was* the deceased ? "

" To the best of my belief it was he."

"You are not certain?"

"I am quite certain."

"Are you aware of the fact that the doctor who examined the body gave it as his opinion that death took place not later than eight o'clock?"

"I am aware of that fact."

"Yet you are certain that you saw the deceased alive an hour later than the hour at which, according to medical testimony, he was dead?"

"I am."

"You are a doctor yourself, are you not?"

"Yes."

"When you examined the body did you find anything incompatible with death having taken place within the past half-hour?"

"No."

"You may stand down, Dr. Merewether."

"Are you interested in carpets, Mr. Christmas?" Hembrow paused in his whistling to ask, with a twinkle in his eye.

"Carpets? What sort of carpets? Why?"

"Oriental. Because I'm going along to see some, and should be glad to have your company, if you care to come too. I'm not so much interested in the carpets, myself, as in the fellow who deals in them. This is the place. Coming in?"

They had turned down a small quiet street off Lower Baker Street, and Hembrow had stopped outside a small but expensive-looking shop which displayed in its window one beautiful old Persian prayer-rug with a grey and purplish bloom, and a vase of Japanese chrysanthemums. Over the shop-front Christmas read the name: "O. Lascarides. Carpets and Oriental hangings."

" My man tracked the owner down to an address in Golders Green," explained Hembrow. " And we've found a cabman in the rank near Circus Road who says that he drove a man wearing a fez out to Golders Green on the night of the murder. He's a Greek, this Lascarides, not a Turk, by the way."

They entered the shop, and a young girl who was engaged in darning a fine tapestry over the counter rose and bade them good morning.

" Mr. Lascarides in? " asked Hembrow.

The girl looked a little surprised.

" I am not sure," she replied courteously. " I'll see. . . . Do you particularly want to see Mr. Lascarides? "

" If I may."

She vanished among the rugs that hung around the walls, and after five minutes or so, which John spent happily in admiring the contents of the shop and Hembrow spent impatiently looking out of the window, a man appeared noiselessly brushing aside one of the wall-hangings and advanced into the shop.

" Good morning, sare. You wish to see me? "

A small, stoutish, olive-complexioned man with a small, grizzled moustache, dapper and suave, with plump, white hands clasped before his immaculate grey waistcoat. He smiled, displaying a row of even teeth of which one was crowned with gold. He looked interrogatively from Hembrow to Christmas.

" You wish to consult me about a carpet? "

" Could I see you privately, Mr. Lascarides? No, it isn't about a carpet. It's a private matter."

The carpet-dealer's eyebrows rose until his low fore-head was a mass of fine horizontal ridges. He glanced quickly from one to the other of his visitors with a narrow, calculating glance that accorded curiously with the bland, deferential smile on his lips. His eyes were dark and narrow and close-set to his large, curved nose, and his left eye had a curious obliqueness of direction that gave a sinister air of secretiveness to his glance. As he noticed this, John felt his heart give a throb of excitement. Were they at last in the presence of the mysterious visitor to Frew's flat? In every detail Mr. Lascarides fitted the description that had been given of him. He watched the man eagerly as he took the card Hembrow held out to him.

He read it through expressionlessly and remained a moment with downcast eyelids, tapping the small piece of pasteboard on his thumb-nail and pursing his thick lips. Then he said blandly, with a slight lift of his shoulders:

"Certainly, certainly. If you gentlemen will step through to my sitting-room? But I cannot imagine in what way I can assist you, Mr.——" (he referred thoughtfully to the card), "ah! Hembrow."

He parted the hangings at the back of the shop and stood aside to let them pass through a small doorway into a dark passage. Then opening another door he showed them into a light and pleasant room which seemed to combine the functions of office and sitting-room. Motioning them to two easy chairs covered with worn but gorgeously-covered rugs, he took a seat in the revolving chair at his desk and waited for Hembrow to speak.

"The matter I wish to see you about is this," said Hembrow slowly. "As you no doubt know, a Mr. Gordon Frew was found murdered on the twenty-fourth in his studio in St. John's Wood. . . ."

He watched the foreigner's face closely as he mentioned

Frew's name, but it remained expressionless—too expressionless to be natural, John thought.

" I saw it in the paper, yes. It was very sad. But it did not concern me. I did not read the details."

" Had you ever met Gordon Frew, Mr. Lascarides? "

" Why do you ask? "

" He was a collector of rugs and Oriental works of art, and it seems to me very likely that he might have purchased some of the items in his collection from you."

The little Greek became very interested in his finger-nail, examining it closely with a slight frown.

" To your question, yes. To your supposition, no. I have met the late Mr. Gordon Frew. But I have sold him nothing, no. Six—eight weeks ago he came to my shop. He wished to buy a fine old Soumak rug I had. But he thought I cheat him over the price. He try to beat me down. But I say: ' This is my price. If you take it, very well. If not, many others there are who will. . . .' He call me a damn old swindler, as if I was a bagman or a cheapjack in your Caledonian market. I am not a dealer in second-hand rubbish. I am an expert, I sell only the best. Nobody dispute with me over the value of a Persian rug. I bow him out. Ten days later he comes again. He asks the price of a silk Tabriz. I tell him one hundred and seventy pounds. But I am keeping it for a good client, for Lord Amberdown. He offer to give me one hundred and eighty pounds if I will sell to him. But it is not with methods like those that I have built the most exclusive business in London. With great pleasure I tell him to go to hell. He walk out of the shop, but I do not know where he went."

The Greek's suave, gentle voice trailed artistically into silence. He clasped his hands on the edge of his writing-table and looked inquiringly at Hembrow with his black eyes to which the squint gave a permanently sinister look. When he dropped his thick eyelids that look completely left his face, leaving nothing but an appearance of amiability, slight melancholy, and great intelligence.

" Another question, Mr. Lascarides, which may seem to you rather trivial. What sort of hat do you wear? "

The dealer's eyebrows mounted towards his thin, grizzled hair, but he replied readily enough, with a faint smile:

" I wear the fez. It is comfortable and I am used to it. Also, it does no harm to a unique business if the head of the business is a little—eccentric in small ways. You understand? If it were not comfortable I should still wear it. It pleases people. And it adds to my prestige. The successful man does not neglect such trifles."

" Mr. Lascarides," said Hembrow gravely, " when were you last in Greentree Road, St. John's Wood? "

" Greentree Road? " echoed the Greek, pinching his lower lip between finger and thumb and gazing thoughtfully at his interlocutor. " I do not know the name. I do not know that I have ever been in Greentree Road—unless, stop! It is the little pleasant road that runs between Finchley Road and Abbey Road somewhere? Then I have been there once, about—let me see. About a year ago. Sir Hubert Strange took a house there, and I went to advise him on its decoration. . . ."

" You have not been there since? "

Mr. Lascarides reflected for a moment, then shook his head.

" No. I am certain."

There was a pause.

" Mr. Lascarides," said Hembrow slowly, " at about

eight o'clock on the night of November 24 a man answering to your description was seen by three separate people walking down Greentree Road. He was also seen by two other people to enter Madox Court, the building in which the murder of Gordon Frew took place."

"I am sorry," replied the Greek mildly. "I am sorry that my appearance is not so unique as I had thought."

He placed his finger-tips gently together and gazed pensively at the ceiling.

"But if I remember right," he added, "it was a foggy night. Possibly the resemblance was not so exact, after all."

"Possibly," answered Hembrow pleasantly. "Still, you will understand that in the circumstances it would be as well if you could give me an account of your movements between seven o'clock and nine o'clock that night."

For the first time a trace of discomfiture appeared in the foreigner's manner. He hesitated, flicking imaginary specks of dust from the table, and seemed to be uncertain how to reply. Finally he said with hauteur:

"I do not know why I should be treated as a suspect. I have told you all I know of the late Mr. Frew."

"Come, come, Mr. Lascarides. You must see quite plainly that we are anxious to establish the identity of the man who was seen in Greentree Road. If you can tell us that you were somewhere else at the time—well, we shall not trouble you further."

"And if I do not choose to tell you?"

"I shall be obliged to detain you until we have investigated the matter without your assistance. Why take this line, Mr. Lascarides? I am making no accusation. I ask you to assist me with information."

The other was silent. John thought his olive face had gone a shade paler.

" That is it," he replied at last with an effort. " I can give you the information. But I do not know if I can prove it."

" You can leave that to me."

There was another long silence. Mr. Lascarides took a handkerchief from his sleeve and blew his nose, at the same time furtively wiping his forehead.

" I—I—— At six o'clock on the night of November 24," he began rather uncertainly, " I was in my house in Golders Green. I was about to begin dinner. The telephone bell rang. I answered it myself. A man's voice spoke to me."

He hesitated, and looked sadly from Hembrow to Christmas.

" I—I did not know the voice. I asked who is it? He would not tell me his name, only that he was a friend and wished me well." Once again the little Greek broke off and looked at Hembrow. " Ah! " he cried. " But what is the use of telling you this? You will not believe me! It is too strange! Yet it is true! Already I see that you do not believe me! "

Hembrow said merely:

" It's not my business to believe or disbelieve. My business is to find out facts. Go on, Mr. Lascarides."

With a slight gulp the other continued:

" He told me to come immediately to meet him at the corner of Circus Road. He will not tell me his business. He says he has something for me. That it will be strongly to my advantage to do as he says. I point out that it is foggy, and getting more foggy. I ask if he cannot give me his address and let me see him there. He says no, it is impossible. I stop and reflect. Half I am inclined not to go. I smell danger. But I am interested. It is my way never to refuse what you call an adventure. I agree. I go."

He paused. Hembrow looked at him woodenly.

"Well?"

"I go. At the corner of Circus Road no one is. The fog by this time is pea-soup. I stroll up and down, never going far. I wait, I wait. No one comes. One or two men pass, but they do not stop. Half-past eight comes. Nearly an hour I have been waiting. I call a taxi and go home. I think, it is some silly trick, some . . . hoax, isn't it? I am hungry, I am angry. But I eat my dinner, I forget my anger, I think no more about it."

He spread out his hands in a revealing, appealing gesture.

"That is all, gentlemen. That is true."

There was a pause. Hembrow looked thoughtfully at the floor. John studied the little man's face. He thought there was real, acute fear lying beneath the surface of that amiable, deprecating mask. The eyelids kept contracting slightly, and the lips seemed to be held lightly apart by an effort of will that made their slight apologetic smile like the fixed smile of a carved figure.

Hembrow asked tranquilly:

"How did you go to Circus Road, Mr. Lascarides?"

"How? I call up a taxi from my house."

"At what time did you get there and dismiss the taxi?'

"At half-past seven, perhaps a few minutes earlier."

"And at half-past eight you hailed a passing taxi and went home?"

"So."

There was a silence, broken only by the sound of the

Greek's hand rubbing nervously along the edge of his desk.

" At what hour exactly did the stranger ring you up? "

" It was just after half-past six."

" You had no idea who it could be? "

" None."

" And no idea what he wished to see you about? "

The foreigner paused a fraction of a second and moistened his lips.

" No idea, Mr. Hembrow."

" I am to understand that a perfect stranger rang you up, refused to give his name or state his business, and that thereupon you, without any idea of his identity or of his reasons for wishing to see you, left home on a foggy night and waited for an hour out in the street before deciding that you had been the victim of a hoax, and going home? Frankly, such a story is not credible for a man of your intelligence and position." Hembrow's voice was like ice. He rose to his feet. " However, I will not question you further at the moment. There will be opportunities later. For I regret, Mr. Lascarides, that I must ask you to——"

What Inspector Hembrow was about to ask, Lascarides did not stop to find out. Christmas at the time suspected his friend of bluff. And the bluff, if bluff it was, was successful. The Greek rose quickly to his feet and moved a step backward from the Inspector, raising his hands in protest and crying :

" No, no! One moment! One moment, and I will tell you all! It was true, it was all true, but it was not all the truth. I will tell you all. . . ."

Hembrow sat down again, saying nothing, and waited, his clear, deep-set eyes fixed inquiringly on the other's face. Mr. Lascarides groped for his chair, sank heavily into it and mopped his forehead with a silk handkerchief. His face was ghastly and he kept moistening his dry lips.

"There is no need to detain me. I can tell you nothing about this murder. I am not a murderer. I had no wish to kill your Gordon Frew. He was a fool. He was a hog. He insulted me. But he was nothing to me. But when I said that I did not know who the man was who rang me up, it was true, and yet it was not true. I was expecting a message. A—business message."

He stopped and sighed heavily.

"Sometimes I buy and sell other things besides rugs, Inspector Hembrow. Amber, jade, old ivories, even more precious things—diamonds, emeralds come sometimes my way. A few days ago I had a message from a man with whom sometimes I make business, to tell me that he has a very fine unmounted emerald for me. He is sending it by messenger, as usually such precious things are sent. When the call came on the telephone I thought it was from the messenger with the emerald. I am anxious to get the gem safely into my own hands. I was a little surprised that he was so secretive on the telephone, but I thought, he has his reasons. I went. No one there was, and no one came. . . . Now what I have told you is the truth, the whole truth, and nothing but the truth, as so poetically you put it in your courts of law."

The Greek seemed to have recovered his composure. He was pale and still breathed rather heavily, but he smiled faintly as he finished his declaration. Hembrow asked:

"Why did you not tell me that in the first place, may I ask, Mr. Lascarides?"

The other hesitated, then spoke in a lower tone.

" To be frank, I do not know the history of this emerald. Perhaps its history would be interesting to the police. I cannot always know the past history of all the things I sell. Therefore I did not wish to tell you the whole truth. I tell you now because I do not care to be detained in connection with a murder I know nothing of. It would be inconvenient. I am at the time very busy."

" Did anybody hear you speaking on the 'phone, Mr. Lascarides? "

" Alas, no! I have no witness. I have no family. I live alone. A housekeeper I have, and servants, but they were far away in the kitchen. The bell of the telephone they may have heard, but not my voice."

" Since then have you heard anything of the messenger you expected to meet? "

" Nothing have I heard, Mr. Hembrow, and I must confess that I am beginning to fear for the safety of my emerald."

" You did not recognize the voice over the 'phone? "

" No . . . but, my dear sir, I did not expect to, for I did not know by whom the emerald is coming."

" Would you recognize it again if you heard it? "

The Greek smiled pityingly.

" No. I am not English. I have no ear for the English voice and accent. It was English, that is all I can say." He mused. " I do think now that perhaps it was a more gentle voice than generally belongs to the kind of man who acts as messenger in these matters. Yes, it might have been the voice of yourself, or your friend. But recognize it again? My friend, just as all black faces look alike to a white man, so do all English voices sound alike to a Greek."

Hembrow remained a moment lost in thought. Then he rose to take his departure.

" I will not trouble you further at the moment, Mr. Lascarides."

The carpet-dealer bowed. He had quite regained his elasticity of manner.

" I shall be charmed to assist you in any way I can. I am generally here from about eleven until about four. My home address you have. Good day, Mr. Inspector Hembrow. Good day, sir."

He bowed them out. Christmas, happening to glance back as they walked down the street, saw him still standing at his shop door looking after them with an extraordinary intensity and malignity in his oblique and sinister gaze.

CHAPTER XIII

A SHEET OF PAPER

WHEN Hembrow, accompanied by John Christmas, arrived at Scotland Yard, he showed Christmas into his own office and left him while he went to report to his Superintendent. Christmas stood looking idly out of the window and thinking. His thoughts chiefly centred themselves on Mr. Lascarides. The vanishing Turk, or Greek, as he turned out to be, had not remained elusive for long. But though he was no longer elusive, he was even more mysterious; or so John thought. He turned eagerly when Hembrow re-entered the room carrying in his hand a slip of paper which he laid on his desk with a satisfied smile.

" Well," said Hembrow cheerily, " what do you think of our friend Lascarides? "

" Well," answered John slowly, " what I'm chiefly thinking about him at the moment is—that he suffers from a certain obliquity of vision. In other words, he squints."

Hembrow looked surprised.

" Well? "

" When I was talking the day before yesterday to my friend the crossing-sweeper at Shipman's Mews, the conversation happened to turn, oddly enough, upon the murder, and especially upon the gentleman who added a touch of romance to Greentree Road by walking down it in a fez. I said to my friend the crossing-sweeper: 'Had he a squint?' My friend the crossing-sweeper replied: 'Not as I noticed.' Could one fail to notice such a squint, Inspector?"

Hembrow looked puzzled.

"We can't expect every one of our witnesses to have noticed every little detail, Mr. Christmas. That would be too much to ask. It was a very foggy night, remember. . . ."

"Yes," echoed Christmas musingly, "it was a foggy night."

"We have several witnesses who saw a man of Lascarides' height, build and complexion, wearing a fez, and having an obviously gold-crowned tooth, walking down Greentree Road at a time when Lascarides was away from home and, by his own account, was not many hundred yards away. Lascarides can only give the flimsiest story to account for his movements at the time. Surely we need not complain because all our witnesses cannot swear that the man in Greentree Road had a cast in his left eye! As I say, it was a foggy night."

"As you say," repeated Christmas, "it was a foggy night." He looked dreamily across the room. "But even on a foggy night I should have thought an intelligent murderer would have changed his head-gear for something less noticeable than a fez before setting forth to do a murder."

Hembrow smiled.

"You're going too far, Mr. Christmas. I never said he was the murderer. I don't think he was."

"Oh, I thought you had the serene, expectant air of one who contemplates making an arrest in the near future."

" So I do. But I don't contemplate arresting old Lascarides. Not for murder, anyhow. But I'm glad we've got our hands on him because it clears the way a bit to the real murderer. So long as he was missing, there was always the possibility that one was going quite on the wrong tack. Now I feel fairly sure that I'm on the right one."

" Oh, you do, do you? " said Christmas. " But if Lascarides is, as they say, guiltless of blood, why should he fabricate that rather thin story about meeting a man at the corner of Circus Road? Why not say frankly: ' Yes, Inspector, I cannot tell a lie, I *did* visit the late regretted Mr. Frew on the evening of the tragedy, yet murderer am I none! ' Why not? It would be much the most sensible thing to do."

" Not in the circumstances," replied Hembrow grimly.

" Surely honesty, as the old adage has it, is the best policy? "

" Depends what you've been doing," said the Inspector. " You see, Mr. Christmas, I've got a pretty good suspicion, in fact more than a suspicion, that old Lascarides sells something else besides rugs. Something which would mean a term of imprisonment for him if he was caught selling it. In a word, opium. And I know beyond a shadow of doubt that the deceased was an opium-taker—a drug-fiend, as they say in novels. I found quite a lot of the stuff in a secret drawer in his writing-table. Now, since Frew collected rugs and such things, and Lascarides sells them, isn't it rather likely, apart from all the other evidence, that Frew got drugs, as well as rugs, from our Greek friend? And if Lascarides visited Frew on the night of the murder, as we may take it he did, isn't it likely that he left with him that unopened packet of opium I found in the writing-table? And isn't it natural that he should risk any kind of silly lie rather than risk his little activities being found out? Trafficking in drugs isn't quite such a serious matter as murder, of course. But it's quite serious enough to account for any lies that Lascarides may take it into his head to tell."

"True," said John pensively, "but—though I'm sorry to be so obstinate, Inspector, it doesn't account for his appalling squint. And it doesn't account for his having asked the crossing-sweeper the way to Primrose Hill."

Hembrow smiled.

"I think we may take it that that crossing-sweeper of yours was mistaken, Mr. Christmas."

John looked back at him thoughtfully.

"To err is human," he agreed, and said no more.

Hembrow picked up the slip of paper he had laid on his desk and held it out to John with an air of some importance. John read: "Gordon Frew, painter, married Phyllis Hilary Templar at the British Consulate, July 14, 1921."

"The message came through from the Paris Sureté this morning, in answer to one of mine. You don't seem very much surprised, Mr. Christmas."

"I'm not," admitted John with a smile. "But I'm delighted, Inspector, at this confirmation of a little guess of my own."

"Oh, you'd guessed it, had you?" said Hembrow with a rather mortified air. "May I ask how, Mr. Christmas?"

"I'm afraid my methods of arriving at the conclusion would make you laugh, my dear Hembrow, so I won't go into details. But I came to the conclusion by these steps —the expression on a man's face when Frew's name was mentioned, a book-plate, the look on another gentleman's face while a song was being sung, the registers of University College, and the information you gave me yesterday as to our friend Frew's weird past."

Hembrow looked a trifle disgruntled.

"Well, I shouldn't stake much on a deduction chiefly built up on the look of people's faces. But it's certainly come off this time. You'll notice that the lady had the same surname as one of Frew's associates in America."

"I should think she's probably his daughter," said John casually.

"Quite possible, of course," assented the Inspector. "But have you any special reason for thinking so, Mr. Christmas?"

"Well," replied John lightly, "she isn't old enough to be his mother or his sister. And I deduce the first degree of relationship from her anxiety to defend the gentleman's reputation. An aunt or cousin would have taken it more philosophically."

Hembrow looked at him curiously for a moment, then laughed.

"I think you're going a little too far in the fantastic direction there, Mr. Christmas. But we can soon find out her relationship, if she's a relation at all. Though personally I don't think it's a point that bears on the case. To get back to facts. Dr. Mordby button-holed me at the court this morning just before the proceedings started, and said he wanted to make a statement. It was about an incident that happened on the evening of the murder. I asked him why he hadn't made the statement earlier, and he said that he had forgotten the incident in the excitement of the discovery of the body, and only realized later that it was his duty to report it."

"I can tell you what it was," said John grimly. "It was about a handkerchief."

"M'm," assented Hembrow. "You're doing a lot of good guessing this morning, Mr. Christmas."

"It wasn't a guess. Mordby had already reported the incident, as you put it, to me and half a dozen other people at Miss Wimpole's house yesterday evening. Old snake."

"Eh? Come, Mr. Christmas, it was Dr. Mordby's duty to report the incident."

"It wasn't his duty to broadcast it at an evening party."

Hembrow was silent for a moment, twiddling his pen with a look of great concentration on his face. Finally he looked up seriously at his friend and said:

"Mr. Christmas, if you're a friend of Dr. Merewether's—I mean, if you've got friendly feelings for him, more than an ordinary acquaintance, I advise you to leave this case alone. I should be sorry, because I like talking things over with you, and often your ideas are useful, you seeing things from a fresh, different angle. But for your own sake, I think you'd best leave it alone. For I've got little doubt in my own mind now that Dr. Merewether was an accessory after, and probably also before, the fact; every new piece of evidence that comes to light goes to build up the case against him."

Christmas looked back at Hembrow with a face as grave as his own.

"Your theory being," he said slowly, "that Frew was murdered by the woman who escaped through the studio window, and that she was assisted to escape by Dr. Merewether?"

"Exactly."

"That makes Merewether an accessory after, but not before."

" There is strong presumptive evidence that he was also an accessory before the fact."

" Then," said Christmas decidedly, " the presumptions on which the evidence is founded are false."

Hembrow sighed.

" There you are, you see, Mr. Christmas. Your personal feelings about Merewether interfere with your common sense at every turn."

" Not at all," said John stoutly. " My common sense and my personal feelings go hand in hand! "

Hembrow shook his head.

" Take my advice, Mr. Christmas. Leave this affair to the police."

John smiled and shook his head.

" Assuming that your theory is correct, Inspector, what do you make of the cry? "

" The cry? "

" The noise which could be heard down in Newtree's studio and sent Merewether up to investigate things in the first place. It couldn't have been given by Frew, for he was already dead. You don't, I suppose, suggest that the woman, an hour after she had murdered Frew, was so overcome with emotion as to cry out loudly and suddenly in a voice which could be heard in the room below and which would jeopardize her escape? Who gave the cry, then? "

Hembrow pushed his chair a little way back from his desk, and leaning on the edge looked gravely and steadfastly at his friend.

" Mr. Christmas," he said, " cast your mind back to the evening of the murder, and the moment that noise was heard. Try to forget that it led to the discovery of a dead man. What did the noise sound like to you?"

John did as he was told.

" Why," he said at last, " it sounded like a cry—a sort of gasping cry. At least, it sounded more like a cry than anything."

" Could you swear on your oath that the noise you heard was a cry of distress? "

John hesitated.

" No, I couldn't swear to the distress. How could I? I don't know that I would *swear* to it being a cry at all. One can't be quite sure with noises from up above. I would swear that it *sounded* like a cry."

" Did it alarm you at the time? "

" No," said John slowly. " It wasn't loud and obvious enough to be alarming. I was interested. But I wasn't alarmed."

" Would it have occurred to you to go up and investigate if you had been alone? "

" No—no, I can't say it would. One needs to be fairly sure that something's wrong before one can go knocking at people's doors and asking if they're all right. I should probably have listened for a bit, and if I'd heard no more curious sounds I should have forgotten it."

" Exactly. It was not until after the murder had been discovered that you really seriously thought of the sound you had heard as a cry of distress. Now, Mr. Christmas, of all the people in Mr. Newtree's studio at the time, Dr. Mordby did not hear the sound at all; Mr. Newtree suggested that it sounded like the feet of a chair scraping over the parquet floor. Sir Marion Steen thought it sounded like a loud yawn; Miss Serafine Wimpole made no remark about it at all; and Mrs. Wimpole asked, so far as I can gather without any symptoms of alarm : ' What was that? ' I know that, after the event, they all agreed that the sound might have been a cry and that the idea of there being something wrong had entered their heads. But one must not attach too great importance to that kind of wisdom after the event. My point is that, when the sound was heard, not one of these people was seriously alarmed or disturbed by it, although afterwards they naturally connected it, just as you did, with the murder. Not one of them, Mr. Christmas, suggested that the matter ought to be investigated—except Dr. Merewether. Dr. Merewether immediately offered to go and see if Frew was all right, and immediately started for the door. Not only that, not only was he determined to go, he was also determined to go alone. Dr. Mordby offered to accompany him, but he very firmly declined the offer. Why? If he was merely going to investigate the cause of a sound which might have meant trouble, and possibly danger, surely it would have been natural to take a companion. But if he knew very well what he was going to find upstairs, if the sound which all of you heard but none of you could identify, had been a signal to him to come—then naturally he would insist upon going alone."

" A signal? "

" Why not? The murderess had to escape before Mr. Newtree and the rest of you came up and found what had happened. Time was running short."

" I still don't see why she should have risked rousing the house just so that Merewether could watch her escape."

" *Help* her escape, Mr. Christmas. She could not risk going down the stairs and out at the front door. Once outside the house she was fairly safe in that fog, but with a party on and people coming in and out of the front door, to say nothing of Greenaway hovering about with refreshments and so on, it would have been too risky to go downstairs and through the hall. There remained the window."

"Well?"

"You climbed out of that window yourself, Mr. Christmas. Did you enjoy it?"

"I didn't mind at the moment. I shouldn't have cared about doing it in cold blood. When I was hanging on to the window-sill by my eyelashes, so to speak, there was a drop of two or three feet on to a sloping out-house roof. Once on the out-house, it was fairly easy to scramble down."

"You are—how tall, Mr. Christmas? Six foot three?"

"Six foot two!"

"The woman who got out of that window on the night of the murder took size four in shoes. She was probably about five foot to five foot four in height. It would have been a risky business her getting out of that window alone. She might well have slipped and injured herself severely, to say nothing of the noise she would make dropping three or four feet on to a galvanized iron roof. She had to escape by the window, and she had to be assisted. Dr. Merewether leaned over the sill and holding her wrists lowered her until her feet touched or nearly touched the roof. The rest she had to do by herself."

"I still think," said John, "that to make a noise, a cry or whatever it was, that might have alarmed the house, was an extraordinarily risky way of getting help from an accomplice."

"Might have alarmed the house," repeated Hembrow slowly. "Why do you keep saying that, Mr. Christmas? It did *not* alarm the house. It was not sufficiently loud and startling, as you yourself just said, to alarm the house. If Dr. Merewether had not answered it, no one else would have done. You said so yourself. And, even if some other person had thought it necessary to go up, Dr. Merewether could effectually have prevented him, as he prevented Dr. Mordby. And, in any case, it's difficult to do a murder without taking some small risk, you know, Mr. Christmas. The alternative, which would have involved Dr. Merewether's going secretly up to Frew's flat under a pretence of fetching something from the hall, or some other pretext, would have been riskier still, if Greenaway or somebody had seen him go up. Also, without some kind of signal, he could not know that the murder had been accomplished. For the woman had to wait her opportunity before she could accomplish it. I'm sorry, Mr. Christmas," said Hembrow kindly and regretfully. "You see how it is. You see why I advised you to withdraw. For it's not just a theory that happens to fit the facts. There's plenty of evidence to prove it, though not quite enough yet to convince a jury against a clever defence."

"Well," said John, "the papers that Cold sent on to Mrs. Rudgwick—where do they come in? Have you any theory as to what was inside that envelope?"

"I have a theory," replied Hembrow slowly, "but it's only conjecture so far. I think there was a will inside the envelope."

"A will? A last will and testament and all that, do you mean?"

"A last will, yes," said Hembrow, with an emphasis on the adjective. "A will which it was in somebody's interest to suppress. Hence the attempt on Cold's flat. Hence the attack which I've been expecting on Mrs. Rudgwick's shop. (It hasn't come off, by the way; I had men watching the place and there's been no attempt at burglary.)"

" But what an extraordinary thing to do with one's will! Why not give it to one's solicitor in the ordinary way? "

Hembrow shrugged his shoulders.

" It's fairly plain that Mr. Frew wasn't an ordinary man. He was an eccentric, and as eccentric in this as in everything else. The will which he did leave with his solicitor was extraordinary enough in parts, after all."

" It certainly was."

" Now, I surmise," went on Hembrow, " that he left a later will. And that we shall find his last will in the envelope now in the possession of Mrs. Emily Rudgwick. I expect to find that in the new will the clause leaving all that property (and it's property of very considerable value) to Dr. Merewether is left out."

" But why? Why set about it in such an extraordinary way? "

" If my theory is correct," said Hembrow, " Frew had some reason for disliking Dr. Merewether. He may have left these two wills on purpose to annoy and disappoint him. I gather that it was quite the sort of thing he would do."

" Quite. He was—well, capable of malice. And you think——"

" I think that Merewether learnt through his accomplice of the second will. (Frew had probably told him about the first.) I think he determined to take the risk of obtaining and destroying the second will, if possible."

" He was the amateur burglar at Gilbert Cold's then? "

Hembrow smiled.

" I have very little doubt of that fact, though the rest of it is pure conjecture, I admit. Consider the clues we have to the identity of the burglar. First, a pair of surgical forceps. Second, footprints in soft ground. When Dr.

Merewether attended to the corpse on the night of the murder he accidentally trod on the bloodstains. The rug was a plum-coloured one, if you remember, and the wet stains on it were not very obvious. He then trod on the parquet floor and left a light but fairly clear print of his shoe there. The prints in Cold's garden correspond in measurement exactly to that print left by Dr. Merewether in the studio. Thirdly, the cigarette-end."

Hembrow pulled open a drawer in his writing-table and took from it an envelope which he opened carefully. He laid a flattened half-cigarette on the table before him.

" A dark smoking-mixture and an A.G. paper. Dr. Merewether rolled his own cigarette with A.G. papers, I noticed on the night of the murder. And he had a dark, sticky tobacco resembling this in his pouch."

" Quite true, I've tried it. And poisonous stuff it is."

" So you see, Mr. Christmas, why I say that if you've got friendly feelings for the doctor, you'd better leave this case alone."

John said nothing for a moment. Then, opening his cigarette-case he replied evenly:

" No, Inspector. I'm determined to see it through."

Hembrow smiled rather pityingly.

" You're determined to turn a blind eye to the evidence, then? "

" I think," said John non-committally, " that the theory you've just expounded is very ingenious and would sound quite plausible to anybody who didn't know Dr. Merewether."

Hembrow looked a trifle annoyed.

" I think the footprints, the forceps and the cigarette-end make it more than an ingenious theory, Mr. Christmas."

" Well," said John with a smile, " I hope that if you

arrest Dr. Merewether, it will only be for attempted burglary and not for murder. I'm afraid you'll come a cropper, Hembrow, if you make it a capital charge."

"I shall certainly not make an arrest until I have a complete case to lay before a jury," replied Hembrow stiffly, and then, as there came a knock on the door: "Come in!"

A plain-clothes man entered.

"Sergeant Douglas is waiting to see you, sir, about this studio murder case. He has a woman with him, a Mrs. Rudgwick."

"Send him up."

"Very good, sir."

"Douglas," explained Hembrow to John, "is the man who's been watching the Rudgwick's place. It will be interesting to see what's inside that envelope. If I find what I confidently expect to find, I think we shall soon be justified in detaining a certain gentleman."

"That," said Christmas amiably, "would be a pity."

Hembrow smiled.

"You can scarcely expect me to agree with you. Come in, Douglas. Let's have your report."

A burly, bearded man of about forty entered and saluted.

"In company with Constable Hawk and Constable Williams I watched the premises of No. 5 Henneker Mews from two a.m. until ten a.m., relieving Sergeant Brushwood. All was quiet during the night. At ten a.m. I entered the premises and questioned the occupants as to a certain sealed package received by them by post. The woman, Emily Rudgwick, positively refused to make a statement beyond the fact that she had received such a package and that it was still in her possession. She offered, however, to accompany me here and make a statement to you, Inspector, personally. She is waiting below and has the package in question with her."

"Right. Bring her up, Sergeant.

In a few moments Mrs. Rudgwick entered the room. As she greeted the Inspector and took the seat he offered her, Christmas was struck again with her likeness to her murdered brother, a likeness not so much of feature as of expression and style. In her outdoor clothes she looked much less slatternly and disreputable than she had looked in the crowded dirty kitchen behind the shop. In her black draperies and large black hat, with her commanding height and coarse, handsome face she achieved, in fact, a certain distinction. The hat-brim was broken, and the voluminous silk scarf around her neck was torn and spotted with grease, but she wore them with an air.

"Well, Inspector," she said without preamble, "I've brought along this precious envelope you seem to be so anxious to get hold of. Though I'm sure I don't know why I should take the trouble, never having been what you might call friendly with the police. I suppose it's no use asking you why you're so anxious about it, but just out of curiosity I'd rather like to know."

"I've no objection to your knowing, Mrs. Rudgwick," replied Hembrow with a smile. "I think its contents may throw light upon the murder of your brother."

"Think so? Well, it hasn't got the name of the murderer written inside it, or anything like that."

"I hardly expected anything so definite as that."

"It seems to come from my brother Gordon," said Mrs. Rudgwick, opening her shabby handbag with a great air of doing a favour, "but as there's nothing private about it I don't mind your seeing it."

"*Seems* to come?" echoed Hembrow with surprise.

" Well, it's his writing. I'd know his queer crooked-up writing anywhere. But it hasn't got his name to it."

Hembrow looked a trifle disconcerted. A will without the name of the testator was scarcely within the bounds of possibility! He leant eagerly and impatiently over his desk. Mrs. Rudgwick, as if enjoying her moment of importance and determined to spin it out as long as possible, slowly groped among the various objects in her large bag and drew forth an extremely grimy handkerchief on which she proceeded to blow her nose. Then she carefully replaced the handkerchief and took out of her bag a foolscap envelope of a very strong, good quality, bearing the blue chalk lines and red sealing-wax dabs of the registered post. This she handed across to the Inspector, and folding her hands on her lap and leaning back in her chair, waited to enjoy the dénouement.

Hembrow, in spite of his eagerness to know what it contained, was true to his instinct and training, and turned the envelope carefully over and over, examining it in detail. The writing was certainly Gordon Frew's, the ink was black and had the look of having been dry for a long time, and the envelope was slightly rubbed and soiled at the corners. It was also queerly faintly indented at the back here and there in a way that puzzled Hembrow for a moment, until he remembered that Cold had hidden it for safety under his mattress. The wire springs probably accounted for those indentations. Having examined the envelope in detail he opened it and drew out a twice-folded sheet of thick stiff paper.

Hembrow gazed attentively at the sheet of paper for a short moment that seemed to John a long one. Mystification, disappointment, disgust and mystification again chased one another across his face. He handed the sheet to John. At first glance it appeared to be a perfectly blank piece of paper. But in the very middle of it, in the small cramped hand of the murdered man, there was a single line of writing. It read :

" *Thus conscience doth make cowards of us all.*"

John turned the paper over. There was nothing else. Only that one line, exquisitely, evenly written, as though the writer had enjoyed inscribing the words. Nobody spoke for a moment. Then Hembrow remarked in tones of deep disgust :

" Well, I'm dashed! "

" That's just how I felt," said Mrs. Rudgwick placidly. " Speaking for myself, I never was one to let my conscience trouble me much."

CHAPTER XIV

OPHELIA IN HAMPSTEAD

SERAFINE shut the front door of her Hampstead cottage behind her and glanced regretfully at the bare black boughs and sunny blue skies which invited her so temptingly to take a walk over the wintry heath. Then she turned her steps in the opposite direction, down towards the High Street. Imogen had suddenly decided to be prostrated by the shock of Gordon Frew's murder and was lying in bed with the blinds drawn, suffering from neuralgia.

"Darling auntie," said Serafine, when she went in to say good morning to her, "you bore the shock so wonderfully at first. Do go on being wonderful. It's so much more interesting and unusual to be wonderful than to be prostrated."

"Do you really think so?" murmured her aunt, opening wide her lovely eyes and considering this view for a moment. Then she remembered her neuralgia, and her lids dropped wearily. She sighed.

"Have some aspirin."

Imogen looked at her reproachfully.

"Serafine! When you know it always makes me sick *immediately*."

"Well," murmured Serafine, who was not at her best

in a sick-room, vaguely, " a hot-water bottle, some tea . . ."

" Got some," sighed Imogen, moving her head languidly to one side.

" Beef-tea."

" Don't be disgusting."

" An osteopath."

" It can't be that. I was adjusted only a fortnight ago. But if you *would* do something for me——"

" Love to."

" Take this prescription down to Halliday's and get him to send it up as soon as he can."

" Won't the chemist at the corner do? "

" Darling! It's not *drugs*. It's a herbal prescription. Of course you have to go to a herbalist."

" I can get most of these out of the garden," said Serafine, running her eye down the prescription. " Oh, sorry! I didn't mean to be flippant. Of course I'll take it to Halliday's with pleasure."

" You don't look very well yourself," murmured Imogen, opening her eyes again and regarding her niece with a lively interest not altogether in keeping with the part of an invalid. " You've been looking horribly washed out ever since that dreadful night."

" Thank you, Aunt Imogen, I am in excellent health."

" Oh, of course you always *say* that! I used to do Coué myself at one time. But one gets so tired of keeping everything to oneself. I'm not surprised it's died out."

" Neither am I. As a subject of conversation, health can't hope to compete with illness. It's too monotonous."

" I don't know what you're talking about," murmured Imogen placidly. " All I say is, you're not looking well. Why don't you marry that nice young Christmas and settle down? Of course he's a little young for you, but——"

"I should think so. My dear aunt, I'm thirty-seven."

"Are you really? Well, that's not much nowadays. I should so like to see you fall in love and marry."

"At thirty-seven," said Serafine, "one does not fall in love and marry. One makes a suitable alliance. Or not, as the case may be."

"In my opinion," said Imogen, "a woman should marry at twenty. I was twenty myself when I married."

"At twenty, my dear aunt, most of us have not attained the age of discretion."

"Oh, if you wait for that," said her aunt, "of course you don't marry at all. . . ." Suddenly remembering that she was an invalid she closed her eyes and sighed. "But your life is your own, my darling. Do as you like."

"I expect I shall," said Serafine amiably, and tiptoed out of the sick-room.

She sauntered down the High Street. The soft November sunlight, filtered through thin mists that made the blue sky whitish, hurt her eyes. She was paying the penalty of sleeplessness with a raging headache. No need to lie awake at night because one man had been murdered and another would be arrested and hanged. It had happened before. It happened, in fact, with lamentable frequency. But not so near at home. Dreadful to feel so restless, dreadful to be so helpless, dreadful to think that already George Merewether might be under arrest. There was little comfort in telling oneself that, even so, he might be proved innocent, must surely be proved innocent. In her heart Serafine had as little doubt that Merewether was the murderer as she had that the murder was justified. Stopping to look with unseeing eyes in a picture-framer's window, she thought: Imogen would say I had fallen in love at first sight. Gazing raptly at a framed oleograph called "The Sailor's Home-coming," Serafine pondered the matter and came to the conclusion that her aunt would be, roughly speaking, right. One would not take this painful interest in the murderous activities of a gentleman to whom one was indifferent. . . .

At this point Serafine became aware of a woman hovering near her, passing and re-passing close to her, as though she wanted to speak to her but had not the courage or the decision to do so. Some down-and-out waiting her chance to beg; or perhaps a possible purchaser for "The Sailor's Home-coming" anxious to obtain a better view of it. Serafine turned away from the shop-window and found a woman in black standing on the kerb and looking at her with an anxious and appealing expression. Not a beggar, not an ordinary beggar, anyhow. Her clothes, though carelessly put on and much in need of brushing, were costly and becoming, and she carried a morocco handbag and an umbrella. She looked at Serafine uncertainly and piteously as if she wished to ask for help but were afraid of a rebuff. Serafine did not pass on, but stopped and looked back at her, struck by the singular beauty of her small, oval face. It was a pale face, barely flushed on the cheeks, modelled with such delicacy and precision as far transcended any beauty of mere colour. From broad forehead to rounded chin there was not one blurred or uncertain line. Under thin, black eyebrows two deep-set dark eyes gazed submissively and nervously at Serafine. The thick, dark lashes curled back like a child's. It was an unobtrusive and yet exquisite beauty, a beauty which did not quickly take the eye, but which, having taken it, held it and would not let it go.

" Did you speak to me? " asked Serafine.

The stranger moved a step nearer, and still gazing with that childish, half-frightened look at Serafine's kindly and humorous face, said in a very low voice :

" I wondered . . . I thought . . . You see, I have forgotten the address."

" Yes? " asked Serafine encouragingly. " What address? "

The woman moved still closer to her, as if she had decided to trust her, and repeated, still in that quiet, confidential way :

" I have forgotten the address. I know it was in Hampstead somewhere. So I came to Hampstead. But now I don't know what to do. . . ."

Her lip trembled absurdly on the last word. Her eyes were tragic. A certain clouded obtuseness in their look gave Serafine a queer, uncomfortable sensation, as if she were dealing with a being not quite human.

" Tell me," she said, instinctively speaking very clearly and slowly as if to a child, " who it is you want to see. Perhaps they are in the telephone book."

The other shook her head slightly. A small hand crept out and laid itself on Serafine's arm, as if to make sure she did not lose patience and go away. Serafine, who by now felt fairly sure that she had to deal with a lunatic, asked gently :

" Well, what is your name? Where do you come from? "

" I was at an hotel. I—I wanted to go away. I was frightened. . . ." She passed a hand across her eyes. " I took my luggage and went to a station—to Victoria.

But then I didn't know where to go. And I remembered Dr. Merewether——"

At Serafine's instinctive start she stopped short and shrank a little away from her as if frightened.

"So I came here on a bus," she went on nervously. "I wish—I wish I hadn't. I'm so frightened out of doors. But when I'm indoors I'm frightened too, and want to come out; isn't it funny?"

Her voice sank to a whisper. Serafine took her hand in a firm clasp.

"Well, there's nothing to be frightened of," she said cheerfully, but inwardly greatly confused and puzzled. "I'll take you where you want to go, if I can. Or you can come home with me. Is it Dr. Merewether you want to go to?"

The strange woman nodded, looking submissively at Serafine as if at the arbiter of her destiny.

"He told me his address, but I forgot it. Something—something made me forget. . . . I was frightened. . . ."

Her brows knitted as though in painful thought, and her lips drooped with an expression of vague distress. She shook her head.

"I can't remember."

"We'll take a taxi," said Serafine, tucking the small hand under her arm. "I know the address."

She had, in fact, looked it up in the telephone directory the night before, when she had had an abortive impulse to ring him up and warn him—warn him of what? She did not know, so she had not rung up.

They walked together down the hill. Serafine's heart warmed to the queer, beautiful stranger who walked so confidingly at her side. She wondered whether Dr. Merewether and his sister supplemented their incomes by taking patients with mild mental troubles off the hands of their relations. It seemed a reasonable explanation of this queer encounter.

" Poor little Ophelia," murmured Serafine, pressing her hand to her side.

" No, Phyllis," murmured the stranger automatically, and then stopped short and looked up at Serafine with distressed and clouded eyes. " Phyllis," she repeated uncertainly. " Is that my name? I—I feel as if it must be. A little while ago I couldn't remember. But now . . . Phyllis. Phyllis."

She rubbed her little hand clumsily over her eyes as if there were cobwebs there.

" Don't worry," said Serafine. " What does a name matter? Dr. Merewether'll remember it for you."

" Yes. Yes," said the stranger, with a sudden enchanting smile that narrowed her dark eyes into bright crescents. " He will, won't he? "

" Here's the taxi-rank. Hullo, that's Mordby's car. I suppose he's on his way to my prostrated aunt."

A large, mulberry-coloured limousine swung round the corner, and Dr. Mordby raised his hand in greeting as it passed. Then, to Serafine's astonishment, he leant out of the window, stared at her and her companion with extraordinary interest for a second and spoke to his chauffeur. The car drew in and stopped a little way up the hill.

" What the dickens," said Serafine to herself, with her hand on the door of her taxi, " does he want, I wonder? I suppose we'd better wait and see."

To her surprise her companion gave a little wail.

" No, no, no! Take me away! "

Turning sharply, Serafine saw that the beautiful face

was white as paper and drawn into an expression of horror. The limousine door swung open and Mordby stepped on to the pavement. Inwardly bewildered but outwardly decisive, Serafine bundled her companion unceremoniously into the taxi, gave the driver Merewether's address and stepped in herself. As she shut the door she heard Mordby's voice from the pavement: "Miss Wimpole, one moment. . . ." The taxi started and left him standing there. Looking through the little window in the back Serafine saw him staring after them with an expression of surprise which gave way immediately to a look of determination. He swung round on his heel and walked quickly back to his car.

"Good Lord," murmured Serafine to herself, "I believe he's going to follow us! I do wish I understood the meaning of all this. I suppose"—she turned tentatively to the woman cowering at her side—"you can't explain?"

"Don't let him see me," whispered the other brokenly. "Take me away. . . . Don't let him come! I hate him! I hate him!"

Serafine looked back. The limousine had turned and was gliding after them down the hill. She glanced dubiously at her companion, inclined to believe now that her Ophelia had escaped from some private asylum of Dr. Mordby's. In that case she ought to stop the taxi and deliver her back into custody, for her own sake. But——

"Oh, blow!" thought Serafine aloud. "I never did like old Mordby. Here goes!"

She leant out of the window and spoke to the driver.

"I'll give you ten shillings if you can shake off that big maroon car that's following us. Take any route you like. Go round and round in circles. Only lose the maroon car before you take us to the address I gave you."

" Right you are, Miss," replied the driver laconically, " how much start've we got? "

" About a hundred yards. You can't possibly outdistance it. You must just turn down every corner and up the next till it's lost."

" Very good, Miss," replied the cabman woodenly, and the cab shot with surprising suddenness round a corner into a side street, along the street for fifty yards, round another corner and out into the High Street again. Taking a business-like silk handkerchief out of her coat-pocket, Serafine offered it to the weeping woman at her side, slipped an arm round her slight shoulders, and settled down to enjoy the extraordinary twists and turns taken by their cabman who, it seemed, liked to do things thoroughly. After an eccentric and expensive journey, during which they explored thoroughly Hampstead, Swiss Cottage and St. John's Wood, the taxi drew peacefully up before a small, quiet house in a road full of small, quiet houses.

" Here you are, Miss," he remarked, opening the door. " I done what you said all right, I fancy. Your friend's gone back to bed long ago, I wager."

" Thank you," said Serafine, paying him. " We enjoyed the drive. I congratulate you on your thoroughness."

" That ain't nothing, lady," replied the cabman modestly, pocketing his fare. " Why, I've 'ad a dead body in this very cab. 'Member the trunk murder last year? It was me as drove the trunk to the station. 'Ad to give evidence afterwards, I did." He looked curiously at the woman in black as Serafine helped her out of the cab. " Not arf 'eavy, that trunk wasn't! "

" Well, thanks very much," said Serafine with a smile, opening the garden gate.

" Oh, 'twasn't nothing to me, lady! " replied the driver, gazing earnestly at her as if to impress her image on his memory. " 'Ad to give evidence afterwards, I did," he repeated with relish, and climbed into his seat and drove off.

The strange woman gave no sign of recognizing her surroundings as they waited in the pretty little drawing-room. She looked listlessly about her and then turned and looked out of the window. Serafine began to wonder whether she had not been rather foolish in behaving in this impulsive manner. Suppose Dr. Merewether disclaimed all acquaintance with this lady? What should Serafine do with her? Take her home to Hampstead, she supposed, and try to trace her relations through the police. What would Imogen say? She was still wondering what Imogen would say to this lovely but unbalanced addition to her peaceful household when the door opened and Dr. Merewether entered. He looked pale and stern and the smile he gave Serafine was the formal and guarded smile of habit.

" How do you do, Miss Wimpole? I hope——" Becoming aware of Serafine's companion he stopped suddenly, halting in the doorway, and gazed across the room incredulously.

" Phyllis? " he whispered in the queerest tone of unbelief blended with relief and joy; and then as the stranger turned her head towards him: " Phyllis! Phyllis! I've been waiting for you! Why didn't you come? "

Serafine's protégée stood up with a little sob.

" I forgot! I forgot! " she cried, and stepped forward into his arms.

" But why? " he cried reproachfully. " These three days—it's been agony! Not knowing where you were! Not knowing——"

She burst into tears.

Serafine said expressionlessly:

" She's lost her memory, or something," and turned to the window and stood looking out at the prim laurestinus bushes. A queer little pain sawed at her heart. She started to count the garden palings as if her life depended on numbering them aright. When she had brought them to the same number—one hundred and seventy-four—three times in succession, she suddenly lost interest in them, and turning back into the room discovered that the pain in her heart was almost gone and that she could contemplate with almost complete equanimity the sight of the beautiful stranger clinging, as a drowning sailor to a spar, to Dr. Merewether's arm. She said amiably:

" Well, I'm glad it was I who happened to meet her."

" I can't tell you," replied the doctor gravely, " how glad *I* am, nor what a load of anxiety you've taken away from me, Miss Wimpole." He paused, looking at her seriously. " I don't know how much you know, or guess, nor what this poor child may have told you——"

" Nothing," said Serafine. She added slowly: " I think I would rather not know or guess anything, Dr. Merewether."

" You are a stranger both to her and to me. Perhaps you may never realize how much I am in your debt for what you have done this morning." He gave a sudden wry smile. " Perhaps, on the other hand, you will. Time will show."

" Dr. Merewether," said Serafine, returning his glance squarely and gravely, " I think there is some danger. I can't help you. But if there is anything you can do to help yourself, you had better do it."

" Thank you," he returned equably. " There is one thing you can do for us, if you will, Miss Wimpole, though I am aware that I have no right to ask it of you. Do not mention your meeting with this poor girl. I have a very strong reason for asking you this, but I will not tell you the reason. It is better for you that I should not."

" I won't tell a soul. But Dr. Mordby knows I met her. He saw us. He tried to follow us, but we shook him off."

Merewether looked grave and reflected for a moment.

" Mordby," he said slowly. " H'm. Yes. Thank you, Miss Wimpole." His steady, ironical eyes hid his thoughts.

" Dr. Mordby is not your friend."

He smiled.

" True. He is not."

There was a pause. Merewether looked gravely and tenderly at the woman who still clung to his arm, as if she were a responsibility he gladly bore but found none the less heavy for his gladness. She looked back at him as if he were her hope and strength embodied. Serafine said:

" I'll leave you now. You must have a good deal to think about."

He looked at her and smiled his gravely humorous smile.

" You may hear of us again, Miss Wimpole. I hope

very much that you will not." He added in a lower tone, as if speaking to himself: " At least we are together. And there should be a way out."

" If I could help you I would. If I can ever help you I will. Good-bye, Dr. Merewether, and good luck to you and her."

The doctor moved to see her out of the house, but Phyllis cried out in apprehension at the thought that he was about to leave her, and clung to him, so he stayed. Serafine let herself gently out of the door, taking away with her the image of the tragic lovers as she had last seen them standing side by side and hand in hand. She felt a little awed and resignedly conscious of limitations to herself, as the comic spirit must feel measured against the scale of tragedy. She walked up to the high road and took a taxi to Hampstead. " My God! " said Serafine to herself, " I hope they get out of this safely. Oh, God, let them get out of this safely."

The taxi drew up outside her cottage gate, behind the mulberry-coloured limousine of Dr. Mordby. Serafine's spirits rose at the sight of it. She felt that a duel with the enemy would appease a little the restless and helpless longing for activity which had taken hold of her. The chauffeur was standing by the car reading the lunch edition of an evening paper, and at the sight she thought: Oh, the newspapers of the next few days! The faint hope of Merewether's innocence that she had managed to keep alive was now finally extinguished. His escape could be only accomplished by the triumph of one man's wits over the entire police organization of England. A forlorn hope, indeed. She remembered how he had said: " There should be a way out," and shuddered, even while she prayed that he might be able to take it.

Dr. Mordby came down the stairs as she entered the hall. He looked unruffled and self-possessed as ever, treading lightly as a cat, swinging his eyeglass by its broad ribbon, distinguished, prosperous and at peace with the world.

" Good morning, Dr. Mordby. How do you find my aunt? "

He enveloped her hand in his white, boneless fingers and smiled.

" She will be all right after a sleep. A slight shock to one of the nerve-centres. She is anxiously awaiting your return."

" I passed your car in the High Street not long ago," said Serafine blandly.

" I was on my way here. You had a lady with you whose face is quite familiar to me, a former patient of mine, I fancy, though I cannot quite place her."

" Friend of mine," said Serafine, beginning to enjoy herself. " Just come back from South Africa. A Miss Sykes."

Not a muscle of Mordby's face moved.

" Ah! " he said negligently. " Then I must have been mistaken in thinking I knew her. I had only the most fleeting glimpse of her as my car passed."

" The world," said Serafine sententiously, " is a very small place. A charming girl. I hadn't seen her since our school days until I met her by chance in the High Street just now. But I knew her at once."

" I am not surprised. From the glimpse I had of her she appeared to be an exceedingly beautiful young lady."

" Don't suppose I shall see her again for another twenty years. She told me her address, but I've unfortunately forgotten it."

Mordby's eyes twinkled.

" Too bad. I was hoping for an introduction." He looked benignly at Serafine with his large head on one side. " What a delightful witness you would make in the law-courts, Miss Wimpole."

" Yes, I was always a good liar."

" The penalty for perjury is rather cramping to a talent for mendacity, though."

" That is why I spend so little of my time in the law-courts. I prefer to practise mendacity as an amateur."

" An amateur," repeated Mordby amiably, " one who works for love. . . . Good-bye, Miss Wimpole. Let me congratulate you once again upon the possession of an exceedingly well-balanced mind. A rare gift, as you would know if you followed my profession."

" Good-bye, Dr. Mordby. Do you take the longest way round or the shortest way home? "

" I shall inquire the way at the taxi-rank," replied Dr. Mordby blandly.

Serafine shut the door gently.

" Hell-fire and damnation," she said thoughtfully. " Suppose he does. . . ." She hesitated a moment and then went quickly to the telephone.

" Hullo! Is that Primrose Hill 1397? Is Dr. Merewether in? "

Faint and far away, a woman's voice replied:

" Who's speaking, please? "

" Miss Serafine Wimpole."

" I am Dr. Merewether's sister. Dr. Merewether is away. Dr. Smythe is taking over his practice until he returns. Dr. Smythe arrives this afternoon."

" Oh! I didn't know Dr. Merewether was going away! "

" No. It was rather sudden. Dr. Merewether's brother has been taken ill."

" Can you tell me when he will be back? "

" I'm afraid not." There was a faint catch in the small ghostly voice at the other end of the wire. " It all depends. I'm leaving myself to-morrow, when Dr. Smythe has arrived. Can I give Dr. Smythe a message from you? "

" Oh, no. No thanks. It doesn't matter. Good-bye."

Serafine hung up the receiver. Her heart was beating fast, and putting her hands to her flushed cheeks she found them hot as fire. So the hopeless contest had begun! The doctor had not wasted much time since she had seen him little more than an hour ago. His plans, she supposed, had been laid for flight ever since the night of the tragedy, and had been held up by the disappearance of the woman he loved—his female accomplice, as the newspapers would call her. Serafine shuddered, and went slowly up the stairs to Imogen's bedroom.

Imogen, sitting up in bed and dabbing eau-de-Cologne on her neck, murmured reproachfully :

" Serafine! Where *have* you been? I've been lying here just thinking of all the dreadful things that might have happened to you."

" You haven't. You've been talking to your psycho-analytical adviser and enjoying yourself no end."

" I don't know what was the matter with Dr. Mordby this morning," murmured Imogen discontentedly. " I had to tell him the dream I had last night three times over, and then he didn't take it seriously. I think I shall give it up, I don't believe there's anything in it. After all, one can buy a twopenny dream book and get interpretations of one's dreams that are much more agreeable than Dr. Mordby's, and just as likely to be true. . . . Serafine! " she exclaimed suddenly, as if inspired: " I wonder whether you oughtn't to have your tonsils out."

" What for? "

" Probably they're septic. You're not looking well. Not as well as you generally do."

" I'm not as young as I generally am," replied Serafine with a sigh, and turned away from the window and the sight of a newsboy running up the street. How would she bear to open a paper to-morrow and the days after?

" I do think," said Imogen plaintively, " you might remember that I'm twenty years older than you are and not keep talking about your age."

CHAPTER XV

ANALYTICAL INTERLUDE

HEMBROW'S first thought, when he had recovered from his chagrin at the sight of Frew's posthumous message, was that the envelope had been tampered with, either by Mrs. Rudgwick or by Gilbert Cold. But the most minute examination failed to reveal any signs of forgery. He was forced rather reluctantly to the conclusion that this absurd inscription was genuine and must be accepted in place of the incriminating will he had confidently hoped to find.

" Like most familiar quotations," said Christmas thoughtfully, " it's true."

" True? " growled Hembrow, for once a little out of humour. " I dare say it is. But that doesn't explain why anybody should commit a burglary to get hold of it."

" Oh, but it does," said John. " It explains the burglary as much as the burglary proves its truth."

" You'll be telling me next," said Hembrow rather sourly, " that it's exactly what you expected to find in that envelope all along."

" No, it isn't what I expected to find. I expected to find what the burglar expected to find. And now I seem to hear the shade of our late lamented friend Gordon Frew laughing at me just as he would have laughed at the burglar. He was fond of practical jokes, like most uncivilized people. But he didn't reckon on this practical joke going quite so far. He never thought the victim of his practical joke would be practical enough to stick a knife in him."

"You think——" began Hembrow, staring with a moody frown at the paper under discussion.

"I think that the burglar expected to find in this envelope his own discreditable past. He didn't expect to find it quite so pithily expressed. Nor did I."

"But why the mystery?" asked Hembrow in exasperation. "Why the registered post, and the secrecy and all the rest of it?"

"Did you never, Hembrow, when you were a small and wicked child, celebrate April Fool's day by sending to one of your long-suffering relations a large, elaborate and interesting-looking parcel consisting entirely of brown paper and string? And did you not, on such occasions, use much ink, sealing-wax and care to make the parcel look like a real parcel and arouse the expectations of the victim? In the same way, though not for such innocent reasons, Frew tried to make his blackmail look like real blackmail. The Shakespearean quotation he wrote out with such care is just a rather apt way of saying 'Sold!' to any victim who might be driven by fear into risking his safety to get hold of the envelope. You may be sure that he let his victim know of the existence of the envelope. It would be an added anxiety to the poor wretch to know that not only was his enemy in possession of the more shady facts of his career, but that those facts were also stowed away in the keeping of a third person."

"But they weren't."

"How was the poor wretch to know that? Frew made him believe that they were. Perhaps they weren't even in

Frew's possession. Perhaps the whole thing was a bluff from beginning to end. Frew was clever enough for anything."

"Your idea being, Mr. Christmas," said the Inspector slowly, "that Frew himself was a blackmailer?"

"Of a kind. A refined form of blackmailer. Not a blackmailer for money, but for love—or rather hate. He managed to make some unfortunate person believe that he could blackmail him if he chose. Probably he kept the victim on tenterhooks by a perpetual threat to publish his past misdeeds. He was writing his reminiscences at the time of his death."

"Pointless sort of blackmail if there was no money in it," muttered Hembrow.

"Not at all. There are other satisfactions besides the possession of large quantities of money. There are satisfactions that no amount will bring. Frew didn't want money, he'd got plenty. He wanted the satisfaction of feeling that he had an enemy in his power, and he wanted his enemy to feel it too. I don't suppose he really had the slightest intention of publishing anything libellous. The continual threat was enough. Enough to keep the poor wretch in a state of perpetual suspense. Enough to keep the amiable Frew in a state of perpetual amusement. Enough, in the long run, to slip a knife between Frew's shoulder-blades. Frew knew a good deal about the shadier side of human nature, no doubt. But he didn't allow for what Mordby calls the breaking-point."

"You think that, having silenced Frew, the murderer then attempted burglary at Camperdown Terrace in order to get possession of documents incriminating himself and prevent Mrs. Rudgwick from stepping into Frew's shoes as blackmailer?"

" No. Not the murderer. Another of Frew's victims."

" Come, Mr. Christmas! I don't see that there's any need to suppose that there were more than one of them! "

" Don't you? I do rather," said John quietly.

Hembrow looked at him shrewdly.

" I can guess why, Mr. Christmas. The evidence being so strong, you can't help believing that Merewether had a hand in the burglary at Camperdown Terrace. But you can't bring yourself to believe that he had a hand in the murder as well. So you invent a second person to be the murderer. Am I right? "

" More or less," admitted John amiably, rising to his feet.

Hembrow shook his head.

" You'd far better stand out of this affair."

" Not I. I'm just beginning to get really interested. Good-bye, Hembrow. I can see I haven't much time to lose if I'm to find the murderer for you before you make an ass of yourself by arresting Dr. Merewether."

Hembrow laughed.

" I shan't make an arrest until I'm quite certain I'm right."

" I trust you won't reach that dizzy pinnacle of complacency until I've had time to prove you're wrong," replied John with a smile, and departed.

Outside the Yard he called a taxi and directed the man to drive him to Temple Court. Arrived there he strolled through the peaceful precincts where the rustle of brown leaves under his feet and the twittering of sparrows seduced the ear from the roaring and hooting of the traffic that was so close and yet shut out, as if in another world. Passing under a dim stone archway into a sort of cloistered darkness he rung at a door which carried a small brass plate: Mr. Sydenham Rampson. The door was opened by an elderly man-servant who recognized John and smiled.

"Mr. Rampson is in his work-room, sir."

"Right. I know the way."

He went up the dimly-lighted stairs and entered a small light room fitted up as a laboratory. His friend Rampson, a short, stockily-built man of about thirty-five with thick fair hair for ever standing on end and a fresh-coloured, humorous face, was standing at a bench with his eye to the microscope, manipulating a tiny slide. He said without taking his eye from the instrument:

"Hullo, John. Take a chair if you can find one. I shan't be a second."

"How did you know it was me?"

"Solomon wouldn't have let anybody else come bounding in here like that. He'd have left them down below while he made inquiries, as he jolly well ought."

"Am I to understand that I'm a favourite of yours?"

"Of Solomon's. Not of mine, particularly," replied his friend, turning with his wide grin from his instrument and perching himself on a high wooden stool. "However, it's quite pleasant to see your amiable and idiotic face occasionally. What've you been doing all these months? Frittering away the precious hours of your youth, as usual, I suppose."

"Yes," assented John meekly. "And I suppose you've had your eye glued to that microscope ever since I saw you last. However, it seems to suit you. You look horribly healthy. How you manage it in the complete absence of fresh air and exercise beats me."

"I still keep up my football. But it's getting rather a bore. I shall drop it next winter. Too much to do."

John smiled. He liked and admired Rampson and was endlessly amused by the contrast between his appearance and manner and his anchorite's mode of life. With the physique of an athlete and the cheerful friendliness of a young man about town, Rampson combined a passion for analytical chemistry which made all other interests negligible or tiresome. He was a remote cousin of John's, and John had first known him as a solemn and good-natured Sixth-Form boy, making extraordinary messes and smells and endangering life and limb with chemical experiments in an attic in his father's house which he had fitted up as a laboratory. Having inherited a comfortable income he had devoted himself soon after leaving the university to research work, and for the last eight years had lived in these rooms in the Temple with his old servant Solomon, pursuing studies which brought him much prestige but little money, free of all necessity or desire to follow other interests, a kind of cenobite of science and a completely happy man.

"And how's *le monde ou l'on s'amuse,* John?"

"Not very amusing at the moment."

"It never is. I can't think why a chap with your brains doesn't use them. You'll die of premature senile decay if you go on trying to amuse yourself without working much longer."

"I hate the very sound of the word work," replied John gently. He always adopted his most dilettante pose in the company of this earnest and single-minded friend. It amused them both.

"You can't live for ever without an interest in life."

" My dear Friar Bacon, I have an interest in life. People."

Rampson looked at him with vague surprise.

" Ethnology? Now that's rather an interesting subject if you've got time for it. I was talking to Professor Nilssen the other day, and——"

" No, no. Just people. Any people who happen to be lying around, as one might say. Even you interest me no end. You've no idea, Sydenham, how mysterious, romantic and incalculable you are."

" Am I? "

" Yes. Don't you feel the same about me? "

" Not in the least," replied Rampson brutally. " To me you're just a chap who blows in at terribly frequent intervals and interrupts me at my work. But then I'm not what you call interested in people. They're always wanting one to do something one doesn't want to do."

" Jolly good guess," said Christmas. " I want you to do something for me. You needn't put on that cautious expression. It's something quite in your own line, and you can do it without setting your foot outside your hermit's cave."

" Well? "

John took from his breast-pocket a small tissue-paper package and unwrapping it laid on the table a little piece of thin gold.

" I want you to tell me all there is to know about this object. What made of, where been, what touched lately, if anything, and, in short, as much of family history as the microscope will disclose."

" You want a good deal," said Rampson. " You amateur detectives seem to think a microscope is a kind of telepathic medium and psychic investigator rolled into one. I can only find what's there, and if there's nothing there I can't find anything."

"Quite. Well, you just see if there's anything there, there's a good chap. That's all I want."

"Right you are, John. Why do you want to know?"

"Somebody has committed a murder."

Rampson looked both disgusted and bored.

"People are always doing silly things," he observed. "But of all the silly things people do, killing other people is the silliest. And that's what you call an interest in life!"

"I know, of course," said John humbly, "that people are not anything like so sensible as molecules. Do you want me to tell you about this murder?"

"I do not. When do you want the report on this scrap of metal?"

"Soon. To-day, if possible."

"Now, if you like. Stay to lunch. I've had mine, but I dare say Solomon will do you up something wholesome and nourishing."

"No thanks. I've got too much to do."

Rampson grinned.

"All right. I'll send old Solomon along with the report this evening. He likes a blow on a bus occasionally. If anything else turns up that you want analysed, John, command me."

"Thank you, Sydenham, I will. Any suspicious objects I may collect shall be forwarded straight to you in plain vans. No deposit. Money back if not satisfied. Good-bye. I must be off e'er the scent cools, as they say in sleuthing circles."

"Well, don't go running your fat head into danger. It's not worth it. I can't understand this morbid interest in murders. If a person's murdered, he's dead, and the only reasonable thing to do is bury him."

" I haven't got time to argue, Sydenham, so I'll simply say that your anti-social tendencies sadden me, your lack of imagination rouses my pity, and your inhumanity fills me with misgivings as to the welfare of your soul. With this veiled rebuke I will take my leave. Don't bother to come down. I'll let myself out with the help of the gentle Solomon."

CHAPTER XVI

IN WHICH A LADY LOSES HER TEMPER

JOHN CHRISTMAS dismissed his taxi at Oxford Circus and walked west along the crowded pavement past the crowded shops. He could think better when he was walking than when he was sitting restlessly in a taxi that crawled along behind other taxis and buses and stopped every few hundred yards in obedience to the large white hand of a traffic controller. And he wanted to think. He wanted to think about Mr. Lascarides, and chiefly about the extreme flimsiness of the alibi offered by that gentleman. A mysterious telephone-call, an assignation in a thick fog, a stolen emerald—it savoured too much of fiction. It savoured so much of fiction that John felt sure that it was true. For he knew that when a clever man invents a story, he is very careful to make it savour of truth.

He turned up into the comparative peacefulness of Duke Street, and crossed Manchester Square. He paused outside the Wallace Collection, reading the notices on the board in the inattentive, negligent way in which a man who is thinking deeply will occupy his eyes with print. He was just passing on, without having assimilated one word, when a light hand touched him on the shoulder, and turning he found Sir Marion Steen looking at him quizzically.

"Not going in, John? I am. And when I saw you studying the notice-board so attentively, I thought perhaps you would accompany me."

"Afraid I can't, Sir Marion, I've got something much less pleasant and peaceful to do."

The financier raised his eyebrows with a half-humorous, half-deprecating look.

"Criminal investigation still? Every man to his taste." In a serious, confidential tone he went on: "Our friend Merewether? Has anything turned up to clear him of suspicion?"

"Not in the eyes of the police. But I hope it won't be long before they're convinced of the truth."

"The truth being?"

"That whoever did this thing, it was not Dr. Merewether."

Sir Marion looked grave.

"It is not very easy to convince people of a negative truth. If only we could make our assertion a positive one, and convince them, not of who did not do it, but of who did it!"

"That is what I hope to do. Do you happen, Sir Marion, to know anything of a man called Lascarides?"

"A Greek name," murmured Sir Marion, poking thoughtfully at a crevice in the pavement with his malacca cane. "No, I have certainly heard the name before. It is not an uncommon one, I imagine. But I don't think I have ever met anybody of the name. Why, if I may ask?"

"He's an acquaintance of the late Mr. Frew's who's cropped up in connection with the case, that's all. And I want to know as much about him as possible—more than I'll ever get him to tell me, I'm afraid. He keeps a carpet shop not far from here, and seems to be rather a swell in the carpet dealing line, so I thought you might have come across him."

"No," said Sir Marion, looking thoughtful. "Sorry I can't help you, John." He looked pensively at his young friend in silence for a moment, as if he were wondering whether it would be tactful to ask for more information. "Is this Lascarides by any chance the man in the fez who accosted Dr. Merewether and myself in Greentree Road? I only ask out of curiosity, so if you would rather keep your counsel, John, you have only to say so."

"I don't mind telling you at all, Sir Marion. In fact, I was rather hoping to see you and ask you about one or two little details that trouble me rather. Yes, it seems fairly obvious that my friend Lascarides was the man you met, although he strenuously denies it and offers an alibi."

"What kind of alibi?"

"Feeble," replied John. "Almost too feeble to be an invention, if you know what I mean. That's one of the little things that worry me. When people invent alibis, they usually invent something with at least a pretence of solidity."

"And in what way can I help you, my dear boy? I am only too glad to be able to do so."

"Well, would you mind describing again the man you met in Greentree Road, Sir Marion, in as much detail as possible? I am on my way to him now, and should like to have your description of the stranger fresh in my memory."

"Certainly." The old man smiled. "Where is your note-book, John?"

"In my head."

" The best place for it, to be sure. Well, to describe our mysterious friend. He was below the middle height; in fact, about my own height. His eyes were about on a level with my own as he spoke to me. He had a dark, sallow complexion and a small, grizzled moustache. He was wearing a dark overcoat buttoned closely up to his chin, and a fez. I didn't particularly observe his features, but they seemed to me to be the sort of features one associates with a fez. The fez looked very much in place on his head. He was a stoutish man." Sir Marion spoke slowly and carefully, looking over John's shoulder as if seeking to conjure up on the pavement an apparition of the man he was describing. " He had a gold-crowned tooth. Yes, one of the canine teeth in the top row was crowned with gold. It showed very much when he smiled."

" Nothing more? "

" Nothing more. I think that's a full report of all I noticed about the gentleman."

" Are you sure, Sir Marion? "

Steen raised his eyebrows, and a shade of that asperity which his aquiline features could so readily assume crossed his face. He spoke good-humouredly enough, however.

" Yes, my dear John, I think I may say I am sure."

" Forgive me for being persistent, but it is a point which troubles me rather. Did you happen to notice whether the gentleman suffered from a squint? "

Sir Marion gave a slight smile, and hesitated.

" That was certainly my impression at the time, but I may have been deceived. He had peculiarly close-set, dark eyes of the kind which sometimes appear to have a slight cast when they have really nothing of the kind.

As I told the Inspector, my impression was of a slight cast in the left eye, but I am not positive. Dr. Merewether did not notice any such thing."

"Yet," said John slowly, "surely a squint is one of the most noticeable peculiarities a man can have. When a stranger speaks to one, it is at his eyes that one looks."

"Well," said the elder man patiently, "as I say, I am quite ready to believe that I was mistaken about the squint. On such a foggy night, one cannot vouch for the accuracy of one's observations. . . . And yet," he added thoughtfully, "it seems to me that he *did* have a squint. or something peculiar about one of his eyes. Why does this matter trouble you so, John? Has your Mr.—Lascarides, wasn't it? a squint, or has he not? Am I the better observer, or is Dr. Merewether?"

"He has," replied John. "What troubles me is that his eyes, when he looks straight at you, are so peculiar and so—well, in fact, unpleasant, that I cannot understand how Dr. Merewether could fail to notice them, or you to be uncertain about them. It troubles me because it makes me feel that, after all, I may be on the wrong track."

Sir Marion gave a small, whimsical smile.

"Peculiarly unpleasant!" he echoed. "Why, this sounds most interesting and sinister, John. But you must remember that when the gentleman spoke to us, he spoke in the character of a harmless fog-bound wayfarer: when he spoke to you, he was in the position of a suspect defending himself. Mightn't that account for the unpleasantness you noticed in the way he looked at you?"

John laughed.

"Perhaps. But he really has such an extraordinarily horrible squint!"

" Really? Well, I wish you luck, John, in clearing our friend the doctor of this horrible suspicion. I'd offer to come with you and help you if I felt at all certain that I could identify the man I met. But I had such a casual glimpse of him, and the night was so dark and foggy, that I am afraid I should not recognize the gentleman if I saw him again, not with any certainty. But I mustn't keep you gossiping here. Good-bye, John. You to the worship of Hecate, and I to the temple of Apollo! "

So saying, the old philanthropist turned in at the gate of Hertford House, and John went on his way towards the exclusive shop kept by Mr. Lascarides.

Arrived there, however, he was informed by the pale girl who spent her time rounding her slim shoulders and straining her pretty eyes over repairing damaged treasures that Mr. Lascarides was not on the premises. He had gone home to lunch, and would not return to the shop until the evening.

" My business," said John, " is rather urgent. Could you give me his home address, or, better still, his 'phone number? "

" Certainly, sir. His home address is Oakdene, Ramsay Hill, Golders Green, and his telephone number is Hampstead 9497. Would you care to leave a message in case he is away from home and you are unable to reach him? "

" No, thank you. In that case I will call again this evening. Good afternoon."

Christmas left the girl to her delicate and wearisome task, and took a bus to Greentree Road. In Newtree's studio he was surprised to find Serafine Wimpole, sitting in a rather lackadaisical attitude on the edge of the throne and smoking. She was looking gloomily across the studio as if her thoughts were in some far-away and rather unpleasant place, and Newtree was making pencil sketches of her with great rapidity and concentration, in complete silence. The moral atmosphere struck John, coming briskly in, as being rather heavy. He was not surprised at Newtree's silence, but taciturnity was not as a rule a characteristic of Miss Serafine Wimpole. They both looked up as he entered, and Newtree with a brief greeting returned to his sketching. Serafine gave a rather lifeless smile and said:

"Hullo, John. I'm suffering torture. My right foot has pins and needles, and Mr. Newtree won't let me get up and see what he's doing."

Dropping his pencil hastily, Laurence protested in some embarrassment:

"I say, I'm awfully sorry, Miss Wimpole! But really there's no reason why you should sit so still. I'm only making quick sketches. I'd much rather, in fact, you moved a bit. I don't seem able to get the expression."

Serafine gave a small, malicious smile at his confusion.

"I'm sorry, Mr. Newtree. I'm afraid I'm not feeling very expressive to-day. I've got rather a headache, and what is worse, so has my aunt." John, who knew Imogen well, smiled at this. Serafine went on: "And really I don't think my constitution is built to stand murders at close quarters. I used to think it would stand anything, from forty cigarettes a day to the remarks of such critics as don't appreciate my remarkable works. But murder, apparently, is a different matter."

"I'm awfully sorry," repeated Laurence humbly. "I wish I could have made the sitting to-morrow. But they want the finished drawing to-night."

"Who does?" asked John, looking at the large sheet

of paper on which Laurence had endeavoured to reproduce Serafine's vigorous and incisive personality while suppressing his own lively instinct for caricature.

"Some bally women's paper or other—*Fireside Notes,* or something."

"Didn't know you went in for contributing to the domestic press, Laurence."

Laurence looked rather uncomfortable and cleared his throat.

"I don't as a rule. But—h'm! I rather wanted to do some studies of Miss Wimpole. And so . . . so when Ferguson tackled me about a portrait for his rag, I—I thought it'd be rather an opportunity of getting a sitting."

"I feel honoured, Mr. Newtree," said Serafine, strolling over to inspect the drawings. "But I wish you hadn't made me so pretty."

This being the kind of remark to which Mr. Newtree was quite incapable of finding a reply, he flushed slightly, began to say something incoherent, and subsided, looking at John for help. John laughed.

"She only says it to annoy because she knows it teases," he said. "I expect *Fireside Bits* won't think they're pretty enough."

Hastily changing a subject he felt incapable of treating with the grace it demanded, Laurence asked:

"Have you found the murderer yet?"

"No. But I'm on a trail."

"The right one?"

"I hope so."

At his confident tone Serafine glanced quickly at him and away again. John, noticing that glance and her sombre look, said rallyingly:

"You don't look as if you shared my hope, Serafine. Have you lost confidence in your sleuth?"

With an averted face, knocking the ash off her cigarette with great care, Serafine muttered:

"Of course not. . . ."

"Who's the man?" asked Laurence, taking up a pencil and beginning to make a sketch of Serafine's averted head.

"The obvious one, of course," replied John teasingly, and was amazed when Serafine turned on him a face gone suddenly white and hard.

"John!" she said in a strangled voice. "You wouldn't—— But you'll let him go! Surely your friends are more to you than this—this detective game of yours!"

Her eyes were fierce, and two spots of carmine, appearing suddenly in her white cheeks, gave a sort of bizarre and hectic beauty to her worn face. Laurence, in the background, began another sketch. Completely taken aback, John stammered:

"My dear! What do you mean?"

Controlling herself with an effort, Serafine said in a strained, cold way:

"You said that you liked Dr. Merewether—that he was your friend."

"I did, I do. But what—— My dear girl, you don't imagine that I'd have anything to do with arresting Merewether, even if—— But of course he didn't. The thing's absurd! When I said the obvious one, I meant our friend in the fez."

The sudden fire and colour died out of Serafine's face. She looked at her friend in silence for a moment, and then made an attempt to laugh.

"Of course. I'm sorry!" She drew a long, unsteady breath. "For a moment I thought . . . As I say, my constitution won't stand murders at close range. Sorry to be such an excitable idiot, John."

She got up from her place on the model's throne and went over towards the great window, over which the leafless boughs of an ash tree made a black tracery in the white light of afternoon. John looked after her in silence, perturbed and puzzled. Laurence with a sigh abandoned his pencil and perched himself on the piano stool.

"Do you mean to say, Serafine," said John slowly at last, "that to you Merewether is the—obvious one?"

There was a pause. Then without turning round, Serafine said in an unsteady, muffled voice:

"No—I . . . I don't. Why should I? I thought—thought you did, that was all."

John stood looking thoughtfully at her inexpressive back. He knew that she had worried a good deal over Dr. Merewether's apparent connection with the mysterious crime. But her manner now seemed to point to something a good deal more serious than distress at the fact that Merewether should be suspected by the police. He walked over to her and linked his arm in hers.

"Serafine," he said seriously, "I feel as if you knew or guessed something about Merewether which you haven't told me. Wouldn't it be better to tell me? Even if it's something which seems to go against him? The sooner I can find the real murderer, the better for Merewether, and the more I know the more likely I am to solve this puzzle. I am afraid that you have some special reason for thinking poor Merewether did it. But if you tell me, we may find that it is a special reason for thinking that he didn't do it. After all, he didn't do it. The thing's impossible. And so the more we know, the sooner we can clear him."

Without returning the pressure of his hand on her arm, Serafine said sombrely:

"I think you're an optimist, John."

"My dear, you can't believe——"

Serafine gave a high, discordant laugh which set John's teeth on edge.

"Oh, can't believe this and can't believe that," she cried. "What's the use of can't believe, if you *have* to believe it?"

"What do you mean, Serafine?" asked John gravely. "Come! Hadn't you better tell me? It can do no harm, in any circumstances. I'm not a Yard officer. I can drop my footling investigations when and where I like."

Serafine drew a long, unsteady breath.

"Yes," she said. "I suppose I'd better tell you. It'll be a relief to tell somebody who feels the same way about it as myself. It—it only happened this morning. I suppose that's why I'm behaving like an hysterical idiot this afternoon." She glanced uncertainly at Newtree.

"I'll sling my hook," remarked Newtree, rising, "for a bit."

"No, don't go, Mr. Newtree. Unless you'd rather. Why should you?"

"All right," said Newtree, sitting down again. "I'll stay, then. But nothing'll make me believe Merewether had anything to do with this affair. I can't think why you're all getting so bothered about it. If he told me he'd done it, I shouldn't believe him."

Serafine sighed.

" I wonder," she said. " Sometimes one has to believe what one would give the world not to."

She went over to the throne and sat down again, and began to tell John all that had happened during the morning, from her encounter with the strange woman in Hampstead High Street to the passage-at-arms with Dr. Mordby in her own hall. John listened in silence, and Newtree, taking advantage of the animation on his sitter's face as she told her story, made drawings of her and listened at the same time.

" At any rate," Serafine finished, " he's got away. Perhaps . . ."

John said nothing. In his opinion, the chances of Dr. Merewether getting farther than a railway station were extremely remote. He knew that for the last two days the doctor had never been out of sight of one of Hembrow's men.

Serafine, watching his grave face, asked pitifully:

" Do you think he has a chance? "

" Of getting out of the country? Frankly, my dear, not the slightest. A Yard man's been watching him ever since Hembrow first suspected him. Probably already . . ."

John left his sentence unfinished.

" Best thing that could happen," observed Newtree tranquilly. " Now we'll have an explanation and the matter'll be cleared up. Idiotic to run away just because you're suspected of murder and haven't got a cast-iron alibi. Worst thing he could do, in my opinion."

" Oh, how can you be so ridiculous! " cried Serafine, jumping to her feet, and looking at her host as if he were beneath contempt and fit only for instant extermination. Her tortured nerves found a queer relief in this violent rudeness to an inoffensive person. "I never heard such obstinate tommy-rot! You say you're a friend of Dr. Merewether's. But to talk like that isn't friendship, it's just blind laziness!"

Newtree's glasses dropped and he blinked at the virago, flushing slightly and feeling extremely at a loss. Yet queerly not altogether displeased at being made the subject of a fierce attack; it was a new experience.

"Isn't it obvious, if Dr. Merewether's gone, that he has some reason for going?" went on Serafine. "And what can the reason be but——" She stopped abruptly.

"Dunno," said Laurence gruffly. "I'm not a detective. Ask Christmas."

John, who had been thinking deeply and had hardly noticed this little passage, asked slowly:

"This woman, Serafine. You say she was mad?"

Serafine hesitated.

"More or less. Mad sounds a little too strong. She wasn't raving, or anything like that. She seemed to have lost her memory and to be incapable of looking after herself."

"She couldn't give an account of herself, at any rate?"

"No. She'd forgotten her own name. She was quite vague about everything."

"And she said she was frightened?"

"Yes. She seemed to have had some dreadful shock. She talked about something that made her forget, something that made her frightened. . . ."

"Laurence!" said John, turning abruptly to his friend. "Can you lend me Greenaway for the afternoon?"

"Certainly, as long as you return him intact."

"Then I'll be off, and take him with me. The less time I lose the better. May I use your telephone?"

" Of course," murmured Laurence, looking a little surprised at this sudden access of energy.

Serafine asked huskily:

" John, tell me first. . . . Can you help? Is there any chance—any hope? "

" Of Merewether's getting away? None. But I'm going to try and save him the trouble of proving himself innocent."

Serafine looked at him helplessly and shrugged her shoulders as he took up the telephone receiver.

" Hullo. Is that Hampstead 9497? Is that Mr. Lascarides? Can you be at the corner of Circus Road, Wellington Road, at a quarter past three this afternoon? I've got the stuff. Yes. Yes. Don't come if you don't want it. . . . What's that? No. I say, I've got the stuff. Isn't that enough for you? You won't? All right. Good-bye."

As John took the receiver from his ear a faint spluttering noise, like the objurgations of an enraged elf, could be heard in the studio. John hung the receiver up and smiled, looking at his wrist-watch.

" Got nearly three-quarters of an hour," he observed. " I'll go and tell Greenaway I want him as an assistant."

" Why," asked Newtree curiously, " did you talk in that extraordinary wooden voice to your blasphemous friend? "

" Didn't want him to recognize me. Wanted to remain incognito."

" You don't think he's coming all the way from Hampstead to meet an incognito, do you? "

" Yes," said John lightly. " I'm rather inclined to think he will. There's nothing like arousing people's curiosity to make them do what you want."

CHAPTER XVII

THE ORIENTAL GENTLEMAN

"ARE you an observant man, Greenaway?"

"I trust so, sir. Reasonably so, that is."

"Do you remember," asked John, as they strolled together out of Madox Court a few moments before three o'clock, "the foreigner in the fez who came to the studios the night Mr. Frew was killed?"

"I should say I do, sir," responded Greenaway with emphasis. "He wasn't the sort of customer whose looks one is likely to forget. I remember every little thing that happened that dreadful night, sir, as plain as if it was happening now in front of my eyes. I can't hardly believe now that my boy is safe from being thought a murderer. It all seemed to go so terrible against him at first."

"I don't think the police'll trouble your son further," said John.

"I always thought the oriental gentleman had done it, sir. Polite and smiling as you please, but looked as if 'e'd stick at nothing."

"Do you think you would know him again if you saw him?"

"Yes, sir," replied the old man promptly. "I can see him plain in my mind's eye now, and if he was to come along this road now, I should know him at once."

"Apart from his fez?"

"I could pick him out of a dozen gentlemen in fezes, sir. It wasn't the fez. It was the ole look of the man as he stood there in the doorway."

"Well," said John, smiling slightly at this dramatic declaration, "this is what I want you to do. I am going to meet somebody at the corner of Circus Road at a quarter past three. I want you to hang about not far away, without seeming to have any connection with me. When the man I'm waiting for turns up, we shall stand there and have a little conversation, he and I—rather an amusing one, I fancy. I want you then to stroll slowly past us, without giving any sign of recognition or seeming to look at us particularly, and then wait for me round the corner out of sight, or in the Wellington Arms, if you like. When I've finished my little talk with my friend, I shall come and meet you, and I shall expect you to be able to tell me whether the man you see me with is the same man who came to Madox Court three days ago or not. See? I want you to identify him for me, if possible."

"Right you are, sir," said Greenaway, looking rather pleased at being asked to take a hand in this drama. "I shall identify him fast enough, if it is the man."

"Good," said John. "Here we are at the corner of Circus Road, and it's nearly ten past three. I shall just wait here. You wander off by yourself and watch for a man to come and meet me, but remember you and I are strangers for the next half-hour or so."

"Very good, sir," said the old servant with deep satisfaction, and walked slowly off with the air of one who has nothing to do and all the afternoon to do it in.

John took up a position at the corner and waited. He determined to give Mr. Lascarides half an hour's grace, and then, if he had not turned up, go and beard him in his bijou lair at Golders Green. At ten minutes past three John felt fairly certain that he would come, whether his previous story had been true or not: for if the story were true, he was in the habit of making assignations with unknown people; and if it were not true, and he had something to conceal, he would come to see how the land lay.

At a quarter past three John was inclined to think that he would come if his story had been true, but not if he suspected a trap.

At twenty past three John cursed himself for wasting time over a twenty to one chance, and wished he had gone straight and unannounced to Golders Green.

At twenty-three minutes past three a taxi-cab drew up about five yards away from him, and his heart gave a little throb of excitement as Lascarides stepped on to the pavement and paid the driver. In the grey light of out-of-doors he looked a very much more noticeable figure than he had seemed among the oriental rugs and tapestries in his carpet-shop. John noticed that several people turned to look at him with mild curiosity as he stood on the pavement turning over the coins in his hand. Besides his crimson fez, which was sufficient in itself to make his appearance remarkable, he wore a long overcoat with an astrakhan collar and carried a very large and sumptuous umbrella with an ornamental crook handle of gold. John thought: If we converse long in this public spot we shall collect a crowd. He noticed, as the Greek turned in his direction, that the fur-collared overcoat was open at the neck in the ordinary way.

John stepped forward with a smile, but before he could speak the other said serenely:

"Good afternoon. We have met before, I think. But your name I do not know. On the telephone you prefer not to give your name. Why, I do not know. To have a name is more convenient, I have always found, even if it is the name of one's choice rather than of one's fathers."

"My name is Christmas," said John, rather taken aback.

"It is a good name," said the Greek with grave politeness. "You have a saying: Call a dog by a bad name, and hang him. But in these so civilized times you have first to prove that he deserves the bad name you give, isn't it?" He smiled, with a glint of white teeth and gold.

"You are not surprised to see me, Mr. Lascarides?"

The carpet-dealer clicked his tongue softly against his teeth, and slowly shook his head.

"Not in the least, Mr. Christmas. I will not say that it was yourself personally I expected to have the happiness of meeting. I thought it might be the excellent officer from Scotland Yard who was with you this morning when you called at my shop. You need not have kept your name from me. I should in any case have been enchanted to offer you an interview, although I should perhaps a more private place have chosen for it. However, you like this place for its associations, eh?"

John laughed.

"You are quite right," he said. "I mentioned this spot because I thought it was a favourite meeting-place of yours. And I refrained from giving my name on the telephone because I understood that people who made appointments to meet you were in the habit of remaining incognito."

The Greek smiled.

"The people who make appointments with me," he

replied calmly, "are in the habit of remaining incognito only when an officer from Scotland Yard shows an impolite interest in their doings. Are you an officer from Scotland Yard?"

"No. I am a private investigator."

"An amateur. I thought so. And what can I do for you, Mr. Private Investigator Christmas?"

And with a grotesque effect the little man put his head on one side and rubbed his expensively gloved hands together, his umbrella hanging over his fore-arm.

"You can tell me the truth," replied John with a grin. "But I don't suppose you will."

"You are mad, my young mister," observed Lascarides equably. "It is a madness of an amiable sort, but one that has already wasted much of my valuable time."

"I am sorry. But an arrest on the capital charge, or even detention pending inquiries, would waste a great deal more of your time than I shall."

"You are bluffing," said the other, looking at him narrowly. "You have no power to make an arrest. And if you had, I am not the man you want. To be arrested for the murder of your late ever-to-be-regretted friend would be an inconvenience to me, but not a tragedy. For I did not kill him, and I could prove it, though at some inconvenience to myself."

"It would be difficult to prove it," murmured John tentatively. "You were with him at the time he was killed, were you not?"

"But I tell you I was not. I was here, in this very place where I stand now, and nearer to your Madox Court than this I did not go."

"Mr. Lascarides," said John gravely, "was not Mr. Gordon Frew a client of yours?"

The Greek looked impassively at the pavement.

"Mr. Christmas," he replied gently, "he was not. Though, if he had been, I do not know why you should suppose that I should visit him at eight o'clock in the evening to sell him rugs. I am not a pedlar."

"I was not suggesting," replied John slowly, "that you sold him rugs, Mr. Lascarides."

The dealer's heavy eye-lids gave the faintest flicker.

"What then?" he inquired smoothly.

"Drugs," said John, and saw the other give an uncontrollable start and press his small hands closely together as if to keep command of himself.

There was a long silence. The Greek appeared to be meditating his answer to this charge, wondering, perhaps, whether John had proof of his illegal dealings or whether his accusation had been shot in the dark. Watching the dark, impassive face, John saw out of the corner of his eye old Greenaway strolling past them for the third time.

"You would suggest," said Lascarides at last, "that I supplied Mr. Frew with drugs, and visited him on the night he died for that purpose?"

"That is my suggestion."

A sort of puzzled frown crossed the other man's face and he gave a short, impatient laugh.

"Oh, no, no, no," he uttered softly. "If your friend took drugs, it was not I who supplied him. There is something here I do not understand."

He glanced up quickly at John, and then back at the pavement again. He seemed to be aware of the fact that he appeared a great deal more prepossessing when his eyes were not in evidence.

"Listen, my young friend," he said at length, more amiably and naturally than he had spoken before. "This morning I told your Inspector Hembrow the story of all I had done on the night this murder was. It was all true —all but one little detail which does not affect the story and which I would prefer to keep my own business. I will tell you, if you wish, that it was not an emerald I went to receive on that foggy night. The emerald was a little story, as I think you have guessed, but all the rest was true. Now I can tell you something more, which may be of service to you. My friend from whom I was expecting the messenger has now arrived in England. Yesterday evening he arrived. After your clever Inspector and your respected friend had gone out of my shop this morning, quickly I take a taxi to my friend's place of business, which is—never mind where! I go to warn him to be discreet, should by any chance your Inspector Hembrow trace him. I should not tell you this, perhaps, if you were an official detective, Mr. Christmas; but being an amateur, I think you are only interested in your murder and will not interfere in a matter that does not bear upon it. As I was saying, to my friend I went, and tell him everything, begging him to be upon his guard. How surprised I was, then, to hear that my friend had sent no messenger to England, but had brought the—emerald, himself! Who it was that spoke to me on the telephone that foggy night I do not know, but my friend's messenger it was not."

The little man spread out his hands and lifted his shoulders.

"Is there no one else who might have 'phoned you a similar message, Mr. Lascarides?"

"No one that I know of. It is a complete mystery to me, young sir."

John found himself wishing that fate had not seen fit

to give Lascarides that appalling squint. It made it impossible to judge his character from his physiognomy. When he looked down at the pavement the gently-cynical, intellectual look of his fleshy olive face queerly inclined John to like him; but when he looked up that sinister, obliquely-staring eye caused an immediate revulsion of feeling and seemed to lay his every word open to the suspicion of being false.

"Have you any enemies, Mr. Lascarides?"

The Greek smiled.

"I do not know. Many I may have. I do not trouble my head. I do not think that I have any, but one cannot see into the hearts of all one's friends." He gave a sudden smile. "You are wishing, are you not, that you could see into my heart and know whether I speak the truth? You cannot, Mr. Detective Christmas. You can only search and test and prove. And now I will leave you to your searching and testing, for I have an appointment at four o'clock. And I see that your friend is waiting for you down the street."

He waved his gloves blandly to where in the distance old Greenaway was strolling away from them, and then signalled to a passing taxi-cab.

"If I had so much interest in your doings as you have in mine," went on Lascarides gently, as the taxi turned, "I should think you had brought your friend here to see if he could identify me. Up and down, up and down, he has walked while we have been standing here. You should tell him, Mr. clever Detective Christmas, that if he does not recognize a man at the first glance, he will not recognize him at the third—no, nor the fourth! Good-bye, Mr. Christmas. My address you know. I will not run away."

He climbed into the taxi and disappeared, leaving John

smiling ruefully to himself on the pavement. As Greenaway came to meet him, he noticed that the old servant looked somewhat dejected.

"Well, Greenaway," said John, as they made their way homewards, "you had a good look at my friend. What did you make of him?"

"I 'ad several good looks, sir," replied Greenaway sadly, "and the rest of the time I've spent wishing I 'adn't been so cocksure, sir, when you spoke about me being an observant man."

"I noticed you walked past us several times."

"Yes, I did, sir, but if I'd walked past a 'undred times it would 'ave been the same, sir."

"Then you didn't recognize the gentleman?"

Greenaway sighed heavily.

"Well, I did and I didn't, sir. When I saw the gentleman get out of the cab, I thought all excited-like: That's him! And then I walked past and saw him a bit clearer, and I 'ad quite a turn, sir, because it wasn't him after all! And then I looked again, and I thought, Well, it might be, remembering that people always look a bit different in colour and that, sir, at night-time. And he was very like the gentleman as called the other night, sir. Same colour, and build, and height and that, and the same darkish moustache, and the same bit of gold in 'is teeth, sir. But the long and short of it is, sir, I couldn't swear as it isn't the gentleman, and I couldn't swear as it is him. There's only one thing I can swear to, an' that is that the gentleman as called at Madox Court never 'ad that dreadful cast in 'is eye—at least," amended Greenaway, rendered cautious by his experience of the difficulties of bearing witness, "I could swear as I never noticed it, if 'e 'ad, sir."

And once again old Greenaway gave a heavy, disappointed sigh.

" I am to take it, then, that you can't identify the gentleman, but that on the whole you are inclined to think it is the same man? "

The servant paused and then slowly shook his head.

" Inclined to think it isn't, sir. Like 'im, very like 'im. But different in a way it isn't easy to explain, sir. 'E seemed—well, thicker than the gentleman I saw before. Thicker in the body and neck and in the features too, sir. It being a different light might make that difference, I can't say. But my feeling is, sir, that it isn't the same man, though I wouldn't swear it isn't."

" Thank you, Greenaway. This looks as if it were going to be interesting."

" Begging your pardon, sir, but didn't you *want* it to be the same man? "

John laughed.

" All I want is to find out the truth, Greenaway, and I must thank you for helping me. Half a minute. I want to have a word with our friend the crossing-sweeper."

That ragged philosopher was sitting in his old place at the corner of Shipman's Mews, with his brooms beside him, contemplating his crossing, and smoking an evil-smelling pipe. He saluted as John came up, and greeted Greenaway, who disapproved of him and his methods of earning a living, with extreme politeness.

John cut short his long and blasphemous discourse on the state of the weather.

" Do you remember," he interrupted, " that I asked you the other day about a foreigner wearing a fez who came down this road the night Mr. Frew was killed? "

"Ah!" assented the other emphatically. "You gave me 'arf a dollar."

"I'll give you another if you can just cast your mind back to that night and remember something for me."

"I'd remember anything for 'arf a dollar," replied the old beggar with a grin.

"You shall have the half-crown anyhow. But I want you to be quite accurate. It's rather important."

The crossing-sweeper composed his features into an expression of portentous solemnity.

"The truth, the 'ole truth and nothing but the truth, so 'elp me bob!"

"Well, first. Can you swear that the man who came into the mews and was so startled when you spoke to him had a cast in his left eye?"

"Fust I've 'eard of it, sir." The old man pushed his hat back and scratched among his long, greasy locks. "I'd almost swear 'e 'adn't anything of the sort, but that there night being so foggy, one can't 'ardly swear to noticing anything. I'll swear I never noticed it if 'e 'ad sir, if that'll do you."

"That'll do. Secondly, can you say positively that he had a gold tooth in the upper row?"

The crossing-sweeper looked mildly surprised.

"Are you sure it's the same gentleman yore thinkin' of, sir? No, my gentleman didn't 'ave no gold tooth!"

"Are you sure?" asked John, and became conscious of Greenaway at his elbow protesting:

"But he *did,* sir! I saw it quite plain."

"No, that 'e didn't!" maintained the old man, wagging his head. "And I can swear to that, foggy night or no foggy night, sir. Cos why? Cos when I spoke to 'im and 'e turned round sort of gibbering with fright, as if the bogey-man was after 'im, 'e gave a kind of silly grin when 'e saw it was only me, an' I noticed as 'is false teeth 'ad come a bit loose, sir. I should say all 'is top teeth was on a plate, by the look of it, an' 'ad come loose in 'is excitement, sir. Cos you could see the top part that wasn't meant to show. An' I laughed to meself, and thanked Gawd I'd managed to keep me own teeth in me 'ead all these years."

"That can't be right," protested old Greenaway plaintively, looking at their ragged informant with extreme disfavour. "I saw distinctly, sir, that the man had a beautiful even row of teeth and that one of them was crowned with gold."

"Beautiful teeth, all right," assented the crossing-sweeper with a grin. "Beautiful as the dentist makes 'em. But white as tomb-stones, every one of 'em. Thank *you*, sir."

"Oh, and just one more thing," said John as they were about to pass on. "Did you notice anybody else pass this way at about the same time as our friend in the fez?"

"Same time, sir? No, I didn't notice anybody passing at the same time, but then I was too ockerpied tellin' the gentleman the way to a place 'e didn't want to go to, to notice anything else, sir. A little while before 'e came shootin' in 'ere, there was a tall gentleman passed, with a walkin'-stick and a white muffler, sir. And soon after 'Is Nibs of Anwell 'ad gone off there come a shortish gentleman in a nopera 'at, nippin' along like a little cock sparrer, sir. An' that was all I see, cos I put up the shutters, as they say, soon after that, sir."

"That can't be right, Mr. Christmas, sir," repeated Greenaway when they had taken leave of the old model. He looked rather distressed that John should appear to place any reliance on what such an old ragamuffin had to say. " I mean, that about the gentleman's teeth, sir. It can't be right."

" It may be, you know, Greenaway," said John cheerily.

" But think, sir, what it would mean! " urged the old man with respectful earnestness. " The gentleman you took me to see to-day 'ad a gold tooth, sir, but I feel almost certain 'e isn't the right gentleman. If we're to believe this person, that means there must 'ave been *three* gentlemen in fezes mixed up in Mr. Frew's death, sir. It don't sound likely or reasonable somehow, do you think, sir? "

John laughed.

" It certainly doesn't, Greenaway. I should fix the likely and reasonable number of gentlemen in fezes at two, at the most."

CHAPTER XVIII

THE STOP PRESS NEWS

WHEN John returned to Madox Court with Greenaway he found that Serafine had departed. Laurence was standing in front of his drawing-table surveying with a rather discontented expression the drawings of that lady's head which covered a large sheet of Whatman paper.

" Not bad, Laurence," commented John, looking over his shoulder. " Serafine pensive, Serafine cheerful, Serafine melancholy, Serafine enraged. By the way, I hope you are feeling chastened by the opinion she expressed of your intellectual capacities! "

Thoughtfully correcting a line in one of the drawings, Laurence replied rather indistinctly that he liked a woman who said what she thought.

" Oh, you do, do you? " said John with some amusement, and was about to comment on this volte-face when there was a loud, urgent rapping on the studio door, and to the surprise of both John and Laurence, Dr. Mordby burst into the room. He looked pale and haggard, and his urbane, professional manner had completely deserted him.

" Oh, there you are, Christmas! " he said abruptly, without so much as glancing at his host. " I rang you up at your flat and they told me you might possibly be here! "

"What is it, Dr. Mordby?" asked John, looking curiously at the unusual spectacle of the suave psychologist in a state of extreme agitation, and offering him a chair. Mordby sank into it with a sigh, but immediately, as though he found inaction impossible, rose to his feet again and paced restlessly across the room.

"Do you know the truth about this murder?" he inquired in a high, excited voice. "For God's sake put my mind at rest! Have you seen this?"

With a shaking hand he took a folded newspaper from his pocket and, unfolding it, flung rather than handed it to John.

"In the stop press news," he uttered brokenly, and watched John's face avidly as he read the item.

STUDIO CRIME. MAN AND WOMAN ARRESTED

"A man and a woman have been arrested at Liverpool Docks in connection with the murder of Gordon Frew in St. John's Wood on November 24."

"Good Lord!" exclaimed Laurence, who had been reading over John's shoulder. "This can't mean that Merewether——"

"I was expecting this," said John quietly, folding the paper and dropping it on the floor.

"But you can't mean, John," protested Laurence, "that you think Merewether——"

"Oh, Merewether!" interrupted Dr. Mordby violently. "Damn Merewether! Damn him eternally! What do I care for Merewether? Let him hang! But she——"

Laurence stared at the doctor in amazement. With his fists clenched and his eyes staring, he looked as though he were on the verge of insanity.

" But she——" went on Mordby more quietly, addressing John. " The woman they mention—*she* had nothing to do with it. It's impossible! For God's sake tell me what you know, Christmas! I feel as though I were going mad! What possible connection can she have had with Frew? And to think that I——"

He dropped into a chair and covered his face with his hands.

" She was his wife," said Christmas quietly. " Laurence, fetch Dr. Mordby a brandy and soda."

" His wife! " echoed Mordby, staring at Christmas as if he were a ghost. " But——"

" And it is the police theory that she is the murderer," went on John.

Mordby looked at him wildly.

" Then I am Judas," he said in a queer, strained voice.

There was a silence.

" Come, Dr. Mordby," said John at last, evenly. " Hadn't you better tell us all about it? And quickly, because I must get down to Fleet Street before six o'clock."

The doctor looked vacantly about him.

" What's the use? It is too late! And it was I—I who betrayed her! "

" You need not worry about that, Dr. Mordby," said John in a matter-of-fact voice. " I do not think any action you may have taken can have made much difference to the course of events. But it would be as well perhaps if you would give me the facts in your possession. I may say that I do not believe for an instant that Mrs. Frew is guilty of the murder."

A faint gleam of hope appeared in Mordby's eyes. He grasped the glass Laurence held out to him and took a gulp from it.

"God grant you may be right!" he said unevenly, with a queer theatricality that yet did not seem inappropriate to his character and to the occasion. "If—if she is convicted I shall never have another moment's peace of mind! If I had guessed for a moment that she was under suspicion I should have let her go, even though it meant letting Merewether go too. Damn him!"

"You had better tell me all you know about Phyllis Frew," suggested John quietly. "And as quickly as possible, Dr. Mordby, if you please. She was before her marriage Miss Phyllis Templar, was she not, and a medical student at University College at the same time as you and Dr. Merewether?"

"Yes, but——"

"At that time she was the cause of a bitter rivalry between you and Merewether. But she left the University without completing the course or taking a degree and went to live in France, did she not?"

"Yes," replied Mordby, looking at John with a puzzled stare. "But how do you know all this? I remember that I told you of an old rivalry between myself and Merewether. But I did not mention her name, and I did not even know that she had become the wife of Gordon Frew, nor that she was in England, nor——"

"That does not matter just now, Dr. Mordby. To identify the lady you spoke of as the wife of Gordon Frew did not require any very elaborate deduction. Will you carry the story on from where I left off, please?"

"She went to live in France," said Dr. Mordby, sitting upright in his chair and speaking more calmly than before, as if he had become infected with John's matter-of-fact briskness. "And for a year or two I neither saw nor heard of her. But I could not forget her at once. She—

she was the most beautiful woman I have ever seen. There is no one like her, even now. I believe she corresponded with Merewether for a while after she went to France," went on the doctor, and added with a sort of stony bitterness: " He was more favoured than I. Two or three years after she left England I took my degree and went for a short rest and holiday to the south of France. I did not go to seek her out, it was pure chance that took me to the town where she lived with her father. For by that time I was more or less cured of my—unfortunate attachment, though it had made so much impression on me that no other had come to take its place. I saw her again, Christmas, and in an instant it was as if the three years interval had never been. I was as madly in love with her as ever. It was a strange obsession," said the doctor meditatively, the psychologist in him rising for a moment above the man, " for there had never been any real friendship between us, and we had not a taste nor an ideal in common. She had always, in fact, disliked me, and made no secret of her aversion. It was a kind of possession, like witchcraft. She is a woman to make one believe in the legend of Helen of Troy. For although I fancied many years ago that the affair had at last become no more than a sentimental memory, yet when I saw her by chance in Hampstead this morning the old magic came back like a dream, although she had lost all her brilliance and a great deal of the beauty she had.

" But to go on with my story. I discovered that she was living quietly in the south of France with her father, to whom she was much attached. And I found out, never mind how, it is not material to the story, that her father was a discharged convict who had taken another name and settled down in this small country town to start a new life as an honest and respected man. His real name was Michael Templar, but to his neighbours he was known as Martin Hilary, and his daughter had dropped her surname and become Phyllis Hilary. Well, I tried to use this knowledge to force the girl to consent to becoming my wife, God forgive me! I threatened to make Templar's discreditable past known to all the people who knew him and respected him as Michael Hilary. I think she would have consented in the end, rather than allow her father's peace to be wrecked, for he had come out of prison a broken wreck of a man, and his hold on life and sanity was not very strong. But I came to myself in time, and realized what it was that I was contemplating. I am not really a villain, although I so nearly behaved like one. I left France immediately, putting temptation behind me, and after travelling round Europe for a while, decided to remain in Vienna to study, and to abandon surgery for psychopathy. In the course of time I came to England and started a practice which has, I think I may say, been not unsuccessful."

Christmas repressed a smile. It was amusing to hear the familiar Mordby emerging, under the spell of his own eloquence, from the agitated, hardly-recognizable human being who had begun to recount this story.

"Since then," went on Simon Mordby, "I had not seen Phyllis Templar until this morning. And in the course of years I had completely recovered from the affair, although to this day I cannot see her Christian name written nor hear it addressed to another woman without the stirring of painful memories. But my old dislike of my rival dies harder than the love which caused the rivalry—a not uncommon phenomenon in such affairs, I am afraid. Dr. Merewether and I would in any case have been antipathetic to one another, I think. With the memory of our hatred between us—and the hatred of youth can be very bitter, as no doubt you know—friendship, or even tolerance, between us has been impossible. You see, I am frank with you, Christmas.

" When I saw Phyllis Templar by chance in Hampstead High Street this morning in company with Miss Serafine Wimpole, the ghost of the old fascination returned to me. But no more than the ghost. Ten years is a long time. However, my curiosity overcame me so far that I attempted to follow the cab they got into and discover their destination. But I was not able to follow them far, owing to Miss Wimpole's ingenuity." Mordby gave the shadow of a grim smile. " I inquired later at the taxi-rank in Hampstead and the man who had driven them was fairly easily persuaded to part with the information that he had driven them to a certain address in Swiss Cottage—an address which I knew to be Merewether's. The old demon of jealousy was upon me in an instant. It seemed monstrous that, while this woman whom we had both loved should fly from me in the street as though I were the plague, she should trust herself to a man whom I knew to be a murderer."

" You knew nothing of the kind, Dr. Mordby," interrupted John. " However, that is beside the point."

Mordby looked up in astonishment.

" My dear Christmas, I had the best reasons for supposing what I take to be the fact, that Merewether is responsible for the death of Gordon Frew."

" To suppose," replied Christmas, " is not to know. And I think you will find that you were mistaken in your supposition."

" But do you mean to tell me," exclaimed Mordby in

astonishment, "that Merewether has been wrongfully arrested?"

"Just as Mrs. Frew has been wrongfully arrested, yes, I think so. I was hoping that Hembrow would not make the arrest until I had had time to complete my case, but of course Merewether's flight made an arrest inevitable."

"And it was I," said Mordby dispiritedly, "who gave Inspector Hembrow the information that Merewether had gone. When I left the taxi-rank I went straight to Merewether's address. His sister informed me that he had been called away suddenly to see his brother, who had been taken ill, and that a locum-tenens was arriving in the afternoon. I went straight with this information to Scotland Yard. I told myself that it was to save the woman I had loved from association with a murderer. But I knew in my heart that it was nothing but blind, instinctive jealousy and hatred. I was glad to have an excuse for putting the police on Merewether's track."

"If it is any comfort to you, Dr. Mordby," said John, "I think I can assure you that your information to the police was quite superfluous. Dr. Merewether and Mrs. Frew would have been arrested in any case, without your intervention. I must thank you for being so frank with me. And now I have to make a little journey to Fleet Street."

"But," cried Mordby, springing to his feet as John rose and looked at his watch, "can you assure me, Christmas, that Phyllis—that she——"

"That she is innocent of this charge? Undoubtedly, Dr. Mordby. If you will come here to-morrow, I hope to prove it to you, and to all of Merewether's friends. I shall be back in about two hours, Laurence, and I hope to bring with me the last links in the chain of evidence."

So saying, he took his departure, followed soon by Dr. Mordby. Laurence wandered meditatively around the studio for a while, unable to settle down to work, feeling in no very cheerful frame of mind. The news brought by Dr. Mordby had disturbed him deeply, and although the suspicion that Merewether might be guilty did not cross his loyal mind, he did not altogether share John's optimistic hope of a speedy discharge. However, John had promised to return in two hours, and he realized that until then he must possess his soul in patience, and settled down to work as the surest antidote to melancholy.

He had just completed a fresh, and, as he himself observed with some surprise, highly-idealized portrait of Serafine Wimpole, when Greenaway entered and announced that Sir Marion Steen had called. Laurence, who did not feel at all in the mood for discussing the turn events had taken with anybody but John, muttered, to Greenaway's shocked surprise:

" Blow Sir Marion Steen! " and contemplated for a moment saying that he was out. His natural truthfulness and amiability, however, got the better of his inclination, and he added that Greenaway might show Sir Marion in. The old man still hesitated in the doorway.

" Is it true, sir," he asked at last, " that Dr. Merewether's been arrested for the murder of Mr. Frew, sir? My son says as it is, sir, but surely it can't be! Dr. Merewether always seemed such a——"

" Oh, go away, Greenaway! " said Laurence irritably. He perceived that he would have to endure a good deal of harping on this string before long, and felt his nerves weakening already at the prospect. " We shall no doubt know quite as much as we want to when we open our morning papers."

Greenaway vanished with an apology, and Laurence immediately regretted his own ill-temper. It was plain from Sir Marion's grave face as he entered the studio that he also had read the stop press news, and he began without preamble, dropping into a chair:

" I was hoping I might find Christmas here in your company, Mr. Newtree. Have you seen the—ah, I see you have! And I see by your face that the worst has happened. I've been hoping against hope as I came along here that the arrested man would turn out to be a stranger."

" There seems to be no doubt," said Laurence, sitting down on his working-stool and bracing himself up to endure the inevitable questions and condolences as best he could, " that Merewether has been arrested. But I shouldn't call it the worst. Christmas says he'll soon be discharged."

Laurence was surprised at the amount of confidence he managed to infuse into his voice, and went on, encouraged by the sound of it: " He says that he knows who the murderer is, though he hasn't quite completed his case yet."

" God grant that he may be right," said Sir Marion quietly. " Are you expecting him here soon? If so, perhaps I might wait a while and see him, if my presence doesn't worry you in these tragic circumstances, Newtree. I should like in any case to know the name of Merewether's solicitor, for if this matter should come to the worst I shall make it my business to procure him the best defence that can be got."

"Oh, I don't think there'll be any need for that, Sir Marion!" said Newtree with a cheerfulness that sounded positively blatant in his own ears, in contrast to the heaviness of his heart. "Christmas says he'll be discharged to-morrow."

There was a pause. Sir Marion's lined and pensive face seemed to express a kindly tolerant scepticism of John's powers to bring about this wished-for result.

"It is difficult to understand," he said diffidently at length, voicing Newtree's own heavy thoughts. "What can have made an innocent man take to flight? I suppose that he saw that appearances went against him, and lost his head. But it seems extraordinary that a man of Merewether's obvious intelligence and strength of mind——"

The philanthropist finished the sentence with a lift of the eyebrows and a shake of the head. Before Newtree could think of an adequate rejoinder (and, indeed, there was none) brisk footsteps sounded on the gravel, and after a moment or two John Christmas entered, carrying a bundle of papers under his arm and looking both grave and tired.

"Ah, Sir Marion!" he said as the great financier greeted him with a sympathetic smile. "I half expected I should find you here. I knew your interest in Merewether's fortunes, and guessed that it would bring you here for news. Oh, Lord! I'm tired! Get me a drink, Laurence, there's a good chap."

He took a long draught from the glass Laurence handed him and dropped into a chair with a sigh.

"The last four days must have been very crowded ones for you," said Sir Marion sympathetically. "Especially if, as Newtree tells me, you have collected sufficient evidence to vindicate Merewether's innocence of this dreadful charge."

"It has been rather a crowded hour of life," replied Christmas. "I won't say 'glorious life.' For though it is pleasant to feel that one holds the power to vindicate a friend, it is not pleasant to have to do so at the expense of someone else."

"Do I understand then," asked Sir Marion, leaning forward with a look of keen interest on his fine, gentle features, "that you not only hold proofs of Merewether's innocence, but also of the real murderer's complicity?"

"Yes, Sir Marion. I do not say that my case is sufficiently strong as it stands to convince a jury. But I think that by to-morrow it will be strong enough to procure Merewether's discharge and to turn Hembrow's attention towards establishing the real identity of the man I have in mind."

"But this sounds almost too good to be true," said Sir Marion. "I suppose my curiosity must remain unsatisfied until to-morrow. But I cannot refrain from asking you now whether the solution has anything to do with the mysterious Turk who spoke to me in Greentree Road?"

John looked dreamily across the wide studio.

"That is not altogether an easy question to answer, Sir Marion," he replied gravely. "He figures in the solution. He appears in the story as that lay figure over there appears in an artist's pictures."

And he pointed to the featureless wooden figure draped in a mandarin's robe which, with its arms bent stiffly under the wide sleeves and its gleaming bald head bent, appeared to be listening earnestly to the conversation.

"In one of Laurence's pictures that wooden figure

might appear as a Chinese priest. In another, as a woman dressed in the height of fashion. In another, as a—let us say as a man in a fez. But apart from Laurence's pictures it has no life. It is only a lay figure."

There was a pause. Sir Marion, who had been listening attentively to this exposition, continued to gaze contemplatively at John's grave face for a moment, then, coming to himself with a start, exchanged a rather puzzled glance with Newtree.

"You might just tell us where you've been this evening," said Laurence, hoping to draw his friend from the realm of fancy to that of fact. "And what those two papers are you're nursing so carefully on your knee."

"Certainly," replied John with a smile. "I have been to Fleet Street, Covent Garden and Bloomsbury. And these two papers are copies of last month's *Collector*."

Laurence took one up and began idly to look through it.

"You could have got a copy of this at a bookstall without chasing down to Fleet Street," he remarked.

"Until I had chased down to Fleet Street, my dear Laurence, and looked through the files of this and several other similar publications, I did not know what paper it was I wanted. I only knew that I wanted one in which a certain photograph had appeared. Ah, I see," he added, as Newtree uttered an exclamation, "that you have discovered the photograph in question."

"Good Lord!" ejaculated Laurence. "Is this the man who passed you on the night of the murder, Sir Marion? It seems to answer exactly to his description."

Sir Marion put on his glasses and took the magazine from Laurence. The photograph showed the intellectual and rather melancholy face of a middle-aged Greek wearing a fez and having a slight cast in his left eye. He was looking at a small ivory carving which he was holding up against the light, and his lips were parted in a pensive smile. A gold-crowned tooth, showing dark in the white row, had not been touched out by the art of the photographer. Underneath were written the lines:

"Mr. Oscar Lascarides, whose shop in Ainslie Street is much frequented by collectors of fine Oriental works of art, examining a newly-acquired treasure."

"I can save Sir Marion the trouble of answering your question, Laurence," said John quietly, as the financier was about to speak. "It is not the man. It is the model. I have seen the man and this is a very good photograph of him, though flattering. It is carefully taken to minimize the effect of the truly appalling squint from which he suffers."

"You are very uncommunicative, John," complained Laurence, laying the paper on the table with a last fascinated glance at the interesting face of Mr. Lascarides. "At least you are very mysterious in your communications."

"On the contrary," said John gravely, "I am being very communicative and not in the least mysterious. And to prove it I will show you this, which I found waiting for me at my flat in Bloomsbury."

He drew from his pocket a small cardboard box and took from it a tiny object wrapped in tissue paper, which he unwrapped and laid upon the table.

"Why," exclaimed Newtree, "it's the little piece of metal old Brett the crossing-sweeper gave you the other day! You don't mean to say that you found out anything from that?"

"I took it to a chemical analyst who is an old friend of mine," said John with a sigh, "and this is his report upon it: 'The object is a thin piece of eighteen carat gold and is engraved on one side with an elaborate floral pattern such as is frequently found on old-fashioned lockets and watch-cases. The edges have been cut with a strong pair of scissors or clippers. The fragment shows traces of mud and road-dust, and there is a minute trace of human blood upon one of the roughened edges.'"

John sighed as he replaced the lid of the little box and put it in his pocket.

"And what did you find in Covent Garden?" asked Laurence, with a puzzled but hopeful air. "Though I can't make head or tail of your discoveries at present!"

"In Covent Garden," said John rather wearily, "I obtained an interesting piece of information at the premises of Messrs. Ryebody and Pratt, theatrical costumiers. And as I walked back here along Greentree Road I noticed, not for the first time, that there is a long, narrow passage about ten yards the other side of Shipman's Mews, which leads through into the recreation ground. And now," he added, disregarding his friend's exclamation of bewilderment, "do you think you could persuade Greenaway to produce some food? I haven't had a meal since breakfast."

"I'll leave you to your rest and refreshment," said Sir Marion, rising, "with many thanks for bearing with my curiosity so long. I am afraid I have fatigued you a good deal. . . . I suppose you do not happen to know the address of Dr. Merewether's solicitor?" he added, turning to Newtree. " You do? I should be glad to have it. For, should our friend Christmas by some evil chance be unable to convince the police of Merewether's innocence, I shall make it my business to procure him a good defence."

CHAPTER XIX

EXIT

JOHN, who had stayed the night at Madox Court on the feeble pretext that he had an objection to going home in the dark, came to breakfast the next morning looking so heavy-eyed and pale that Laurence exclaimed in concern at the sight of him.

" You don't look exactly brilliant yourself," remarked John, drawing up a chair.

" To tell you the truth," replied Laurence, looking somewhat ashamed of himself, " I hardly slept all night, thinking of poor Merewether,"

" I didn't sleep much either," confessed John, looking with an unfavourable eye at his eggs and bacon and pouring himself out some strong black coffee. " But I wasn't thinking of Merewether."

His eye strayed speculatively to the newspapers that still lay folded in a pile upon the floor. Newtree subscribed to all the daily papers, under the impression that this catholicity was likely to give him good ideas for cartoons. But he rarely opened more than one or two, and the long-suffering Greenaway struggled in vain to find domestic uses for the never-ceasing accumulation of news-print.

" I haven't had the pluck to open the beastly things yet," said Laurence, picking up one or two with a wry smile. " I suppose we shall find Merewether's name sprawled all over them. Which one shall I open first? "

" The *Times*," said John, " if you want the news broken gently. The *Daily Wire*, if you want to get the shock over quickly."

Laurence chose the latter, and having finished his breakfast, leant back in his chair, lit a cigarette and stoically unfolded the paper. At his sudden stifled exclamation, which seemed to hold even more of surprise than horror, John looked up quickly. Laurence's face looked at him over the print, as white as the paper itself.

" My God, John! Look at this! "

John jumped up and went round to his friend's chair. The headline stared gigantic across the page. " SUDDEN DEATH OF MILLIONAIRE-PHILANTHROPIST." And crossing three columns below in letters which seemed small only by comparison: " SIR MARION STEEN FOUND DEAD IN HIS STUDY."

John straightened himself with a sigh.

" I couldn't tell from his parting remarks last night whether he intended to kill himself or me," he said. " I am glad, not only for personal reasons, that he was wise enough to choose himself."

Laurence, scarcely listening, went on to read:

" Sir Marion Steen, the millionaire, was discovered lying dead in the library of his house in Mary Street, Mayfair, at eleven o'clock last night. The cause of death is thought to have been strychnine poisoning, and the circumstances point strongly to suicide. The dead financier's butler states that Sir Marion arrived at his house at about eight o'clock last night, apparently in good health and spirits, and retired to his library. About an hour afterwards he rang the bell and gave the footman who answered it an envelope which he required him to take by hand immediately to the office of Mr. Henry Marchant, a solicitor in Bedford Row. He gave orders that a tray of refreshments should be brought to him in the library at eleven o'clock, as he intended to work late. On entering the library at the stated hour, the butler was horrified to perceive the body of his master extended upon the floor. Death appeared to have taken place an hour or two previously. The dead millionaire is stated to have been a man of cheerful disposition, and to have suffered no nervous derangement or illness which might account for this tragic occurrence. A self-made man, he was well known for his charitable activities, and the Steen Homes of Rest now number upwards of thirty."

Laurence laid the paper on his knees and looked up at John with a sad and puzzled face.

" What an extraordinary thing! " he remarked. " You take it very calmly, I must say, John! Why, the man was perfectly sane and cheerful when he left here last night, and yet within three hours——"

" Oh, he had courage," said John, with a sigh. " He knew how to make the best of a bad business."

" Just listen to this," said Laurence with disgust, taking up the paper again. " ' A tragic feature of this sad affair is that the dead man was to have opened to-morrow the new Steen Home of Rest near Primrose Hill, which will now be inaugurated under such sad conditions.' The way these people write! That's what they call a tragic feature, is it? "

" Well," replied John quietly, " as it happens there were elements of tragedy in that fact, for Sir Marion Steen . . . There's Hembrow walking past the window. I thought we should see him here this morning."

"This is an extraordinary affair, Mr. Christmas," began Hembrow as soon as he had entered and briefly greeted Newtree. "Ah, I see you've read your paper! I hardly know what to make of this affair!"

He sat down on the edge of the model's throne and frowned in a perplexed and disgruntled way.

"The whole thing seems impossible," he said irritably. "I thought the case against Merewether and Mrs. Frew quite good enough to justify an arrest, although perhaps I shouldn't have been in such a hurry if they hadn't forced my hand by trying to leave the country. But now!" He ran his hand through his hair and looked from Laurence to John. "Would you say there was a possibility that Sir Marion Steen was insane? I can't find any support for the idea, but it seems he must have been!"

"He was perfectly sane when he left here last night at about half-past seven," replied John.

Hembrow's eyebrows drew together in a gloomy frown.

"Well, he must have gone suddenly off his head almost immediately afterwards. I had a solicitor, a Mr. Marchant, round at Scotland Yard first thing this morning, fairly frothing with excitement and demanding Merewether's immediate release on the grounds that he had received a confession of murder from Sir Marion Steen. Found it in his letter-box when he arrived at his office this morning. I thought it was a hoax at first. But, damn it, it's perfectly genuine, as I found out when I rang up Sir Marion's household. And then to go and do away with himself like that! He *must* have been insane. What other explanation can there be, except——"

"Except that he was the murderer of Gordon Frew," finished John quietly, "and wished to save himself the unpleasantness of a trial and conviction. Newtree will tell you that he was here yesterday evening, and that I presented him with one or two clues to the identity of the murderer."

"Yes," agreed Laurence. "That is so. But, good God, John, you don't mean to say——"

"He took the hint, like a sensible man," said John. "There is no doubt that he was a sensible man. For consider how admirably sensible his behaviour has been ever since the murder, how natural and detached his interest in the affair has seemed. Yes, the murder itself was the only foolish thing he did. And what an unnecessary piece of folly!" John sighed and smiled. "When a man becomes obsessed by the morbid craving for respectability, there is no knowing to what lengths he will go! He might have known that he was safe, if only his vanity had not destroyed his sense of proportion. Gordon Frew would never really have given him away. For he had the same obsession, and the same stake, as it were, in silence. But I suppose the uncertainty became unbearable. And Gordon Frew was a cruel devil. Suffering amused him."

"My dear John!" and "Mr. Christmas!" began Laurence and Hembrow simultaneously. "Will you please explain what this is all about?"

John looked at the two rueful faces and laughed.

"Didn't Sir Marion explain it all," he asked, "in the letter he sent to Mr. Marchant, Solicitor?"

"No, he didn't," returned Hembrow. "It was quite a short statement. I've got it here. At least, old Marchant wouldn't leave me the original"—a slight bitterness in the Inspector's tone seemed to imply that his feelings had been somewhat ruffled during his interview with Merewether's solicitor—"but I've got a copy."

He unfolded a sheet of paper and cleared his throat, and began to read in a rather sceptical tone:

"I understand that your client Dr. George Merewether has been arrested on a charge of being concerned in the murder of Gordon Frew at Madox Court, St. John's Wood, on November 24. As I shall in a few hours' time be out of reach of the law, and as I see no reason why Dr. Merewether should be inconvenienced by my affairs, I wish to make the following statement:

"I myself, and no one else, am responsible for the death of my objectionable relation Gordon Frew. For reasons which I do not feel inclined to enlarge on here, I stabbed him in the back as he sat at his writing-table at eight o'clock precisely on the evening of November 24, and I do not in the least regret the action itself, although I regret the consequences. If details are required, no doubt Mr. John Christmas will be delighted to supply you with them.

"I may say that I had no intention of incriminating Dr. Merewether, but had provided as a scapegoat a man whom I well knew to be a pest to society, although I had no personal animosity against him. I should very much like to know (1) what made Dr. Merewether tell that thundering lie about having seen Frew alive at nine o'clock, and (2) what happened to the remarkably beautiful woman who arrived in Frew's studio about five minutes before his death and went into an inner room to await my departure. However, I am afraid that my curiosity will have to go unsatisfied.

"Marion Steen."

Hembrow folded the paper up with a grim look on his face and put it into his pocket.

" He says you can supply the details, Mr. Christmas," he remarked. " And perhaps you wouldn't mind doing so. Have I really made a mistake in arresting Mrs. Frew and Dr. Merewether? "

" I'm afraid you'll have to let them go again, Hembrow. I was hoping very much that the arrest could be staved off until this morning, when it need never have taken place. But of course in the circumstances you had no alternative. Better luck next time, Hembrow. Anyway, you're a bit young for promotion yet, aren't you? "

Hembrow grinned philosophically.

" Well, let's have these details, Mr. Christmas, if you don't mind. How did Sir Marion Steen manage to go up to Frew's flat and get down again without being seen? Why, he overtook Dr. Merewether in Greentree Road at about twenty-five minutes past eight! He couldn't possibly have got round the block in the time, so unless he flew over the houses, he must have passed Dr. Merewether face to face before he could turn and overtake him. To say nothing of the cabmen on the rank and the crossing-sweeper at Shipman's Mews. Yet none of these people saw him going down the road away from here."

" Pardon me, Hembrow," said John with a smile, " Dr. Merewether and the crossing-sweeper not only saw him but conversed with him. He deliberately asked Dr. Merewether the way to Golders Green. And in a moment of mental aberration he asked the crossing-sweeper the way to Primrose Hill. It was unfortunate for him that in his excitement he should have let slip the name of a place he was really interested in, instead of a place he wanted to appear interested in."

" But Good Lord! " broke in Laurence, staring blankly. " It was the Turk who met Dr. Merewether and asked him—— And, dash it, John, he met Sir Marion too! "

John laughed.

"There's no particular difficulty about meeting oneself, you know, Laurence. It's quite easy to be most convincingly circumstantial about it. One has special facilities for observation and can describe oneself minutely afterwards to the police. But one should be careful not to describe oneself too minutely. One should be careful not to observe details which no one else observed. Of all the people who saw the man in the fez that night, only Sir Marion noticed that he had a cast in his left eye. It was when I first realized that, that a glimmering of the truth first crossed my mind."

"But," objected Hembrow, who had quickly assimilated this idea, "there's old Lascarides. Now he certainly has a cast in his left eye. Where does he come into it? "

"He doesn't come any farther into it than the pages of the *Collector*," replied John, producing that magazine with its elegant studio portrait of the Greek, "and the corner of Circus Road. He was only the model and the scapegoat. It was unwise of Sir Marion to make up from a photograph. If he had had a glimpse of his model in real life he would have realized the stumbling-block. For as soon as I saw Lascarides I felt pretty sure that he was not the man we wanted. Nobody who saw him could have failed to notice that diabolical squint."

"The squint is quite noticeable here," observed Hembrow, examining the portrait.

"It is q ite noticeable as a slight cast," agreed John. "And a slight cast is not a very noticeable thing on a foggy night. Sir Marion thought he was quite safe in ascribing a slight cast to his other self, even though nobody else could have noticed it. Unfortunately for him, the fashionable photographer who took this picture knew his business."

"What made you think of this photograph, Mr. Christmas?"

"When I saw Lascarides I knew, or I had a strong suspicion, that he was not the man we wanted. But, except for the squint, he was so like the man we wanted in every way, that the corollary seemed to be that somebody had impersonated him. And once the theory of impersonation had settled firmly in my mind, there was so much to support it that I had no doubt about the matter. There was, for instance, the way the mysterious Greek had broadcasted his intention of going to Golders Green, where Lascarides lived: a likely, though not very subtle, procedure on the part of a man who wished to incriminate Lascarides. There was Lascarides' own story of having been called into the district by a telephone call. And you will remember, Hembrow, that Pandora Shirley, when she was tying her shoe-lace outside Frew's front door, heard Frew say to his visitor: 'You've mistaken the date, old man!' Now the night on which Frew was murdered was the night before the Arts Club fancy dress ball at the Albert Hall. In the light of that fact and of the theory of impersonation, those words of Frew's took on a significance they had not seemed to have at first. Further, although Greenaway, Merewether, and Sir Marion himself all noticed that the stranger had a gold-filled tooth, the crossing-sweeper at Shipman's Mews swore positively that he had no such thing. And this small article was picked up just inside the mews and handed to me. I am told that under the microscope it shows slight traces of blood. And you will observe that the edges are slightly bent as if to take a purchase on some other small article of the same size—possibly a tooth."

Hembrow took the little piece of gold and turned it over and over.

"Rather an amateurish way of faking a gold tooth," he remarked.

"True. But no doubt Sir Marion thought it would be safer not to take his dentist into his confidence. And the gold tooth had to be removable at a moment's notice. Unfortunately for him, it was so easily removable that it removed itself prematurely. But to continue. When yesterday I gave old Greenaway a sight of Mr. Lascarides and he was unable to identify him as the man he had seen in the doorway here, my theory of impersonation was complete. But it was obvious to me that the impersonator could not have seen Lascarides in the life, or he would never have attempted to impersonate him at all. Therefore, he must have taken a photograph or other picture of the gentleman as his model. It only remained to hunt up a paper or magazine with a photograph in it of Mr. Lascarides. Bearing in mind the Greek's business of dealer in works of art I looked first through the collector's periodicals, and it was not long before I found the magazine I wanted."

"I thought," remarked Laurence thoughtfully, "that Sir Marion seemed very silent and unenthusiastic when you showed him that photograph yesterday evening."

"I suppose," said Hembrow, who had been thinking hard, "that he went into Shipman's Mews for the purpose of removing his make-up. He can't have had much on, by the way, to be able to remove it so quickly."

"False eyebrows, a false moustache, a fez and a little bronze powder will do wonders in a fog," said John.

" Yes, I have no doubt that was why he dashed into the mews as though the devil was after him, to use my friend the crossing-sweeper's own words. Startled at being spoken to, he then asked the crossing-sweeper to tell him the way to the first place that came into his head, to account for his apparent benightedness, and went on quickly along the road to the passage that leads into the recreation ground. Sheltering there, he removed his make-up, took off the fez and put it in his pocket, put on the opera-hat he had been carrying under his coat, and hurried along the road to overtake Merewether. By the way, he made a bad slip when he told you that he had met the mysterious stranger just *this* side of Shipman's Mews. He overlooked the little episode with the crossing-sweeper when he said that. For the sweeper saw Sir Marion Steen pass the mews a little while after the excitable stranger in the fez had passed on."

There was a pause.

" I should like to know," said Laurence at last, " what there was between Frew and Steen. I didn't know they even knew one another."

" I fancy they knew one another only too well," said John, " and that there was a good deal between them which Sir Marion would willingly have forgotten, but which Gordon Frew, in his jealousy and hatred, was determined to keep alive. You remember, Hembrow, that the delightful Mrs. Rudgwick told us that Gordon Frew had followed his elder brother to America, and that there had always been dislike and jealousy between the two? By the way, in my opinion that woman is an excellent judge of character. I thought her remarks on the characters and potentialities of her brothers most interesting and instructive."

" Well? " asked Laurence, as John paused.

" I have no doubt in my own mind," said John, " that James Frew and Sir Marion Steen were one and the same person. And I'm inclined to stretch the personality to include Frew's quondam business associate Henry Winter, who managed to escape the penalty of the law while Frew himself paid it in full."

" But Henry Winter died," objected Hembrow. " At least——"

" Your New York confrères didn't seem very positive on that point," returned John. " All they knew positively was that he had disappeared. And I find that Henry Winter's disappearance from America's too-hospitable shore preceded by little less than a year the setting-up of the small hardware shop in an East Anglian town which formed Sir Marion's first stepping-stone to fortune. I've been looking him up in *Who's Who*. He's rather proud of that hardware shop, but I think he should have suppressed the date of its opening. However, I suppose when he made that entry he thought the past was safely buried, and his brother safely down-and-out. He did not allow for the fact that his brother's business acumen and determination to cut a figure in the world were equal to his own. He did not think that his brother's affection for him was not likely to be increased during seven years' penal servitude. Ah! " said John with a sigh, " what a terrible thing the competitive spirit is! When it appears as jealousy, I think it is the worst thing in the world. They each had what they wanted. Why couldn't they have left one another alone? "

There was a long pause. Then Hembrow got to his feet briskly.

" Well, it's all wrong, you know, Mr. Christmas," he

observed with a smile. "Your methods, I mean. It looks more like lucky guess-work than anything else to me."

"I admit," said John, "that I am capable of building a very high edifice on a small foundation of proved fact. But the observation of character isn't guess-work, although by its very nature it isn't capable of what you would call proof. I knew as soon as I saw his studio that Gordon Frew was a vain man. And with that kind of vanity jealousy goes hand in hand. Besides, you will remember that there was a book on the libel laws among the sumptuously-bound and scrupulously uncut art-books on Frew's shelves. And that he was in communication with the Herald's Office when he died."

"I wonder," said Laurence pensively, "what name he was thinking of taking. I suppose we shall never know."

"I have no doubt in my own mind," replied John, "though, of course, Inspector, I haven't a shadow of proof, that it was Steen. You will remember that it was at Frew's suggestion that his charming sister changed her name. And I don't imagine that the name Steen was chosen for that disreputable shop-front entirely by chance. It was all, I imagine, part of the amiable Frew's scheme for the persecution of his brother."

"There's one small thing that puzzles me," said Hembrow thoughtfully, "though it's not important. What was that the girl Shirley overheard about 'a coffin for one'? It sounds as if it ought to have had some bearing on the murder, but I'm blowed if I can see what, unless Frew was threatening Sir Marion."

"Not exactly, I think," responded John with a smile. "I fancy that the words she overheard were not 'a coffin for one,' but 'coffee for one.' You remember that Frew's own thumb-print was found on the knife that killed him, running at an angle towards the handle, as though he had held the weapon with the point towards himself? Well, my idea is that at some point in the argument with his visitor Frew took the knife down from where it was hanging on the wall and held it out to the other man, saying with a sort of grim jocularity: 'Daggers for two and coffee for one!' "

"Yes," said Laurence. "It's just the sort of thing he would have said. I've heard him use that little epigram in conversation more than once."

"Yes, I suppose that's the explanation," assented Hembrow. "For Frew's next remark was that 'he thought it would save argument,' which fits in perfectly. Well, I'll be off, Mr. Christmas. Lord, what a morning! I must say that in one way I'm not sorry to find I've arrested the wrong man. For Dr. Merewether seems a very likeable gentleman, though he hasn't got much to say. What beats me is why he behaved in such a suspicious way all through, seeing that he's perfectly innocent!"

"I think," said Christmas, "that the explanation lies in Mrs. Frew's present state of mind. And I have no doubt that once she is released Dr. Merewether will be quite willing to enlighten you as to the motives for his suspicious behaviour."

CHAPTER XX

THE DOCTOR'S STORY

ONE afternoon a week or so later Serafine Wimpole, entering her house in the company of John Christmas after a private view of some new artist's works, found Dr. Merewether descending the stairs from her Aunt Imogen's bedroom. Imogen, who was suffering from a bad cold in the head, had abandoned psycho-analysis for the homely ministrations of a general practitioner, and was at the moment lying in bed much soothed by the doctor's assurance that the cold she was suffering from bore no resemblance to the latest epidemic, Russian influenza.

"Good afternoon, Dr. Merewether," said Serafine. "How do you find my aunt?"

"She has a nasty cold," replied the doctor, "but that is all. Her temperature is quite normal. She will be all right after a day in bed."

He took up his hat and coat, and hesitated, looking from Serafine to Christmas. Then, laying these garments down again, he said with the grave formality that was characteristic of him:

"I feel that I have never thanked you as I should have done, Miss Wimpole, for your kindness to Phyllis on that —that dreadful day. I do so now."

Serafine smiled at his serious face, and hesitated, and then said, greatly daring:

"I should so like to know, Dr. Merewether, what happened on the night Mr. Frew was killed. Why did you give us all such a dreadful three days? Will you tell me?"

"Certainly," said Merewether, with his slight grave smile, and followed Serafine and John into the sitting-room.

"I expect," he said quietly after a moment, "you know, or can guess, at the early part of Phyllis's history and mine. We were fellow-students, and—and we became engaged to be married, although we had the prospect of a very long engagement in front of us. After we had been engaged a few months, she left the college and went to live in France with her father."

Merewether hesitated and glanced at John.

"I expect you know her father's history, and that he is a discharged convict, although his conviction and imprisonment in America took place many years ago. When he changed his name and settled down in a small town in the south of France to start a new life, Phyllis thought it her duty to stand by him. And she soon became very much attached to him." The doctor sighed. "So much so that in the end she broke off our engagement and consented to marry Gordon Frew rather than allow him to make her father's past known to the people who liked and respected him. He was—still is—a weak and nervous man, and I think she feared the shock would kill him. She allowed herself to be blackmailed into marrying a scoundrel. I'll pass over all that time. I did not at the time know her reasons for breaking off our engagement. I suffered a good deal, but not so much as I should have if I had not had the consolation of thinking that she was happy with the man she had chosen. She married Gordon Frew, and I did not see her again for many years."

The doctor paused a moment, looking with unseeing eyes out of the window.

"I had not met Frew," he went on, "and it was not until I was called in to attend him during an attack of influenza last April, that I realized what kind of man it was my poor girl had married. I realized, too, why she had married him. For Frew, who knew me well enough by name and had often taunted Phyllis with her former attachment to me, took care to tell me how it was that she had come to marry him."

The doctor paused and looked from Serafine to John.

"You thought for a while, Miss Wimpole, did you not, that I was guilty of the murder of Gordon Frew? I can tell you that last April I came near to murdering him. However," he sighed and half-smiled, "I didn't do it. I even prevented him from dying, though there was murder in my heart. A few days before he—died, I met Phyllis in the street. It was the first time I had seen her since her marriage, but for me the years were as though they had never been. I implored her to leave the scoundrel she had married. She told me that, although he left her so far in peace as to allow her to live with her father, he would not consent to a divorce. And that she dared not divorce him while he held the secret of her father's past over him like a threat. He had even told her that he had papers proving her father's complicity in other crimes than the one for which he had been imprisoned. I guessed that it was a lie, but the poor girl believed him, and believed him when he said that the envelope containing these papers was in the possession of a third person, whose name and address he gave her. I think he hoped that she would amuse him by involving herself in desperate efforts to get hold of the papers which, I am inclined to believe, never existed."

"There was an envelope," interrupted John, "but there was nothing inside it. It was a cruel practical joke."

"Well," went on the doctor with a sigh, "she would not listen to my reasoning and pleading. She was obsessed with the idea that Frew could, if he chose, ruin her father's life. She told me that she would at least make one more attempt to persuade him to give up the papers and leave her and her father in peace."

Merewether paused a while, as if collecting his thoughts.

"And so," he said, "we come to the evening of November 24, the night on which Frew was murdered. I knew that Phyllis intended to visit her husband that evening and make her last appeal to the better feelings which he did not possess. I had tried to dissuade her, but it had been no use. You can imagine my anxiety, therefore, when we heard a sound like a cry coming from the room overhead. I imagined—well, the anxiety I felt at hearing that cry need not be described. I ran upstairs to inquire of Frew whether all was well with her. I knocked at the door and could get no answer. There was silence in the studio. I was terribly alarmed. I looked through the key-hole, and could see Phyllis standing rigid in the centre of the room with her hands clenched at her sides and an expression of horror on her face. Still there was no sound, and my fears for her safety began to change into a suspicion equally dreadful. I remembered her overwrought and nervous manner, and the excitability she had shown when I had attempted to reason with her. I called softly to her to let me in. She recognized my voice, and after a moment opened the door. You know what I saw. And you can guess what I imagined. Phyllis would say nothing. Her face was quite white and there was blood upon her bare arm. I wiped it off on my handkerchief and implored her to tell me what had happened. But her reason seemed to have deserted her. She would only say, again and again: 'He's dead! ' and 'Nobody must see, nobody must see! ' in that dreadful, vacant, earnest voice. . . ."

Merewether shuddered and stopped abruptly for a moment.

" She took the key and put it in the lock, muttering that nobody must see, and then prepared to open the door and go downstairs. She seemed dazed, like a sleep-walker. I told her that she could not go out that way, and flinging up the window, saw that it would be possible to help her to escape. I gave her my address and told her to go straight to my house. I do not know how I imagined I was going to hide her from the police, I had no idea at the moment but to help her escape. . . . The rest you know."

There was a long pause. Merewether lay back in his chair with a sigh, as if the memory of that night were too much for him.

" Of course," he said, " in her unbalanced state, poor girl, she forgot my address, and I did not see her again until you brought her to me, Miss Wimpole. My God! I should not care to live through those days again! "

He shuddered.

" When I returned home and found that she was not there, you can imagine my state of mind. I did not know what to do, nor where to look for her, for I did not know the address at which she was staying in London. After futile wandering about the streets looking for her, it occurred to me that she might have made the attempt to regain the papers relating to her father's misdeeds which had been the cause of the tragedy. I knew the address which Frew had given her and I went to the place on the forlorn hope of finding her there. I broke into the house, as I could get no answer to my ringing at the bell. I turned out the drawers and papers in Cold's flat on the off-chance that documents incriminating her father might really exist, for I was afraid that such documents might tell against my poor girl if the police got possession of them. I did not find them. And that," said Merewether, with a wry smile, " is the end of my story. You know all the rest."

" How is Phyllis? " asked Serafine gently, after a silence.

The doctor roused himself to speak more cheerfully.

" She is improving every day under my sister's nursing," he replied. " It will not be many weeks, I hope, before she is able to receive company. And now I must be getting on, Miss Wimpole, for I have quite a round of visits to make before returning home. I have promised Mrs. Wimpole that I will look in again to-morrow morning, though I do not think it will really be necessary. She should be feeling quite herself again by to-morrow, but I should keep her in bed for the rest of to-day."

" I don't think," said Serafine with a smile, " that force will be necessary. My aunt is one of those rare beings who enjoys obeying a doctor's orders."

Merewether smiled and took his departure. Serafine watched him from the window as he went down the garden path.

" I like Dr. Merewether," she observed. " In fact, I

was about to lose my heart to him when I discovered that his affections were already engaged. But luckily I made the discovery very early and the young buds of my affection obligingly retired. What a good thing it is, John, that affairs of the heart, in their early stages, are so easily controlled by the intellect."

"My dear Serafine," replied her friend lazily, "I don't know whether to be more shocked by the shamelessness of your confession or the lack of true romantic feeling implied in your last remark. Are you going to give me any tea? Those pictures, I find, have left me with a feeling of discouragement combined with thirst. Futurist art is like that."

"Afraid not, John," said Serafine. "I promised to take my dish of tea this afternoon at Mr. Newtree's studio. He is making a pastel study of my interesting face. You had better come along with me."

"I will," replied John, with a gleam of amusement in his eyes. "Is this the forty-fifth portrait Newtree has made of you, Serafine, or only the forty-fourth?"

Serafine laughed.

"Somewhere about there," she replied. "Rather a nice little man, your friend Newtree, if he does live in his studio like a hermit-crab in its shell. He amuses me."

"Then you'll probably end up by marrying him."

"My dear John, I'd as soon marry Diogenes."

"Well, you can't," said John reasonably. "He's dead. So powder your nose and come along."

THE END

Printed in Great Britain
by Amazon